Muddy Boots and Mishaps

by

Morag Clarke

Muddy Boots and Mishaps

First published in paperback by Braiswick 2009

Re-printed 2018 by Createspace, an Amazon.com Company
ISBN 978-1986315241

Copyright by Morag Clarke 2009

The rights of the above author to be identified as the author of this work has been asserted in accordance with the Copyright, Designs and Patents Act 1988.

All rights reserved. No part of this publication may be reproduced, stored in a retrieval system or transmitted in any form or by any means without prior permission of the copyright owner.

All the characters in this book are fictitious and any resemblance to actual persons, living or dead, is entirely coincidental.

Prologue

Giles Peterson, businessman, gambler and entrepreneur, was not having a good day.

'What do you mean it's been withdrawn,' he bellowed, waving his catalogue at the poor, unfortunate girl who happened to be sitting in the wrong place at the wrong time. 'It's listed in here.'

He had come to the stallion auction at Newmarket for the sole purpose of buying one particular horse – not just any horse – but the horse whose progress he had been following over the years with mounting excitement and anticipation, knowing that one day he would own him.

Midnight Prince was the proud winner of 15 races including the Coral Eclipse Stakes, the Coronation Cup at Epsom, the Champion stakes at Newmarket and the Prix d'Ispahon at Longchamp. The prize money he had earned as a two to five-year-old had totalled over three million pounds. Since being retired to stud at six he had sired the winners of over two hundred individual stakes. And now he was up for sale and predicted to fetch a record price at auction.

Giles Peterson was prepared to pay whatever it would take. He had wanted this horse for as long as he could remember. As a betting man, he would lay odds on the fact that Midnight Prince was one of the best stallions he had ever seen, both on and off the track, and he wasn't alone in thinking that. Consequently, the stud fees he would be able to charge would be worth a small fortune.

And now this chit of an office girl was telling him he couldn't do it, that the stallion was no longer for sale.

The girl's cheeks flushed as she sifted through the pile of documents and envelopes in front of her on the ornately carved polished wood of the reception desk.

'I'm sorry, Sir,' she said, scanning a sheet of paper quickly. 'The horse was withdrawn from the auction by the owners. I believe it's being sold privately.'

'What! What!' Giles bellowed, beads of sweat pricking his forehead. 'Who to?'

'I'm afraid I can't divulge...'

'Oh, give me that,' Giles snapped, his patience exhausted. He snatched the piece of paper out of her hand. "Hollyfield Stables and Stud" he read, before the girl managed to grab the letter back again with an indignant 'Sir!'

Hollyfield Stables and Stud. Now where had he heard that name before?

'I'm going to have to ask you to leave,' the girl said crisply.

'Don't worry,' Giles muttered, reaching into the pocket of his immaculately tailored camel coat. 'I've got no reason to stay.'

By the time he reached the car park and the privacy of his silver-coloured BMW, he had made several phone calls on his mobile and was starting to reel in people who could help him. Because one way or another, he was going to own that stallion. And he didn't intend to take no for an answer.

Unfortunately, two weeks later, and the likelihood was, that he would have to do just that. Negotiations for the purchase of Midnight Prince had fallen on deaf ears. The woman had no intention of selling him despite his generous offer, (and God knows, he'd offered her enough).

Giles Peterson stood in front of the window of his office overlooking the Thames, and gently swirled an expensive malt whisky round in a cut crystal glass.
He didn't like doing business with women, particularly stubborn businesswomen, and this young lady was proving more troublesome than most.

It was time he tried a different approach, if only to protect his formidable reputation. He was known as a person who got what he wanted - usually with no questions asked – and he intended to get that horse. But he could afford to be patient. There was no rush. It was only a matter of time.

'Mr Peterson?' The intercom on his desk buzzed.

'Yes, Michelle?'

'Jed Harrison's here.'

'Good.' Giles swallowed the whisky in one and put the glass back on his desk. 'Send him in.'

The man, who strolled into Giles' office as if he owned the place, had the lean, rugged look of someone who spent most of his life outdoors. He was wearing black jeans and a thin cotton shirt, rolled up at the elbows. A gold watch glinted on his tanned wrist.

'What do you want, this time?' he said, sitting down and helping himself to a glassful of whisky from the decanter on the desk. 'You know how I'm placed. As soon as I get my money, you'll get yours.'

'Of course. Yes, of course.' Giles bit the end off a fat cigar and lit it, before blowing a cloud of smoke into the overhead extractor fan. 'The trouble is,' he said. 'This gambling habit of yours is turning into a very *bad* habit.' He strolled over to the window and peered outside as if contemplating the murky waters of the river.

'The point being?'

'I'd like to help you.'

The man gave a short, dry laugh. 'You,' he said, 'want to help me? That, I don't believe.'

Giles exhaled slowly. 'It would be a mutual arrangement. I clear your debts and you repay the favour.'

'By doing what, exactly?'

Giles smiled. 'Oh, just a little job. Something I think you're eminently capable of. In fact,' he added with a satisfied smirk, 'something that's right up your street.'

Chapter 1

The shrill ringing of the telephone jolted Ursula Lloyd-Duncan awake from her after dinner nap. A sudden and painful crick in her neck reminded her that she shouldn't make a habit of dozing off in an armchair. She blinked, bleary-eyed at the clock on the mantelpiece as she slowly became aware of her granddaughter's excited chattering. Was it really half past three? Surely not?

'Granny Ursula! Granny! It's Mummy on the phone,' came the young voice from the next room.

'Coming!' Ursula called, levering herself up from the comfy armchair. Trust Ella to call at this time. Why couldn't she wait until after six o'clock like normal people? She straightened her crumpled trousers, and smoothed down the creases in her overlarge blouse, before perching her glasses on the end of her nose and making her way to the breakfast room.

Rosie was kneeling on the cushioned window seat, her head of shining blonde hair bobbing up and down as she talked. She was ten years old and the spitting image of her mother at the same age.

It was like stepping back in time, Ursula thought, as she waited patiently to be handed the receiver. If her memory served her correctly (and it didn't always) Ella had been about Rosie's age when she had become a stepmother to her.

'Mummy's won another cup and a rosette,' Rosie announced proudly. 'Can I have another biscuit, Granny?'

'Just one,' Ursula said, waving her away. She couldn't get used to being called 'Granny'. The more youthful sounding 'Nan' or 'Nanny' would have suited her better, but Joyce Trevelyan had plumped for that one. She had been left with the choice of either 'Grandma' or 'Granny', and both of them made her sound like an old maid. Still, at least she had the grandchildren to look after, even if they were only 'step' grandchildren. Lewis' parents lived in Devon and latterly, had found the long journey too exhausting for any more than the occasional visit.

'Hello, Ella,' she said. 'I gather from Rosie that it's good news.' She perched uncomfortably on the narrow window seat as she spoke. 'Well done. Your father would have been proud of you. Very proud, if he'd been alive to see it,' she added. Her gaze lingered on the framed picture Ella had put in pride of place over the fireplace - Robert Johnson in his scarlet show jacket and cream breeches, standing beside a chestnut gelding – Hazelnut, if she remembered correctly. The photograph had been taken at Hickstead, shortly before he'd been killed in a tragic car accident. And now here was his daughter, Ella, reaching the pinnacle of her career as well. 'You've certainly inherited his talent for show-jumping,' she said. 'And by the way your son was tearing round the course on Blackthorn this morning, I'd say you've got another up-and-coming champion in the family.'

'And me, Granny. What about me?' Rosie said, tugging at the sleeve of Ursula's blouse. A trail of chocolate chip cookie crumbs followed in her wake. 'Tell Mummy I rode Spice.'

'It was only in the sand school,' Ursula said quickly, knowing Ella's views on her children riding newly backed ponies. 'And it was under Thomas' careful supervision as well.' She shook her finger warningly at her granddaughter. Some things Ella didn't need to know about. At least, not yet. 'I'd let you speak to Adam,' she added, deftly changing the subject, 'but he's helping Vanessa out in the tack shop. I'll tell him you called, though. Yes, I will. And give my love to Lewis. Bye, Ella.' She held out the receiver to her granddaughter. 'Say "goodbye", Rosie.'

'Bye, Mummy,' Rosie blew a kiss down the phone, and giggled as she replaced the receiver. 'When are they coming home, Granny?'

'Sometime tomorrow,' Ursula said. 'She didn't say, for sure, but I don't expect them to be too late back. Your Daddy's got to get his things ready for his trip to Paris, hasn't he?' And it would be good if he could spend some time with his children, before he left, Ursula thought. Lewis was always jetting off to some distant part of the world. Ella went with him when she could, but more often than not, she wasn't able to. It was one of the reasons why she had announced her intention to retire from the show-jumping circuit. She wanted to be able to spend more time with her husband and children.

Rosie looked suddenly crestfallen. 'I wish we could go with him,' she said. 'I want to climb the Eiffel Tower. Lucy Benson's done it,' she added, trotting after Ursula. 'She told me so at school.' She sprawled on the floor in front of the television and kicked off her trainers. 'Granny,' she said, in the wheedling tone that most children adopt when they want to know something. 'Why didn't you tell Mummy about the cowboy?'

'Oh, there's plenty of time for that later,' Ursula blustered. 'We don't want your Mummy worrying about little things like that when she's not here.'

Although whether Ella would think that the matter of the 'cowboy' was a "little thing" or not, was open to question.

Hank Jefferson was from Montana, USA, and was an experienced range rider and Western riding enthusiast.

As of this week, he was also Hollyfield Stables newest riding instructor.

'How was the black widow, anyway?' Lewis asked, as he handed Ella a glass of bubbling champagne, and chinked his glass with hers. 'Still single and unattached? Or has she managed to snare another unsuspecting gentleman while we've been away?'

'Lewis!' Ella groaned.

'Well,' he said. 'You know what I mean. Your stepmother's had more husbands than most, and they've all managed to die on her.'

'Yes, but they have been a lot older than her,' Ella reminded him.

'And richer,' Lewis observed, running his finger round the top of the glass and tilting his head to one side as it made a whining noise. 'Don't forget the richer part.'

'Yes, well, if Michael Lloyd-Duncan hadn't left her so well provided for, she might not be sitting so happily at Hollyfields looking after our children,' Ella reminded him. 'You have to admit, it took a few years for her to come to terms with things.'

'Like what?' Lewis snorted. 'The "swindling you out of your personal inheritance"– that sort of thing?' He flopped back on the huge king size bed as he spoke and patted the covers.

Ella pulled a face as she sat down beside him. 'You know she was only doing what she thought was best.'

'For her,' he said.

'Whatever.'

Lewis smiled. It was a thorny subject. Families always were. 'So, my sweet,' he murmured, brushing his lips against her ear. 'Another trophy for the sideboard.'

'Hmm. Good, isn't it. I always said I wanted to go out on a high.' She sipped a mouthful of champagne. 'I think I deserve this. Oh, and guess what,' she added. 'Ursula thinks Adam's going to take after his grandfather as well. She says he was jumping the course on Blackthorn this morning.'

'Did you speak to him?'

'No,' she said, shaking her head. 'He was out. Apparently – now get this – apparently, he was helping Vanessa in the tack shop.'

'And she let him?' Lewis laughed. 'Good grief.'

'Actually, I think she's rather fond of him.'

'Well, he is male, I suppose.'

'Don't be mean,' Ella said, giving him a half-hearted thump on the arm. She had a soft spot for her ungainly stepsister, who had so far failed in all her attempts to secure herself a suitable wealthy boyfriend, or indeed, any boyfriend, for that matter. Unlike her sister Caroline, who was now married to the most obnoxious little weasel of a man Ella had ever had the misfortune to meet. Marcus Milton worked for the Inland Revenue and was the sort of person who had earned a minority of tax inspectors their unfavourable name. He was mean, petty minded, and mercenary; characteristics that were not unknown in Caroline herself. In fact, all things considered, Ella thought their partnership was probably perfect.

For Vanessa, however, the ideal partner was being somewhat elusive.

'You've got to admit, she does throw herself at the most unlikely candidates,' Lewis said.

'I seem to recall she threw herself at you.'

'Threw up on me, more like,' Lewis muttered. 'Believe me, it's not something I'm likely to forget.'

Ella smiled. 'Nor me. She brought us together, you know.'

'I know.' He took the glass from her hand and placed it beside his on the bedside table. 'She does have some redeeming features. I'll give her that.'

'Adam seems to like her.'

Lewis grinned, as he lay back against the heaped-up pillows. 'Adam's only thirteen.'

Ella snuggled into the crook of his arm and ran her fingers over his chest. She loved this man more than she could have thought possible. It was hard to believe they had been together for fifteen years. Fifteen years that had swept past in the blink of an eye. Lewis had supported her through marriage, motherhood, and a return to the career that she loved. And now she was planning to step back and support him, as one of the country's leading producers in the film industry.

'Come with me to Paris,' he murmured, stroking her cheek with his thumb. 'It's only for a few weeks, and I won't be working all the time.'

Ella raised herself up on one elbow and looked down at him. 'You know I would if I could, Lewis.'

'Then do it,' he said. 'Bring the children. Come on, Ella. It's the school holidays. It'll be fun.'

'But what about the stables?' she said. 'I can't just leave everything. Thomas has done more than enough for me while I've been away, but his interest is in the stud, not the riding school. Besides,' she added, 'he's not as young and fit as he used to be.'

She knew, even though Thomas would never admit to it that his arthritis was playing up. His limp, which had been with him since he was a jockey, had become more pronounced over the years, and his wife had been urging him to take it a bit easier. They had only been married a couple of years, and Ella suspected that she wanted to see more of him than his long working hours allowed.

Maisie Wilcocks had been a widow for as long as Ella could remember so it was strange to think of her as Thomas' wife. She used to run the village newsagents and

Thomas had had a soft spot for her for years, but it had been Maisie who had made the first move, inviting him over for a spot of Sunday lunch one weekend, if he wasn't too busy.

The weekend had extended into the following week, and then the next one, and it came as no surprise to anyone when they announced their wedding plans a couple of months later. At their age, Thomas said, there was no point in hanging about.

So, no, Ella thought, she couldn't ask Thomas to take on the running of Hollyfield stables just so she could go gallivanting to Paris with her husband and family. It wouldn't be fair on him.

'You could ask Ursula,' Lewis said, twirling a strand of her silky blonde hair around his finger. 'I mean, it's not as if she hasn't done it before.'

'Yes, and a fine mess she made of it too,' Ella sighed. 'Don't you remember how long it took me to sort out her debts? To say nothing of all the people she'd managed to offend over the years.'

'But that's all forgotten about now, isn't it?'

'Hmm. Well, maybe.' Ella sounded doubtful.

'I think you should give her another chance. What have you got to lose? You've said so yourself. She only did what she thought was best. And it's not as if she's after the money. She's got more than enough in her own right now. I think she'd jump at the opportunity. She's stuck in that huge mansion house on her own all day, rattling around the place with nothing to do except keep an eye on Vanessa.' He leaned over to pick up the glasses of champagne and handed Ella hers before continuing. 'I reckon that's why she bought Vanessa that tack shop in the first place, so it would give her something to do. You know how Ursula likes to organise things.'

'Yes, I know.'

'And she's always willing to look after the children.'

Ella knew exactly what he was implying. If she could trust her stepmother to care for their children, then surely, she could trust her to run the business for a few weeks.

'It's not as if Paris is on the other side of the world,' Lewis said. 'We could be home in a couple of hours, if need be.'

Ella fingered the stem of her glass. 'You've really thought about this, haven't you?'

'Not until now,' he admitted ruefully. 'But now that I have - and the more I think about it - I can't see why not? Come on, Ella. Let's go for it.'

'But you're leaving on Monday.'

'So? That gives you tomorrow to get home and get organised. What more time do you need, woman?'

Ella sighed as she reached for the phone. 'Guess I'd better ask Ursula, then.'

'Is that a yes?'

'It's a maybe, Lewis, just a 'maybe'.

Grinning, he topped up her glass. Ursula wasn't going to refuse, that much he knew for sure. It was Ella who was having misgivings about the trip, and he could hardly blame her for that. But sometimes people needed to be given a second chance to prove themselves, and maybe it was time they gave Ursula that chance.

'Here's to Paris,' he said.

'Yes, all right,' Ella said. 'Though I'll know who to blame if it all goes horribly wrong.'

'It won't go wrong,' Lewis said. 'Believe me. I've got faith in the woman.'

Ursula had just settled herself back down in the armchair in front of the television with a cup of tea and a scone, when she heard the telephone ring for the second time.

'I'll get it!' Rosie said, scampering through into the breakfast room in her bare feet.

Her excited shriek came a few seconds later. 'Paris! Oh yes! Yes!'

Ursula placed the cup of tea on the small side table and stood up.

'Granny, it's Mummy again. She wants to take us to Paris!'

'All of you?'

'Yes, all of us.' Rosie thrust the phone at her grandmother. 'And she wants to talk to you about it.'

So that was it then. They were all shooting off to France, leaving her in charge of everything. Rosie had galloped up the stairs to pack whatever it was that ten-year-olds took on holiday with them, leaving Ursula to ponder over Ella's apparent change of heart. Leaving her in charge of the children was one thing but leaving her in charge of the business was something else.

Ursula munched on a mouthful of buttered scone, as she strolled through into the large, stone flagged kitchen, and gazed out of the window. The beautifully tended lawn sloped down to the stable yard, with its rows of freshly whitewashed stables. Neat, post and rail fencing surrounded the paddocks, and, in the distance, she could see horses grazing. She slurped a mouthful of hot tea and watched the stable girls going about their business, or "her business" she decided, allowing herself a small, self-satisfied smirk. It couldn't have happened at a more convenient time. A few weeks would be just long enough for her to decide whether the ideas she had been mulling over for the 'Great Western Riding Experience' (as she liked to think of it) could be put into practice.

Admittedly, she had employed "the cowboy" as Rosie called him, on impulse but that was neither here nor there. She had been meaning to talk to Ella about him ever since he had turned up looking for casual work a few days ago, but she hadn't got around to it.

Hank Raymond Jefferson was a presentable and likeable young American with stacks of good references. Not only that, but he was an experienced and competent trail rider, who would be ideal for escorting long-distance rides. ('My speciality, Ma'am,' he'd said). Ursula had no intention of letting him be snapped up by one of the other equestrian centres nearby. She had employed him on the spot, with the proviso that she needed to clear his appointment with her stepdaughter. So far, the opportunity to do so had not arisen. Now it didn't have to.

If her plans for the 'Great Western Riding Experience' were the success she hoped they would be, Ella would be the first to hear the good news. If the project was a flop, she could send Hank on his way and Ella need not know anything about him.

That's the way she would play it, she decided, as she swallowed the last mouthful of her scone. And why not? After all, she was the one being left in charge.

* * *

'Adam? Adam!' Vanessa stood at the top of the cellar stairs, peering down the dusty steps to the gloomy basement beneath her. 'Have you found them yet?'

'No. I'm still looking,' came the distant and faintly echoing reply.

'Sorry about this, Madame,' she said, turning back to her customer, the last of the day, if she was lucky. 'You just can't get the staff,' she added, in a vain attempt at jocular conversation.

The woman's implacable expression did not change. 'I can go to Middletons if you haven't got one,' she said, glancing at her watch.

'Oh no, we do stock them,' Vanessa said, refraining from adding that not many people wanted quilted winter stable rugs in the middle of a scorching hot summer.

'Aunty Van! What size do you want?'

'I'm not sure.' Vanessa said, fervently wishing that Adam would stop calling her Aunty Van when customers were present. It made her sound like some kind of car accessory. She turned back to her customer. 'What size would you...'

'Five foot six,' the woman said. 'It's for a pony. And please don't tell me you've only got them in tartan. I loathe tartan stable rugs.'

Vanessa nodded her head agreeably, as she deftly booted the first rug Adam had found back down the stairs. 'Not tartan, you idiot,' she hissed.

The woman gave her an imperialistic stare. 'Do you think he'll be much longer?'

'No. No, he's just coming.' Vanessa leaned into the dark hole and scooped up the black bin bag full of last year's stock, that Adam was trying to balance on one shoulder. 'Ah yes, we've got a green rug, quilted, in that size.'

'Green?' The sneer on the woman's face matched her tone.

'And blue. Oh, and we've got a rather nice burgundy one as well. Blue, or burgundy,' Vanessa announced brightly. 'Thank you, Adam.'

'No probs, Aunty Van.' The youth hauled himself out of the cellar and slid the trapdoor shut over the stairs. A faint cloud of dust settled on the polished wood floor behind the counter.

'Burgundy, I think,' the woman said, reaching for her purse. 'I don't need it wrapped.'

Since Vanessa had no intention of wrapping it, that was just as well.

She could hardly wait for the woman to leave before she locked the door and flipped over the 'closed' sign. But her agitation had not gone unnoticed by her young nephew, Adam.

'What's the rush, Aunty Van?' he asked, as he fiddled with a display tray of plastic ponies. 'Are you going out, or something?'

'No. And I'm not rushing.' Vanessa scooped the money from the till drawer and emptied it into a small cotton sack. 'Now get your jacket and I'll give you a lift home.'

'Duh. It's only down the lane.'

'I know, I know. But I don't mind dropping you off. Now hurry up.'

Vanessa glanced at her watch. The current object of her affection would be finishing his work round about…now. Vanessa tossed the sack of money into the small safe and turned the lock.

'Come on, Adam.'

'I can walk, you know.'

'Yes, I know. I know.' Vanessa hustled him through the door and jabbed at the alarm. 'Get in the car,' she said, tossing him the keys. 'Go on, get in the car.'

Adam had barely done up his seat belt, before Vanessa had thrust the small hatchback into gear and roared off down the road like a rally driver trying to make up time.

Her eyes darted to the dashboard clock – five forty-seven. He'd be wiping down the tack by now. If she wasn't quick, he'd have left by the time she…

'Car! Aunty Van, watch that car!'

Vanessa jammed on the brakes as a fast-moving estate came speeding across the junction. They missed its rear bumper by a mere fraction of an inch.

'Didn't you see him?' Adam spluttered, rubbing his chest where the seat belt had dug into him. In that moment, Vanessa saw the look of his father about him - cross and implacable, with sun-streaked hair that fell forwards over his forehead – he was Lewis Trevelyan, mark two.

'Course I saw him,' Vanessa lied. 'I stopped, didn't I?' She pulled away from the junction with a scowl. 'You wait till you can drive, young man,' she said.

'I can,' Adam said, matter-of-factly, as he peered into the glove compartment, and started sifting through the stack of CDs he had found. 'Dad lets me drive across the fields.'

'That's hardly driving,' Vanessa said.

Adam ignored her. 'Haven't you anything decent in here?'

'Probably nothing you'd find decent. Here, put that one on,' she said, pointing at the one he was currently holding.

'Greatest Country and Western hits', he read. 'You must be joking.'

Vanessa scowled at him. The trouble with the youth of today was how little they had in the way of taste.

'Have it your way,' he muttered, sliding the disc into the CD player. 'It's your car.'

'Thank-you,' Vanessa said graciously.

By the time they had pulled into the yard at Hollyfields, the foot-tapping tune was almost deafening him, and Adam was fervently wishing he had walked home.

'Bye,' Vanessa yelled, as she wound down the window. 'See you tomorrow. You can help me re-organise the displays, if you like.'

'Yeah, see you, Aunty Van.'

He ran back to the house, and Vanessa turned her attention to the activity – or lack of it – in the stable yard. Where was everybody? A couple of horses were standing tethered outside their boxes, idly flicking their tails and twitching away the flies. The tap had been left running and now threatened to overflow the bucket someone had placed beneath it.

Strange? Vanessa switched off the car engine. The silence was so sudden it was almost startling. And then she heard the giggling. It wasn't childish laughter – the sort she would expect from Rosie- but teenage giggling, and it was coming from the barn. Puzzled, Vanessa stepped out of the car. She was wearing her tailored navy trousers, high-heeled shoes and a smart blouse, the sort of clothes that weren't very practical on a livery yard. Her mousy brown hair had been pulled back off her face and secured with a velvet ribbon at the nape of her neck. She looked, she decided, quite presentable, quite attractive even, which was the whole object of the exercise.

Avoiding the worst of the mud and puddles, Vanessa made her way to the barn and peered through the huge, open doors, into the dimly lit interior. A trio of girls sat perched on hay bales, which had been positioned in a semi circle around the floor, whilst a group of others were lounging against the barn walls.

Hank Raymond Jefferson was giving the stable girls a credible demonstration of Western line-dancing. Every time he dragged one of them to their feet to persuade them to give it a go, the place erupted in fits of giggles.

Vanessa watched, enthralled. Not for the first time, she was hopelessly smitten, and head over heels in love

Chapter 2

'No, Rosie, you can't take all that stuff with you,' Ella groaned. 'You won't have time to play with half of it.' She shook her head as she studied the mountain of bags and luggage her ten-year-old daughter had assembled in readiness for the next days' trip to Paris.

Lewis was going on ahead with his colleagues from Blackwater Films. Their flight had been booked up for weeks. But Ella had decided to take the children by train.

'I really don't want to go, Mum,' Adam complained, playing idly with the toggle on his jacket. 'It'll be dead boring.' He was making half-hearted attempts to pack, but not getting very far. 'It's all museums, and art galleries, and stuffy buildings.'

'Paris is not what I would call boring,' Ella said.

'It's got Euro Disney,' Rosie said. 'We can go there, can't we, Mummy?'

'I don't know, darling. We'll see. Now try and choose between the teddies and the cuddly pony – you can't take all of them. And Adam, try and pack a bag. We're leaving first thing in the morning.'

'Why can't I stay here?' he muttered.

'Because it's supposed to be a family holiday.'

'Yeah, and Dad's going to be working most of the time.'

Which was true enough, Ella supposed. She glanced across at her son, and the way he slouched, arms folded, against the wardrobe door. He really didn't want to go, she realised. It wasn't just a bad mood. He would much prefer to stay at home. Mind you, she could understand that much. She wasn't all that keen to go herself.

Ursula, however, was ecstatic. Over dinner that night she could hardly contain herself. 'Oh, you must go. You must. How long has it been since you've all had a holiday together?'

'Well, it won't exactly be a holiday for Lewis,' Ella said, as she passed him the bowl of salad. 'He's got to work, remember.'

'Oh, I know, but in Paris – the city of romance – it won't be like normal work. No, you must go, Ella. You'll have a wonderful time. I'm sure of it.'

'I hope so.'

'She's concerned about the business,' Lewis said. 'I've told her she doesn't need to worry about it. She doesn't, does she?' He glanced sideways at Ursula as he spoke. The expression on his face was as clear as day. Mess up this time, and you'll never be forgiven.

'No, of course she doesn't,' Ursula assured him. 'Honestly, Ella, you have my word. I won't do anything that will jeopardise the reputation of Hollyfields stables. All I plan to do is keep the place running smoothly till you get back.'

'I could stay and help,' Adam said, heaping his plate up with a second portion of buttery new potatoes.

'Oh, for goodness, sake,' Ella sighed. 'Do you really not want to go to Paris, Adam?'

'Yes, Mum. I really do not want to go to Paris. Look, it's all right for you and Rosie. She's happy pootling around shops and things, and she'll probably enjoy going to the museums. But I'd be bored stiff. And with Dad working, well, I just don't think it'll be much fun.'

'It will be if we go to Euro Disney,' Rosie said. 'We are going there, aren't we, Mummy?'

Ella glanced wearily over at Lewis. 'Yes, maybe,' she said. 'Look, Adam, why don't you come with us tomorrow, and if it's so boring, then you can come home again, maybe in a week or so. But at least make the effort, hmm?'

'If I must,' he sighed, stabbing his fork into a potato.

'Let me make a suggestion,' Ursula said, as she lathered her salad with mayonnaise. 'If the boy's going to be miserable, he might as well stay here with me. I mean, it's not as if he's any trouble. He's got friends in the village to play with, and if he's bored, he can help Vanessa in the shop.'

'Yeah, and I can ride,' Adam said, his voice immediately sounding brighter. 'I can't do that in Paris. They eat horses in France.'

'Ugh!' Rosie groaned.' They don't, do they? That's awful. Mummy, I don't want to eat a horse.'

'You won't have to, darling,' Ella said, glaring at Adam. Trust him. His sister would probably have nightmares for weeks now.

'You're sure you don't mind looking after him?' Lewis said.

'Not at all,' Ursula gushed. She could afford to be generous. Because if she didn't do something quickly, she had the distinct impression that Ella wouldn't be going to Paris either.

'Thanks, Gran.' Adam presented her with a beaming smile.

'My pleasure,' Ursula said.

'Well, it looks like that's decided then,' Lewis said, pushing his plate to one side. 'Adam's going to stay here, and it'll just be you, me and Rosie going to France.'

'Yeah!' Rosie said happily. She liked having her parents to herself. 'You won't get to climb the Eiffel Tower,' she said, in the singsong voice she reserved to annoy people.

'I don't care,' Adam replied, in the same tone. 'You won't get to play at cowboys.'

'Children,' Ursula warned, clattering the cutlery down on her plate. 'I'm sure your parents don't want to hear you arguing.'

'Yes, Adam,' Rosie sneered.

He brother pulled a face at her.

'It seems a bit of an imposition,' Ella said. 'I mean, we've only just got back. Maybe I should stay at home for a few days.'

'And do what?' Lewis asked, grinning wickedly. 'Show Ursula the ropes?'

Ella drew him a look.

'No, no, you go,' Ursula said. 'I'll be fine here. It's not as if I don't have Thomas to help me, and the stable girls are more than competent. You said so yourself, Ella. In fact,' she added, gathering up the plates, 'I don't expect I'll need to do very much at all.'

'Which is probably just as well,' Lewis whispered, watching Ursula depart into the kitchen with a pile of dirty dishes. 'No, seriously, Ella – if Adam stays here, I can't see us having anything to worry about. He can keep an eye on things.' He glanced over at his son, who almost matched him in height and build despite his young age. 'You'll make sure your Gran doesn't do anything daft, won't you?'

'Like what?' Adam said airily. All he could think about was the long summer holidays stretching out in front of him with no boring school work, no annoying little sister, and best of all, a stable yard full of horses needing exercise.

'Oh, you know, bankrupt us,' Ella sighed.

Lewis patted her hand reassuringly. 'It won't come to that, I promise. But if it makes you feel any better, we'll go and see Thomas and put him in the picture before we leave.'

To say that the elderly groom was less than thrilled with the prospect of Ursula overseeing the running of Hollyfield Stables was a bit of an understatement.

Thomas was mortified. 'Six weeks!' he groaned. 'Tell me you're joking. She'll be taking things back to square one, so she will.'

'Who will?' Maisie said, carrying a tray of tea and biscuits into the sitting room where Ella and Lewis were breaking the unwelcome news to him.

'Ursula Lloyd Duncan!' Thomas almost spat out the name. He had never liked the woman, and he wasn't afraid to show it either. 'That interfering, scheming old busybody. She'll be up to something. You mark my words.'

'She has mellowed over the years,' Ella said.

'Harrumph!' Thomas snorted.

'And it's not as if she's after the money,' Lewis added, taking a biscuit and nodding his thanks to Maisie. Her home baked cookies had something of a reputation about them and he was sure he had room for at least one.

'That's right,' Ella said. 'She's got more than enough to know what to do with. You know how wealthy Michael was, and he didn't have any family of his own.' She declined the offered biscuit plate with a reluctant shake of her head. 'She's only going to oversee the stables, Thomas. I promise you she won't interfere with the stud.'

'She'd better not.'

'She won't,' Ella assured him. 'That will be completely under your jurisdiction.'

'And she knows that.'

'I'll make sure she does,' Ella said, giving in to her craving and picking the smallest biscuit she could find from the heaped-up plateful. 'Ursula will be in charge of the livery yard and the lessons. Oh, and Adam, of course,' she added.

'The lad's staying here, then.' That was some consolation. He was a good help about the place, and with three mares set to foal any day, Thomas would need all the help he could get.

'The lure of Paris isn't quite the same when you're thirteen,' Lewis chuckled, helping himself to another biscuit. 'Can't understand why.'

Thomas stirred a spoonful of sugar into his cup of tea and nodded agreeably. Museums and fancy buildings had never interested him much either. Now if it had been Dublin they'd been going to, that would have been a different matter. But he'd never held much truck with the French – not since he'd discovered they ate snails and frogs legs and suchlike.

'You'll miss the horses,' he said.

'I know, but it's only for a few weeks.' Ella flicked through the pages of her diary as she spoke. 'How's Midnight Prince settling in, anyway?'

The black stallion was her latest acquisition for the stud, having arrived from Newmarket less than a fortnight ago. Even though she had known the previous owners for years (Her father had been a close friend of the family), he'd cost her a small fortune. However, she anticipated that it would be money well spent. Hollyfield had a reputation for providing quality bloodstock, and Midnight Prince was going to further that reputation, of that she was quite sure. His breeding and bloodline were second to none.

'Champion,' Thomas said. 'We'll not go far wrong with him.'

Ella nodded, pleased.

'I take it you've not heard anymore from that syndicate,' he added, leaning forward to pick a couple of biscuits from the plate.

'What syndicate?' Lewis asked.

'Oh, just some businessmen who wanted to buy Midnight Prince,' Ella said. 'They phoned before I went to Gloucester, but I told them he wasn't for sale.'

'You never said.'

'I forgot,' she said through a mouthful of delicious crumbs. 'These are gorgeous Maisie. You must let me have the recipe. No, it was something and nothing, really,' she added. 'They'd been after buying him at Newmarket, so were a bit annoyed when he was taken out of the sale.'

'Aye, well, he's a fine-looking horse and that's for sure,' Thomas said.

'He certainly cost enough,' Ella admitted ruefully. 'But we'll get that back in no time once we start advertising him. Sally's already put his details on the website, so I'm expecting a lot of interest. And let's face it,' she added, 'we need another stallion now that we've got the new block for the visiting mares.'

'Aye, that's true,' Thomas said.

Lewis decided to stay out of it. What he knew about horses and breeding could be written on the back of a matchbox. This sort of thing was best left to the experts. He leaned forward and took another biscuit from the plate.

'Thomas says he's a good little rider, your boy,' Maisie said.

'Less of the little,' Lewis chuckled. 'He's almost six feet and still growing.'

'Really? My goodness. He's not that old.'

'He'll be fourteen in August,' Ella said. 'Rosie's ten.'

'My, don't they grow up quickly. It doesn't seem five minutes since they were both babies.'

'Tell me about it,' Ella laughed, putting her diary back into her bag. 'Anyway, we'd best be off now. Thanks for the tea.'

'Aye, well, you'll have a lot to do, so you will,' Thomas said, standing up and brushing biscuit crumbs from his cord trousers onto the rug, where a small wire-haired terrier that had been lying by his feet instantly devoured them. "Specially if you're leaving "her ladyship" in charge,' he added.

'Don't you worry about Ursula,' Ella said. 'You just concentrate on the stud.'

'I will, that,' he murmured, seeing them to the door. 'You take care, now.'

The fixed smile that had been anchored to his face, rapidly slipped as he clicked the latch and turned back to his wife.

'Thomas?' she queried.

'Tis madness, so it is,' he sighed. 'They're leaving that woman in charge when she's nothing more than a manipulative and scheming old shrew.'

Maisie rested a reassuring hand on his arm. 'Ella says she's changed.'

'Humph!' Thomas grunted. 'Seeing is believing, and I haven't seen anything to make me think otherwise. Come on Sandy,' he added, clicking his fingers for the dog. 'It's time we checked on the horses.'

Maisie followed him through into the kitchen, her expression one of kindness and concern. 'Don't think the worst, dear,' she said. 'It might never happen.'

'Believe me, my darling,' Thomas muttered as he pulled his cap on and headed for the back door. 'It already has.'

By nine thirty the following morning Lewis was at the airport waiting for his flight to Paris and Ella was bundling Rosie and her belongings into her friend Kate's car.

'When I said we should get together for a chat I didn't think it was going to be en-route to the station,' Kate complained. 'Honestly, Ella, you've only been back five minutes, and now you're heading off for France.'

'I know. Great, isn't it.' Ella slid into the front seat and grinned at her dearest and closest friend. (In the back-seat Rosie was showing Charlotte, Kate's seven-year-old daughter, her collection of luminous pink and yellow toy ponies.)

'I thought we'd at least be able to spend some of the holidays together,' Kate grumbled. 'Especially now that Charlotte wants to start riding lessons. Who else am I going to trust her with?'

'She'll be fine with Tammy,' Ella said, waving at Adam, who was slouching by the front door with a mug of tea in one hand and a piece of toast in the other.

Ursula was standing half way down the garden path, clad in a towelling dressing gown, and with pink fluffy slippers on her feet, trying in vain to stop the dog – a black and white collie - from jumping up at her.

'I hope he's going to be all right.'

'His choice,' Kate said, swinging the car – a sensible people carrier - in a wide arc on to the main road. 'But Paris, I ask you. It'll be steaming hot in the city. Everyone says so. I think Adam's got the right idea.'

Ella craned her neck around for one final view of her son, the house and the stables. 'This is ever so good of you, Kate,' she said. 'I was going to call a taxi.'

'They'd charge you the earth for it.'

'Since when did you start worrying about money?'

Kate glanced sideways at her. 'I'll have you know, I've always been careful with money. Or at least,' she smiled, 'I have since I've given up work.'

'You've given up work!' Ella gasped. 'When?'

'Last week.'

'Why? Oh, come on, Kate,' she urged. 'What happened?' Kate had been a career girl for as long as Ella could remember, putting her job and work commitments ahead of her family from day one. There was no staying at home and enjoying a few months of maternity leave for her. She'd worked until the week before her baby was born and was back at work as soon as she could find a suitable nanny for Charlotte. For Kate to give it all up now could only mean one thing, she must have been made redundant, or sacked, or worse.

'Nothing happened,' Kate said, easing her foot off the accelerator as they cruised through the village. 'I just decided that I wanted to spend some more time with Charlotte.'

'But you loved your job.'

'I know. But I love my daughter more,' she said. 'And, to be honest, I couldn't face having to find another au pair for the summer holidays. Last year was bad enough. I swear Graham was ogling Petronella over his cornflakes every morning - so I thought, why not take a break – and that's what I'm doing.'

'Blimey!' Ella said.

25

'That's why I arranged for Charlotte to start having riding lessons,' she added. 'Honestly, Ella, I've been dying for you to come back so I could tell you, and now you're swanning off again, and taking Rosie with you.'

'It's only for six weeks.'

'That'll be the summer holidays, then.'

'Kate, I'm so sorry,' Ella sighed. 'I had no idea. Look, maybe I could come back earlier and not stay the full time in Paris. Like you said, it's bound to be hot and Rosie will get bored, and...'

'Don't you dare,' Kate warned. 'No, you make the most of it, Ella. It's not often you get a chance to travel with Lewis. I don't want you rushing home on my account. Honestly, I don't.'

'I know.' Ella glanced sideways at her and smiled. 'But it would be fun if I could. I might even get you on a horse.'

'There's no chance of that happening, sweetie. Never in a million years.'

'Not even for Charlotte?'

'Not even for her,' Kate said, glancing in her rear-view mirror. The two girls were chattering away quite happily in the back of the car. 'She'll miss Rosie, you know. I mean, I know she's a lot younger than her, but they get on well together.'

'They do, don't they,' Ella said. The germ of an idea was starting to grow in the back of her mind. 'I've just had a thought,' she said. 'If you're not working, maybe you and Charlotte could come to Paris for a few days.'

'Hmm. Now that sounds like a good idea. I don't know if Graham would be too impressed though. I tell you what, let me think about it and I can always give you a ring.'

'Great. And once I know when and where Lewis is working, we can decide when will be the best time.'

'And in the meantime, Charlotte will have to struggle on with her riding lessons without an expert instructor on hand.'

'Tammy is an expert instructor,' Ella said.

'Possibly. But she's not the best.' Kate swung the car into the forecourt of the small village station. 'What time's your train?'

'Nine fifty-five, with a connection for London at ten twenty.'

'Best get a move on, then.'

The train was waiting as they trundled onto the platform, complete with armfuls of bags and luggage.

'I'll miss you,' Kate said, giving Ella a hug. 'It's been ages.'

'I know. I feel guilty about going now.'

'Don't. You'll have a wonderful time. Besides, you need someone to keep an eye on Ursula and Adam.'

'Too right,' Ella sighed, ushering her daughter into the first carriage 'Thanks for the lift, Kate.'

'No problem, and I'll give you a ring when I've talked things over with Graham.'

'Yes, you do that.'

'Have fun in Paris.'

'I'll try,' Ella said. Though, not for the first time, she was wondering whether she should be going there at all.

'Paris!' Vanessa echoed, her jaw dropping open in a most unladylike manner as she hooked the phone receiver under her chin and tried to sign a docket for the waiting delivery driver. 'What do you mean they've all gone to Paris?'

'Just what I said,' Ursula told her gleefully. 'Apart from Adam, of course. He's staying here with me.'

'At the house?' Vanessa waved the man away with an irritated flick of her wrist. 'Wait! No, put the rest of the boxes over there,' she added. 'Hang on a minute, Mother. No, by the storeroom door. Twit,' she muttered under her breath.

'Darling, if you're busy I can call back later.'

'No, it's all right. Yes, you can go,' she said in a loud voice. 'No, not you, Mother.' She held the receiver in her hand for a moment until the shop door closed behind the disgruntled driver.

'Darling?'

'Yes, I'm listening.' Vanessa plumped herself down on a chair behind the counter and made herself comfortable. 'What did you say? Something about staying with Adam?'

'Yes, dear. For six weeks. Ella's left me in charge.'

'Of Hollyfield?'

'Yes, of course, Hollyfield.' Ursula sighed. 'Where else?'

'But you're not going to be staying there, are you?'

'Why shouldn't I?'

'Mother!' Vanessa cried. 'You can't leave me at Grey Lodge on my own.'

'Why ever not?' Ursula said, a trifle irritated by Vanessa's almost hysterical tone. The girl was almost thirty-four, after all, and hardly a child.

'Because…well, because the children usually sleep at our house when Ella's away. There's no need for you to stay at Hollyfield.'

'Ah, but this time I'm being left in charge of the business, darling. I need to be on hand in case of any emergencies. Besides, you've managed without me for the past few nights.'

'Yes, I know,' Vanessa sighed, omitting to tell her that she had slept at her sister Caroline's house after the first night alone in the old house had reduced her to a quivering wreck. 'I don't like being there on my own,' she sniffed.

'Oh, don't be so ridiculous.'

'Michael died there,' she whimpered.

'So?'

'Mother, I can't stay there. Not by myself.'

'Fine,' Ursula snapped, losing patience. 'Then invite a friend over.'

Since Vanessa could count the number of friends she had on one hand, and most of them were not of the close variety, it was hardly a practical suggestion.

'Can't I stay at Hollyfield with you?' she whined.

'And leave Grey Lodge empty and vulnerable to burglars? I don't think so,' came the curt reply. 'You know there's been a spate of robberies in the village. Someone needs to be there to keep an eye on things.'

'I don't know what use I'd be against a burglar,' Vanessa sniffed. 'Please, Mother, let me stay with you and Adam.' She paused and was met by an awkward silence on the other end of the phone. 'We could ask Caroline and Marcus to move into Grey Lodge. They'd love to stay there for the summer, I know they would.'

'I'm sure your sister and her husband are perfectly happy in their own home.'

That's all she knew, Vanessa thought. Caroline did nothing but complain about the tiny shoebox size house Marcus had bought for them on the edge of the council estate. She'd leap at the chance to be lady of the manor for a few weeks, even if it was in a haunted house. (For Vanessa seriously believed that Grey Lodge was haunted, and that the spirit of Michael Lloyd Duncan, amongst others, roamed the long passageways and curving staircases of the old mansion house. She'd heard the creaks of the floorboards and the thud of footsteps often enough during the night to convince her of that, and no way was she going to stay there on her own. Not for a million pounds or more).

'It would be a lovely surprise for both of them,' Vanessa said, in her most wheedling tone. 'I know Marcus can't afford to take Caroline on holiday this year (or any other year for that matter, she thought, miserable scrooge that he was), and this would be a perfect little break for them, a second honeymoon, even,' she said. 'Go on, say yes, Mother, and I'll ring them right away.'

'Oh, all right. If you must,' Ursula sighed. 'But if they don't want to come, you'll have to stay there. You've got Bruno for company, after all.'

A half blind and profoundly deaf Labrador was not what Vanessa had in mind as a guard dog. Besides which, he was getting a touch incontinent in his old age and she didn't like the thought of having to clear up after him each morning.

No, she would do her utmost to persuade Caroline to move in to Grey Lodge for a few weeks. And naturally, she wouldn't be able to stay with them. Two was company but three was a crowd. She would be gracious and accommodating and move into Hollyfield with her mother and nephew for the summer.

A move that, in her eyes, had obvious advantages; the close proximity to Hank Raymond Jefferson being one of them.

Chapter 3

Ursula wasted no time at all in settling herself into the daily routines of life at Hollyfield Stables. She spent hours pouring over the computer going through lists and schedules and details of forthcoming events. It had been fifteen years since she had last done anything remotely like work, and she wanted to prove she was still capable of running a business.

Her selective memory failed to remind her that the last time she had done so it had been an unmitigated disaster, with debt collectors and bailiffs appearing out of the woodwork the moment her fortunes had changed. The fact that total bankruptcy had only been avoided by the timely intervention of Lewis Trevelyan and his sizeable bank account was neither her nor there. Ursula considered herself a shrewd and knowledgeable businesswoman, and she was determined to push Hollyfield Stables to the forefront of the Equestrian world.

Ella had been letting the riding school side of things drift, she decided, peering at the facts and figures heaped up on piles of paper in front of her. The stud was in excellent shape, financially speaking, but that was down to Thomas and his various helpers. But the bookings for livery and riding lessons seemed to have stagnated. Ella had obviously been so busy competing that she'd let the business run by itself. It wouldn't take much to put things back on track, though — a few changes here and there — a reshuffling of staff — nothing insurmountable.

Ursula sat back in her chair and chewed on the end of a pencil as she considered the matter thoughtfully. Six weeks was long enough to make a difference. She'd make improvements that would benefit everybody, and as for her plans for the 'Western Riding Experience' - well, even Ella would be proud of that one. Talk about initiative and motivation. Oh yes — after all this time, she still had it in her.

She smiled gleefully, and then frowned as she caught sight of the puzzled stare from the young woman sifting through the filing cabinet opposite her.

Sally Dickson had been employed by Ella to do reception duties and help manage the accounts. She worked five days a week in the room that had once been the dining room (in Ursula's day) and which had been now been converted into a small office. A new door opened directly into the car park, so that anyone arriving at Hollyfield for the first time would come up to the house, where Sally would be there to greet them with a smile and a cheerful greeting.

Which was good, Ursula thought. Even she couldn't find fault with that arrangement. Prospective clients were made to feel welcome and bookings for riding lessons; stable management tuition or livery could be made face to face or by phone.

The downside of it was, that privacy was hard to come by. A steady stream of visitors was fine, but the constant coming and going of the stable girls, who seemed to have nothing better to do than to drop in for a chat was most annoying.

Or at least, it was for Ursula. She needed to concentrate.

She balanced her glasses on her nose and returned her gaze to the screen in front of her.

'Problem?' Sally said, peering over her shoulder.

'Nothing I can't handle,' Ursula said, clicking away with the mouse.

Sally shrugged and sat down at her desk. She had a bad feeling about this. A very bad feeling. Ursula was hammering away at the keyboard like a woman possessed. She could only hope that Ella had kept a back up of all the information her stepmother seemed so intent on feverishly deleting.

Ursula, meanwhile, was on a roll. Ideas for improvements were coming in fast and furious and she was eager to make the changes as quickly as possible, if only to prove her own brilliance at being left in charge.

Mondays, she discovered, was traditionally a rest day for the horses, many of which had been worked long and hard over the weekend. But it didn't have to be, she decided, not if there was a demand for lessons. A bit of juggling with the staff duty list was all it would take, and they would be covered for all eventualities.

'But you can't do that,' Sally protested, shoving some more paper into the printer. Ursula must have used half a ream since breakfast. The stack of papers on her desk threatened to topple onto the floor at any moment. 'Half the staff don't even come in on a Monday.'

'Not now, they don't,' Ursula said. 'But I aim to change that.'

'Why?' Sally said. 'You'll only have to give them time off on another day and that will mess up the current schedules.'

'I'm aware of that,' Ursula sniffed.

'And what about the horses? Don't they deserve a rest day?'

'Yes, but they don't all have to be idle on a Monday. Nothing's set in stone.'

'More's the pity,' Sally muttered under her breath. One person in particular, she'd like to see wearing a concrete collar, preferably somewhere under the nearest building site. Three days, Ursula had been in residence, and already she'd managed to offend the lady who organised the Riding for the Disabled classes by refusing her the use of one of the groups' most suitable horses. "Duster is needed in the 'beginner riders' class", she had said in her most imperious tone.

It had taken more than a few kind words to smooth over those ruffled feathers. (Mrs Winstanley was not without influence in the local village Women's Circle.)

Sally was beginning to lose her normally calm and unflappable temperament.

'I don't think you should make any major changes without consulting Ella,' she said.

'They're hardly "major" changes,' Ursula retorted. 'They're common-sense ones, and I'm hardly likely to trouble Ella with those. Now be a good girl and fetch me a cup of coffee while I finish what I'm doing.'

Sally dumped the steaming mug on her desk and hoped she choked on it. The timely intervention of the phone ringing prevented her from saying what she thought about being treated like a servant as well.

'Hollyfield stables?' she said, snatching up the receiver before Ursula could reach it. 'Riding lessons? Certainly madam. How old is your daughter?'

By lunchtime the atmosphere in the small office had become chilly to the point of freezing. Sally felt as if a predatory vulture was shadowing her. Every move she made and every word she spoke was being scrutinised and inwardly digested by this unbearable woman. What on earth had possessed Ella to bring her back into the fold?

'You'll be going home for lunch soon, won't you?' Ursula said, glancing up from her stack of paperwork.

'Yes – in about ten minutes.' Thank God, Sally thought.

'Good. You can drop these off at the post office,' she said, waving a pile of envelopes at her.

'But I don't go past the post office,' Sally said. 'And I'm on my bike.'

'Well leave now, then,' Ursula said. 'It can't be more than a few minutes out of your way.'

Not in a car, maybe, Sally thought, somewhat peevishly, as she took the bundle of letters from her and stuffed them into her shoulder bag. 'What are they, anyway?' she asked.

'Publicity leaflets,' Ursula said. 'I'm sending them to all the local shops and businesses. Oh, and there's one for the newspaper as well.'

'But we already pay for an advert in the paper.'

'Not for the 'Great Western Riding Experience' we don't,' Ursula said.

Sally's mouth dropped open. 'The *what?*'

'Western Riding,' Ursula repeated. 'It's the new big thing. I've read up about it, you know. It's in all the magazines. Just think, Sally,' she enthused, 'we can have cowboy trails, and tracking, roping, lassoing. I mean we've got Hank. What more could we ask for?'

'Um, how about Western saddles,' Sally said.

Ursula's gleeful exuberance vanished in a flash.

'And how about horses that know what to do? That would be good too.'

'Well how hard can it be,' Ursula snapped? 'Oh, all right, maybe I was being a bit premature.' She held out her hand for the return of the letters. 'I'll keep these for now. And you might as well take your jacket off,' she added, glancing at her watch. 'You've got about ten minutes working time left.'

Not to be thwarted from her plans, Ursula decided it was time she had words with her new protégée, Hank. He could put her in the picture over what was required far better than a slip of an office girl. First of all, though, she had to find him.

She searched the stables and the barn to no avail, and then wandered up to the ménage and the paddocks. A jumping lesson was in progress, and Ursula watched it for some time, pleased at the standard of the young riders. Tamsin was being very thorough in both her praise and her criticism of them, and all seemed to be going well.

'Can I help you?' Tammy asked, wondering what it was she'd done wrong this time. Distant memories of being a young Saturday helper at Hollyfield when Ursula had last been in charge had never left her. Fifteen years later, and it was like her worst nightmare had come back to haunt her.

'No. No, you carry on,' Ursula said. 'You're doing fine.'

Tammy felt her cheeks redden at the unexpected comment. From Ursula this was praise indeed. Heartened, she turned back to her class.

'More leg, Melanie,' she called. 'Push him on. That's right.' She glanced back over her shoulder. Ursula was marching down towards the stables like a woman on a mission. It appeared that she hadn't come to complain or to criticise her. How odd, she thought. How very odd.

Ursula had more important things to worry about, and finding Hank, the American, was one of them. According to the schedules, he should have been exercising some of the younger horses, but it didn't look as if any of them were being ridden.

Eventually she found him in the tack room, sponging down some muddy stirrup leathers and whistling cheerfully as he soaped and polished them.

'Afternoon, Ma'am,' he said, touching his forehead in a gesture that Ursula found quite endearing.

'Hank,' she panted, breathless from her exertions. She felt as if she had walked for miles. 'I've been looking everywhere for you. I've got a proposition for you,' she said, 'and it's one that I think you might like.'

'Sounds interesting,' he said, rubbing his hands on a grubby cloth. Grinning, he laid it to one side and sat down on the corner of a wooden trunk used for storing rugs. 'Guess you'd better tell me what it is, then.'

Jed Harrison was playing the acting role of his life. Not only playing it, but living it for all it was worth (several thousand pounds being a pretty rough estimate).

Pretending to be an American ranch hand in exchange for the settling of his debts was child's play to an out of work actor and stunt man who'd spent his formative years in the United States. The role of Hank Raymond Jefferson wasn't exactly a hard part to play, either. Jed had played him for real in a Western movie filmed some years ago, so adopting him as an alter ego had been simplicity itself. The mannerisms, the accent, everything; he'd picked up and practiced on set.

One thing was for sure. He had Ursula Lloyd Duncan convinced.

She'd practically jumped at the chance to employ him, with or without her daughter in law's permission.

Admittedly, at thirty-seven, he was a good deal older than the other stable hands at Hollyfield, but it was his tale of living in Montana where his family owned and ran a working cattle and holiday ranch, that had swung things in his favour. When he'd told Ursula that it had been his job to escort the tourists on trail rides through the spectacular scenery, sometimes going off for days at a time, her ears had immediately pricked up.

Hollyfield Stables had a shortage of instructors able to spend hours hacking out with pleasure riders, a fact he had gleaned from conversations in the local bar with one of the grooms. Bookings for lessons in jumping and dressage meant that escorts for hacks were in short supply.

Jed had seen the opportunity and gone for it, offering to help with the rides in exchange for board and lodging.

'I'm trying to drum up a bit of publicity for the holidays my folks run in the States,' he'd explained. 'And there ain't no better place to get it than in a British Riding School.'

Ursula had been tempted. 'Cash in hand?'

'Sounds fine to me, Ma'am.'

And now, here he was - Jed Harrison, currently masquerading as Hank Raymond Jefferson - and a better and more enjoyable role he had yet to find.

Ursula, of course, couldn't help but congratulate herself over what she considered to be one of her better decisions. This young man had film star looks, and a wealth of experience when it came to dealing with horses. He could turn his hand to most things, be it taking off a loose shoe on a lame horse or treating an infected wound on an injured one. And as for charm and charisma, well, he had that in bucketloads. She'd never seen such a fashion-conscious lot of girls on the yard. Normally they were content to slop around in jodhpurs and baggy sweaters, but since Hank had arrived, they were turning up in eye-catching, figure-hugging outfits and plastering themselves in make-up. Even Vanessa had started to take an interest in her appearance, and that wasn't like her. (Although Ursula didn't know if it was a good thing, or a bad thing, considering her daughter's track record with men.)

'Western Riding,' she puffed, then paused for a moment to catch her breath. (All that rushing around wasn't good for a woman of her age, she decided.)

'Uhuh,' Jed said, waiting patiently.

'I want you to start running classes here.'

'Me?' He looked suitably surprised, which indeed, he was.

'I can't think of anyone better to do it,' she said. 'I mean, with all your experience in the States, you'd be perfect.'

'Well, that's as maybe, but...'

'And you look the part, the way you dress, everything,' she gushed. 'Oh, please say you'll do it.'

'Now hang on a minute, Ma'am, 'he said, 'Like I told you before, I'm only here for a few weeks. I can start your classes, sure I can. That's no problem. But I won't be here forever.'

'No, I appreciate that,' Ursula said. 'But if it's a success we can hire someone else.' Her voice was rising in her excitement.

Jed frowned, and jumped down from the trunk he was sitting on. His mind was racing. Western riding lessons. Blimey! How would he be able to pull that one off? He could ride well enough, but his knowledge of teaching was less than zero.

He tried to concentrate on pairing up the stirrup leathers but found it hard to remain focussed with Ursula watching him so intently. 'It'll take a while to organise things, Ma'am,' he said.

'How long?'

The woman was shadowing him round the tack room as he started to hang up the newly cleaned stirrup leathers and bridles.

Jed sighed, and shook his head. 'I can't rightly say,' he said. (There was no easy way out of this. It looked like he was cornered. He would just have to bluff it out.) He glanced up and met her eager stare with a casual shrug of one shoulder. 'It depends what you want your folks to do,' he said. 'Straightforward pleasure riding's easy enough, but if you want to do barrel racing or cutting...'

'Pleasure riding,' Ursula said, seizing the quickest available option. 'To start with.'

Jed wondered if she had a clue what she was talking about, and suspected that she didn't.

'How long will it take to train the horses?' she added.

He gave another shrug and tried to remain non-committal. 'It depends. I mean, a horse doesn't know if it's a 'western' horse or not. It will either move away from pressure or against it, depending on how it was taught. The main difference is that most Western horses are ridden on little or no contact.'

'What?' Ursula looked aghast. 'How do you keep control, then?'

'That bit's easy,' he laughed. It amazed him that this woman was so eager to set up Western riding classes, but obviously had no idea what was involved. Not that he was complaining. He needed all the help he could get. 'Haven't you seen any old cowboy movies? You can't rope cattle if you're fiddling about with your reins. You put them in one hand, see?' He held up a pair to demonstrate. 'And you keep them slack. Then you use your weight and your legs to push the horse into the bridle. It's a bit like dressage,' he said.

Ursula thought it was nothing like dressage, at least, not the dressage she was accustomed to. How could a horse with slack reins be considered safe and under control? Her heart sank. This might take longer than she had, at first, anticipated.

'All you need is a horse that has a mind to please. One that's happy to do what you want it to do, and let's face it, Ma'am, most horses are that way inclined.'

Not in Ursula's experience they weren't. She'd had her fair share of naughty, bad-tempered and uncontrollable animals in the past. She decided to reserve judgement on that one.

'Tell you what,' Jed said. 'Give me a couple of days to try out a few horses, and I'll let you know what I think.' In more ways than one, he mused, as he hung up the last of the stirrup leathers and wiped his hands on a damp cloth. Riding was one thing, but teaching was a whole new ball game. He wasn't convinced that he wanted to be involved in it, either.

'Thank you, thank you,' Ursula said, with visible relief. 'That's all I wanted to hear. I'll get some Western saddles brought over for you.' It was obvious that her mind was running eagerly away with her.

'You've got some already?' Jed's heart sank.

'Oh yes. They won't be a problem,' she assured him. 'My daughter, Vanessa, runs her own tack shop.'

'Neat,' Jed said with a forced smile.

Shit! He wasn't looking forward to this. How could he teach Western, when all he'd ever done was act as an escort? Sure, he knew what to do, but knowing it and doing it was another matter. On the other hand, it was in his own interests for the scheme to be a success. He'd already done a bit of neck reining with one or two of the horses while he'd been out hacking. Having ridden Western most of his life it had come automatically to him, and the horses had accepted his aids without question. It was all a case of pushing the right buttons. It wouldn't be hard for him to find suitable horses on the yard with laid-back temperaments and good paces. Most riding school horses tended to be that way inclined.

What puzzled him most was the reason Ursula was so desperate to get her idea off the ground. After all, as far as he was aware, she wasn't even the owner of the place.

'What do you mean, have I told Ella?' Ursula snapped, as she faced another battery of questions from Sally Dickson, who had returned from lunch in a none too pleasant frame of mind. 'I've only just thought of the idea myself.'

'Well, I think she ought to know what you're planning,' Sally said, stuffing a folder into the filing cabinet and slamming the drawer shut with a bang.

'Yes, yes, well I'll get around to it.'

'When?'

'The next time she phones,' she sighed. 'Honestly, Sally, I don't know what you're making such a fuss about. I would have thought that somebody with your intelligence would have realised that introducing Western Riding to the list of activities at Hollyfield was the way to go.'

'Yes, with a qualified instructor,' Sally muttered. For all she knew, Hank was nothing more than an experienced trail rider, used to herding cattle not a class of learner riders.

'It's not a problem,' Ursula said, giving her one of her most condescending smiles. 'I'm the one taking full responsibility for this.'

Too right, you are, Sally thought, but aloud she said, 'Good.'

'That's why Ella left me in charge,' she added, placing emphasis on the words so that Sally would be quite clear where she stood.

'Fine.'

An uncomfortable silence descended on the small office, broken only by the constant and somewhat irritating tapping of Sally's fingers on the keyboard.

Ursula decided to leave her to sulk. She would go and see Vanessa and sort out the tack they needed for her new venture.

Western Saddles and bridles, however, were not on Vanessa's list of priorities when it came to stocking up her tack shop. She had dressage saddles, jumping saddles and general-purpose leather saddles of all sizes and makes, but the closest thing she could find to anything remotely Western was a second-hand Australian stock saddle that she was trying to sell for a customer.

'It'll have to do,' Ursula said, 'though goodness knows what Hank's going to say. I told him it wouldn't be a problem.'

'Hank?' Vanessa echoed, her cheeks flushing at the mention of his name. 'You're buying this for Hank?'

'No, darling, for the business. He's going to start a Western riding class.' Ursula poked and prodded at the ornate leather of the stock saddle, oblivious to the fact that her daughter looked as if she were about to pass out.

'Cool,' Adam said, emerging from the back room carrying a large cardboard box. 'I'm up for it. Where do you want me to put these, Aunty Van?'

'Um, anywhere. No, there,' Vanessa said, wagging a finger at the shelves on the far wall. Western riding – with Hank. Oh my God – that would be so wonderful. She snatched up the nearest tack catalogue and began flicking feverishly through the pages. 'I can order something, anything. It'll be here in a couple of days. There, look!' She jabbed a finger at the page of colour photographs. 'They've got everything, saddles, blankets, cinches, the lot.'

Ursula peered eagerly at the catalogue. Her face fell. 'I didn't realise they cost that much.'

Adam joined her in looking at the glossy spread. 'Neat,' he said. 'But pricey.'

'Yes, but I'll get them at trade price.'

'How about trying to get one on the Internet?' Adam said. 'I can find a couple of good sites.'

'No. No, I only want the best,' Ursula said. 'Those will do. Two of each for starters, and I'll need a couple of saddle pads, those fancy ones.'

'And split reins? You'll need two sets?' Vanessa's hands were shaking as she jotted down the order.

'Can I have one of those cowboy hats, Gran?' Adam said. 'They're proper riding hats.'

Ursula nodded. Why not? This was going to cost her a small fortune; a few pounds more wouldn't make any difference.

'Can I?' Vanessa asked, as visions of herself and Hank galloping over the fields together in checked shirts and jeans flitted dreamily through her mind.

'Don't be so ridiculous,' Ursula said, throwing cold water over her daydream. 'Who do you think you are, Annie Oakley? Now then, how soon will this get here?'

'I can pay extra, and get it by special delivery,' Vanessa said sulkily. 'They usually say twenty-four hours.'

'Then do that,' Ursula said, 'and I'll take this stock saddle for now.'

Vanessa was on the phone to the catalogue company the moment her mother had left the shop. As well as the items already on the list, she ordered herself a pair of denim riding jeans, a pair of fringed chaps, an authentic cowboy shirt, a hat and some soft leather riding gloves.

'Gran will kill you,' Adam said, grinning.

'Not if she doesn't know.' Vanessa put a finger to her lips and winked at him.

'You're wicked, you are.'

'Yes, and I'm also the boss. Fetch those other boxes up from the cellar, will you?'

'Yes Ma'am,' Adam drawled, tucking his thumbs into the pockets of his jeans and sauntering past her.

Vanessa smiled. This could be the answer she was looking for. Western riding. It would be another string to her bow, and something to show those silly young girls at the yard. With that and her line dancing (her first lesson was booked to take place later that evening in the community hall), she was sure Hank couldn't fail to be impressed.

'I can't believe you've got me doing this,' Caroline complained, as she stuffed her feet into a pair of tan leather boots that she'd last worn as a teenager. 'Line-dancing classes, I ask you.'

'I can't believe you've still got those boots,' Vanessa said, having plumped for a pair of black lace up shoes with a small heel herself. 'Don't you ever throw anything away?'

Her sister gave her a sniff of disdain. 'I'll have you know these were very expensive at the time. Now then, where's this class being held?'

'In the village hall,' Vanessa said, bending down to stroke Bruno's silky black head. 'Do you think Marcus will be all right with him in the house, or shall I put him outside till we get back?'

'He'll be fine,' Caroline said. 'I know he says he can't stand dogs, but Bruno's such a sweet old thing. How could anyone not like him?'

Vanessa nodded agreeably. She'd learn. It had been several years since her sister had slept in the same house as Bruno. He wasn't quite so sweet at three in the morning when he wanted to be let out, nor at seven when no one had heard him.

Caroline straightened up and brushed a dog hair from her beige coloured trousers. 'Now then, boots, bag, jacket, do I need anything else? No? Right, I'm ready. Bye Darling,' she called, standing at the foot of the stairs.

A distant echoing reply came from somewhere along the landing.

'He doesn't mind you going out, then?' Vanessa whispered.

'Why should he?' Caroline said. 'We're married, not joined at the hip.'

'No, I mean, he doesn't mind staying here, on his own.'

Caroline gave her a strange look. 'No. Why?'

Vanessa wondered if she had said too much. 'Oh no, it's just, well you know, it's all so new for him,' she blustered, 'and it's such a big house compared to, well, your house.'

'And?'

'And we're going to be late,' she said, snatching up the car keys. 'Come on.'

The church hall in the centre of the village was the meeting point for all kinds of rural activities. Everything from toddler Groups, to Weight Watchers and amateur dramatics took place on a regular basis. Wednesday nights were particularly busy, with the weekly Yoga class at six, followed by the Line Dancing class at eight.

Vanessa loitered in the porch, alternating between looking at her watch and peering through the slit in the door. As Caroline kept telling her, they had arrived too early. The Yoga class was still in full swing.

Vanessa watched in amazement as the group took up various contorted positions that brought tears to her eyes just thinking about them.

How was that possible, she wondered, staring at a skinny slip of a woman who appeared to have upended herself backwards over an invisible barrel?

'Oh no!' Caroline hissed, jabbing Vanessa in the back with her elbow.

'What?'

'You didn't tell me they'd be here.'

The trio of young girls in skin-tight jeans and skimpy tops standing whispering in the doorway were from the stables. Vanessa recognised them instantly as the ones Hank had been giving a demonstration to in the barn.

Peeved, she looked away. 'So, what,' she said. 'We've as much right to be here as they have. Anyway, look. There's loads of older people in the queue.'

She was right. In fact, the younger girls were in the minority, which caused Vanessa to wonder if perhaps they'd got the wrong night, and this was the Ballroom dancing class. But no, the arrival of 'Donna', complete with red-shirt, Stetson and jeans, signalled that this was indeed the Line-Dancing group.

Five minutes later, and the Yoga group had departed, suitably stretched and relaxed, and the prospective line-dancers were all lined up in the hall in readiness, thumbs tucked into the waistbands of their jeans (or whatever else they happened to be wearing), and feet poised to move.

Donna attached her radio microphone and took centre place on the stage. The music was turned up loud, and the foot tapping began.

Vanessa was in her element. She had listened to Country and Western music for years and had practised the dance steps with a video when no one else was around, so it all came relatively easy to her. She shimmied and shuffled, heel-tapped and turned in total harmony with the music, if not her fellow dancers who seemed to be having a bit of trouble following the steps.

'I can see some of you have done this before,' Donna said, prancing sideways to the left with Vanessa mirroring her precisely. 'And heel tap, and toe, and heel – yes, good…And back to the right – and heel and toe.'

The stable girls had giggled their way through the first couple of routines, and then given up and gone to sit down at the far end of the hall. Caroline was persevering gamely, if only because she felt that she must, and Vanessa was having a wonderful time.

'You didn't tell me you could do this,' Caroline muttered, as she stepped sideways and nearly collided with her next-door neighbour.

'Didn't I?' Vanessa said.

'No, you bloody didn't.' She winced as the bearded man beside her crunched down on her little toe.

'And turn to the right, heel tap, and shimmy to the left…good, excellent.'

'I've had enough,' Caroline panted. She was pink in the face and perspiring from every pore.

Vanessa was bursting with joy. If Hank could see her now, she thought dreamily. If only Hank could see her. Sideways step, turn, step…sideways turn.

'That's it, folks.' Donna clicked the music off and stood grinning down at her audience. 'You did really well. All of you,' she added. 'See you next week?'

'Not bloody likely,' Caroline muttered.

'Oh, go on,' Vanessa said, as they headed back to the car. 'It was fun.'

'Well, it wasn't my idea of fun.'

No, Vanessa thought, smirking to herself, it probably wasn't, but then her idea of fun wasn't the same as her sisters. After all, Caroline was the one who had married Marcus.

'That dog's bloody incontinent,' Marcus complained, coming to meet them at the door. 'Twice in one evening, I ask you. It must have been that lamb stew you gave him. I told you it was off.'

'Well, why didn't you let him out?' Caroline said, breezing past him and into the kitchen. God, but her feet were killing her. Her boots were far too tight.

'I did let him out, but all he did was howl. I didn't want the neighbours complaining.'

'What neighbours?' Vanessa said, laughing. 'There's no one round here for miles.'

'That's a slight exaggeration,' Marcus, said, miffed.

'Bruno doesn't howl, do you darling,' Caroline said, soothingly stroking the Labradors silky black ears. 'You must have done something to upset him.'

'Exist, I expect,' Marcus snapped, who'd had quite enough of the dog's fractious behaviour for one night. 'Anyway, I'm going to bed. I take it you had a good time.'

'It was different,' Caroline muttered.

'Well, I thought it was great,' Vanessa said. She was still on a high having realised that this was something she could do and do well.

'Oh good,' Marcus said, picking up his copy of the Financial Times. 'And let the bloody thing out before you come upstairs.'

Vanessa stooped to give Bruno one last pat before she left for Hollyfield. 'He does seem a bit on edge,' she said, glancing up at her sister. 'I hope he's not coming down with something.'

'Rubbish,' Caroline said. 'It's Marcus. He's never liked animals. I expect Bruno can sense it.'

'Hmm, possibly.' Vanessa picked up her car keys. 'I'll be off now, and thanks for coming with me.'

'Well, I won't say it was a pleasure,' Caroline said, 'but you're welcome. I suppose I owed you one for asking mother if we could stay here. I don't think I could have stood those kids kicking that football against our wall for one more night. Talking to them doesn't help, you know,' she added, tugging off her boots and wiggling her toes gratefully. 'They called Marcus a little prat when he went to remonstrate with them. I ask you. They've no respect.'

'No,' Vanessa said, trying hard to keep a straight face.

She turned her attention to Bruno, who was trying to follow her out of the front door. It wasn't like him to be so restless. Normally he slept for the best part of the day and night, but something was certainly upsetting him.

'He'll be fine,' Caroline said, grabbing hold of his collar. 'Honestly, there's nothing to worry about.'

Vanessa wished she shared her confidence. As she hurried back to her car, she thought she heard a faint clanking and shuffling noise. A cold breeze made the hairs on the back of her neck stand on end. She peered into the inky darkness of the distant lawns and rose garden but could see nothing.

Then she heard it again, a grating, clanking sort of noise, like old chains being dragged across the ground.

Vanessa bolted for the car, dived into her seat and locked the door.

With shaking fingers, she switched on the engine, and turned the volume up on her CD player. A sudden blare of country music blasted out of the car's speakers as she roared off down the gravel drive.

Not for the first time, she was heartily relieved to be heading away from Grey Lodge. Something about that place was giving her the creeps. She was highly tempted to have a word with the local vicar - discreetly, of course - to see if the place really was haunted.

In the meantime, she was glad to be heading back to Hollyfield Stables. She couldn't think of any place she'd rather stay, particularly as the gorgeous Hank was now resident in the 'Groom's cottage' for the summer. The chances of seeing him again would be many and varied.

Vanessa intended to take full advantage of each and every one of them.

Chapter 4

'Ella, darling, how's Paris?' Ursula frantically signalled to Adam that he should tear himself away from his latest computer game and come to the phone to speak to his mother. 'Yes, everything's fine here,' she continued. 'What? Oh, no, I'm leaving most of the office work to Sally. She's very good, isn't she? Yes, nice girl.' Ursula coughed and cleared her throat. 'Adam!' she hissed, with one hand over the receiver. 'Come and speak to your mother. What was that, Ella?' she said. 'Thomas? I haven't spoken to him. No, no foals yet, but I'll let you know as soon as I hear anything. Oh, and Ella,' (She waved her grandson over.) 'We've taken on a casual worker for the summer. Yes. He's called Hank. Hank,' she repeated. 'He's American. Oh, here's Adam now. I'll put him on.'

There! Sorted. Ursula thrust the receiver into her grandson's hand and congratulated herself on the way she had given her stepdaughter the news. A little information was better than nothing, and at least Ella wouldn't be able to say that she hadn't been told.

A little information, however, was often the precursor to bigger speculation. In this case it was Ella who was left wondering what it was all about.

'How very strange,' she said, as she replaced the receiver and looked at Lewis, who had just come out of the shower and was standing, dripping and gorgeous by the bathroom door. A large and fluffy white bath towel was draped around his firmly muscled middle.

'What's strange?' he said, combing his fingers through his wet hair.

'Ursula.'

'Tell me something I don't know.'

'No, something she said.' Ella frowned. 'She's taken on a casual worker for the summer, an American, apparently.'

'Is that a problem?'

'I don't know.' She glanced up at him. 'It could be if he doesn't have the right work permit and stuff.'

Lewis grinned and stepped towards her. 'Stop worrying,' he said, drawing her into his arms. 'I'm sure Ursula knows what she's doing.'

'Ugh, you're all wet,' she laughed, putting her hands on his chest to push him away. 'Lewis,' she giggled, as he ignored her. 'Rosie's only next door.'

'Hmm. Pity,' he murmured.

'And you're supposed to be working.'

'I am working,' he said, tapping his forehead. 'Believe me, it's all up here.' He kissed her fondly before releasing her and reaching for his trousers that were draped over the end of the bed. 'How's Adam?'

'He says he's fine, but you know Adam,' Ella said. 'He doesn't give much away. Although he did say that Vanessa has moved into Hollyfield with them.'

'Vanessa has?' Lewis said, buckling his belt. 'That's odd.' He took a crisp blue shirt from a hanger inside the wardrobe. 'You'd think she'd revel at the prospect of having Grey Lodge all to herself.'

'Hmm. Maybe. But it is a bit of a lonely old house.'

'All the better for having wild parties in,' Lewis said.

Ella sat in front of the dressing table and reached for a hairbrush. She couldn't imagine Vanessa attending a wild party, let alone hosting one. 'Apparently Caroline and Marcus have taken up residence there for the summer.'

'In that case, I'm not surprised Vanessa moved out,' Lewis chuckled. 'That Marcus is a miserable little weasel of a man.'

'Yes, well, Caroline knew what she was getting when she married him.'

'She did, didn't she,' he murmured, coming to stand behind her. He rested his hands on her shoulders and pressed a kiss on the top of her head. 'And I, my love, knew exactly what I was getting when I married you.'

Ella smiled. 'What time will you be back?'

'I don't know. Seven, maybe eight. I'll give you a ring,' he added, reaching for his jacket. 'Have you got any plans for this afternoon?'

'Rosie wants to visit the Eiffel Tower,' Ella sighed. 'I'd rather wait until you were free, but you know what she's like. I won't get any peace until she's seen it.'

'Have fun, then,' he chuckled, knowing full well how persistent his young daughter could be. 'I'm going to talk to Marcel and see when we can move into the apartment,' he added. 'I mean, the hotel's fine for now, but it'll be better once we've got our own place.'

'Yes,' Ella agreed, although she could not fault the suite of rooms they had been given. Everything was of the highest standard, with luxury being the main criteria when it came to the carpets and furnishings. Rosie's room was the size of a small house, and came complete with a walk-in bathroom, dressing room and enormous king-sized bed, which, needless to say, had her in instant raptures the moment she saw it. ('Look how high I can bounce, Mummy,' she said, as Ella and Lewis looked on in dismay.)

The huge sitting room adjoining the two bedrooms had a white settee, of all things, piled high with cushions. Two matching white armchairs and a glass-topped coffee table were equally impractical, as were the pale cream carpets. The television and audio system were the last word in technical excellence – of that, Ella had no doubt - and the pictures and ornaments decorating the room were original and exquisite. But they weren't exactly suitable for a family, or at least, not her family, Ella decided. She'd be petrified if Rosie so much as thought about having a blackcurrant drink or an ice cream. And as for letting her use felt tip pens to draw with, well, that was completely out of the question.

No, Ella was looking forward to moving into the more relaxed and homely surroundings of Marcel's apartment. He had promised Lewis the use of it when he, like most wealthy Parisians, left Paris for the summer.

Let's just hope it has air conditioning, she thought, spritzing her face with a cooling spray of water. The temperature outside had to be in the low nineties, she decided, leaning against the window to peer down at the bustling streets several floors below her. Trust Rosie to want to visit the Eiffel Tower in a heat wave.

She wandered through into her daughter's room, where she had left her reading a book. They had all taken refuge in the hotel during the mid day heat, where the cool freshness of the air conditioning was helping to revive them after a morning spent shopping and sight-seeing. Lewis had engineered a few hours off work but had arranged to meet up with the other members of the crew in the afternoon to discuss the current filming schedule. Ella knew she was going to be spending the best part of her time in Paris alone with Rosie, but she was determined to make the most of it.

'Aren't you ready to go out, yet?' she said.

Apparently not.

Ella stepped closer. Rosie lay curled up in the middle of the huge, king-size bed. Her blonde hair spilled over the pillows, and her eyes were tight shut. She looked so peaceful and angelic that Ella didn't have the heart to wake her.

She'd phone Kate, she decided, tiptoeing out of the room and closing the door behind her. As a self-confessed lady of leisure, her friend would probably be at home with Charlotte right now. They hadn't had much time to talk the other day, so it would be good to have a chat with her.

Kate was delighted to hear from Ella and badgered her with so many questions about the hotel, the food and the sights, that Ella started to wonder if her friend had done the right thing by giving up work.

'I take it you're bored,' she said.

'Out of my skull,' Kate admitted ruefully. 'And it's raining.'

'What's Charlotte doing?'

'Something horrible with papier-mâché,' she sighed. 'Honestly, Ella, if you could see the mess in the kitchen. She's got one of her little friends from school with her. I had promised to take them up to the stables, but I couldn't face it, not in this weather.'

'Oh, you should have gone,' Ella said. 'They could have had a lesson in the indoor arena.'

'Hmm, well, maybe another day.'

'How about tomorrow.'

Kate laughed. 'You're keen, aren't you. What's the matter, short of business or something?'

'No.' She paused. 'Oh, it's probably nothing.'

'If it's nothing you wouldn't be worried,' came Kate's concerned reply. 'Come on, Ella, what's wrong?'

Ella sighed. 'Ursula mentioned that she'd taken on an American guy for the summer. It kind of threw me a bit because I didn't think we needed any more staff, but before

I could talk to her about it, she handed the phone over to Adam.'

'He's all right, isn't he?'

'Adam? Yes, he's fine. We chatted for a bit and then I asked to speak to Ursula again and he said she'd gone down to the yard.'

'And you think she was avoiding talking to you?'

'Possibly,' Ella said, considering the matter. 'But I could be wrong.'

'I doubt it,' Kate said, who knew Ella's stepmother of old. 'Have you spoken to Sally about it?'

'No, and I don't really want to,' she said. 'Can you imagine how Ursula would react if she thought I was checking up on her?'

'Vividly.'

'Lewis thinks I'm worrying too much, anyway,' Ella sighed. 'He says I've got to give her a chance to prove herself, if only for the children's sake.'

'He's got a point. But just because she's good at looking after the children, doesn't mean she's good at looking after the business. You know that from past experience. I think you've got a right to be worried,' Kate added.

'You do?'

'Yes.'

Ella was more worried than ever, now. 'Kate, you don't think she'd do anything stupid, do you?'

'Ursula, stupid?' Kate's voice oozed sarcasm. 'Now let me see.'

'I'm being serious.'

'So am I. Just think about it, Ella. She told you she'd taken on a casual worker. Now then, could this be an illegal casual worker, someone paying no tax, no insurance, that sort of thing?'

'No. No,' Ella repeated. 'She wouldn't do that. Marcus is a tax inspector, for goodness sake. She wouldn't dare.'

The long silence on the other end of the phone was indicative that Kate thought she would.

Ella sighed. 'I'll need to speak to her. That's all there is to it. I can't leave things like this.'

'No!' Kate's shout on the other end of the line startled her. 'No, not on the carpet, darling. Keep it in the kitchen. Yes, it is lovely, but mummy's talking. Sorry,' she said quickly. 'That was Charlotte dripping her gungey creation all over the Axminster. Graham will have a fit if he sees it.'

'I'd better let you go,' Ella said. It was time she woke Rosie up in any case, otherwise she'd never get her to go to bed at night.

'Yes, sorry,' Kate said. 'But don't do anything rash. Let me take a trip up to Hollyfield and I'll have a snout around and get back to you.'

'Will you? Oh thanks, Kate. I mean it, thank-you.'

'No problem. Charlotte can't wait to go there, anyway, so I've got the perfect excuse. Give me a couple of days,' she added,' and I'll see what I can find out.'

'Discreetly,' Ella said.

'As if I'd be anything else,' Kate laughed. 'Don't worry. I'll be careful. There's no way I'm going to let Ursula know I'm snooping on her.'

A wise move indeed, Ella thought, because her stepmother, in a temper, was a force to be reckoned with.

'She's actually quite scary,' Adam said, as he sauntered into Vanessa's tack shop the following morning and hung his denim jacket on a peg behind the door. 'I've never seen Gran so cross.'

'Mother?'

Adam nodded firmly. 'She was spitting blood, Aunty Van.'

'But why?' Vanessa frantically searched the recesses of her brain. Her mother had seemed fine at breakfast. In fact, she'd even offered to scramble her an egg. Vanessa would have accepted it too, if she hadn't had to rush down to the tack shop early in case the Western saddles were delivered first thing. 'What on earth's happened?' she said.

'Search me,' Adam said, with a nonchalant shrug. 'It's something to do with Aunty Caroline, though.'

'Caroline?' Vanessa echoed.

'And...um...gipsies, I think.' Adam stooped to pick up a box of horse treats. 'Can I take some of these for Blackthorn?'

'Gipsies!' Vanessa repeated, vaguely realising that she was beginning to sound like a parrot. 'Yes, yes, take them,' she said distractedly. 'What gipsies?'

'Thanks. Um, the ones at Grey Lodge, I think.'

'Grey Lodge!' Vanessa shrieked, causing her nephew to glance at her in alarm, convinced she was about to throw a hissy fit.

'Um, I think that's what she said,' he mumbled.

'I don't believe it. Adam, watch the shop for me.' Vanessa was snatching up her bag and car keys at a run.

'What? Me! Aunty Van, I'm not old enough to...'

'Just do it,' she said. 'Pretend you're sixteen. You'll be fine.'

'What? No, wait a minute!'

The bell above the door jangled as Vanessa yanked it open.

'I can't sign for the delivery,' Adam shouted. 'What if they've got it wrong?'

'Tough!'

It was hardly the sort of encouragement he was looking for. Adam mooched over to the window and looked outside. His aunt was revving her car engine like a Formula One driver on the starting grid. She drove off like one too, leaving a great black smear of rubber on the road. How cool was that, he thought, wandering back to the display shelves. He helped himself to a bag of horse shaped chocolate sweets and sat down to munch them, before glancing round at the rest of his empire. His shop – and he was in charge - now that was really cool.

Caroline alternated between waves of hysteria and floods of tears. It wasn't fair. It just wasn't fair. Why did things like this have to happen to her?

She'd woken up early that morning in absolute agony. Her knees were so stiff she could barely straighten them and every muscle in her body ached, all because she'd overdone things at that humiliating line-dancing class.

As if that hadn't been bad enough, she'd stumbled downstairs to make herself a cup of tea and discovered the dog had disgraced himself on the kitchen floor, not once, but twice. The whole place stunk to high heaven. It had taken her forever to get the rug clean.

When she'd eventually taken the kettle to the tap to fill it, she'd raised the blind over the window to let some fresh air in, and that's when she'd seen the horse – an extremely scruffy looking skewbald cob - standing munching its way across the back lawn, a long tethering chain trailing behind it.

'Marcus! Marcus!'

Her hysterical screeching had been enough to wake the dead.

It woke her husband up anyway. He came stumbling downstairs in a blue and burgundy dressing gown and blue, striped pyjamas. A stray tuft of dark hair stuck upwards and looked oddly out of place on his thinning scalp.

'What the hell? My God, this place stinks. That bloody dog...'

'Shut up about Bruno,' Caroline shrieked, wagging a finger at the window. 'Look! Look!'

Marcus blinked like a bewildered owl. 'That's a horse,' he said.

'On mother's lawn,' Caroline sobbed.' Oh, Marcus, what are we going to do?'

Her husband looked at her strangely. 'Well, catch it, I suppose. It must have escaped from somewhere.'

'It's tethered,' Caroline sniffed.

'What, you mean tied up?'

She nodded. 'And there's others.'

Now the scene before him was starting to make sense. He pressed his nose to the windowpane, and even without his glasses, could see not one but several horses grazing quite happily on the back lawn.

'What the devil? Hang on a minute.'

'What?' Caroline clutched at his sleeve, wondering what other horrors had befallen them.

'It's gipsies,' he spluttered. 'There's vans and trucks everywhere. Look.' He wagged his finger at the offending vehicles that were congregating on the distant field. 'They can't stop there. It's private property.' He yanked his dressing gown cord tighter round his middle. 'I'm going to have words with them.'

'No!' Caroline shrieked. 'Marcus, they might have shotguns.'

He paused in mid-stride. 'You don't think so, do you?'

'Well, they might have,' she said. 'It's silly to take risks. Maybe we should call the police.'

'Good idea. The police,' Marcus said. 'I'll put some clothes on first.'

'I doubt they'll get here that quickly,' Caroline said as she handed him the phone.

She was right. They weren't in any hurry to come at all.

'Best thing you can do,' the officer on the other end of the line told him, 'is to get in touch with the Council and get an Eviction order served on them.'

'An eviction order!' Marcus spluttered. 'But they're trespassing.'

'There's no law against that.'

'But it's private property.'

'I thought you said it was a field,' came the weary response. 'And not even your field, if I understand you correctly.'

'Now look here, officer.'

'Yes?'

'Look, could you just send somebody round? My mother-in-law doesn't know about this yet, and she's going to be very upset.'

'I should think she will be, Sir, if she's left you in charge of her property and this has happened.'

Marcus sighed. 'Yes, thank you officer.' He banged down the phone.

'Well?' Caroline rounded on him. 'What did they say? When are they coming?'

'God knows.'

'Marcus?'

'Apparently – and I quote - it's not their problem,' he said, 'not unless there's been any criminal or public order offences.'

'But they're trespassing.'

'My point exactly,' Marcus muttered. 'However, trespass, so I've been told, is not a criminal offence, and it's the responsibility of the landowner to remove them.'

'But how?' Caroline wailed.

He handed her the phone. 'I think, perhaps, you'd better phone your mother.'

Had the people from the travelling community known that they were going to be camped out on Ursula Lloyd Duncan's paddock, they might have had second thoughts and gone elsewhere. But it had been dark when they rolled into the village, and the promise of good grazing for the horses, and level ground for the vans had been too good an opportunity to miss.

Now, in the cold light of day, and with Ursula on the rampage, they were beginning to wonder if it had been such a good idea after all.

'I won't have it. I tell you, I won't have it,' she railed, waving a lunging whip at them like a demented circus trainer. Even the dogs were scared and had retreated under the caravans where they could growl and snarl in safety. 'I want you off my land this instant. Do you hear? This instant!'

'Look, lady, we're not doing any harm. All we want is somewhere to stay for a few days,' said the spokesman for the group, a swarthy looking man in his early fifties with a few days dark growth on his chin. 'We're working in the area.'

'Working?' Ursula said scornfully.

The man looked suitably aggrieved at her tone. 'We could fell your trees for you if you like. No charge?' he added.

'My trees are fine.'

'Well, tidy up any brickwork, odd jobs, that sort of thing.'

'I'll tell you what you can do,' Ursula snapped, raising herself up to her full height. She wasn't very tall, but she could look formidable when she wanted to. 'You can get your mangy looking horses off my lawn.'

'Ah yes. Well, that was a bit of a mistake,' said one of the other men, a younger version of the first one, but with a rolling Irish accent. 'It being so big, you see. In the dark, and all, we took it for a field.'

'With a rose garden in it,' Ursula said witheringly.

'Black as pitch it were, last night.'

Ursula's raised eyebrow was enough to send two of the younger men running to untie the tethering ropes.

'We'll put them in the field with the vans, if that's all right.'

'Of course, it's not all right, you stupid man.'

'Oi! Now who you calling stupid.'

'Lads, lads!' The oldest man tried to calm the situation down. 'Can't you see the lady's upset?' He jerked his head in the direction of the caravans, and with muttered grumbles, the group began to disperse. 'We'll not be staying long,' he added, grinning a toothless grin at her. 'Got a fair up at Yarmouth the end of the month.'

'End of the month!' Ursula spat. 'Over my dead body.'

'Mother!' Caroline hissed. 'Don't.'

'Don't what?'

Caroline's eyes almost rolled in her head. 'Antagonise them,' she whispered, tugging at her sleeve. 'Come on, Mother. We're the ones who've got to live here.'

'Too right you are. I don't want you leaving the house while they're camped out in that field.'

Caroline's jaw dropped. 'Mother, I have to go to work.' She couldn't just down tools, not without giving her boss some notice. It may only be a part time job in an office in town, but it was important to her, and she liked to think the company she worked for valued her services.

'You've got annual leave due, haven't you?'

'Yes, but....'

'Good,' Ursula snapped. 'Well, it's the summer, so take it.'

Vanessa arrived in time to see a pair of scruffy looking horses being led off the lawn by an even scruffier pair of men. Caroline was standing sniffing into Marcus' shoulder, and Ursula was looking downright bloody-minded.

'And clear up that muck while you're at it,' she yelled.

'That's good stuff that,' said the younger of the men. 'You ought to put it on your roses.'

'I'll put it on you if you don't...'

'All right, all right, keep your hair on.'

'Oh my God!' Vanessa leapt out of her car and slammed the door shut. 'What's happened?'

'What does it look like,' Ursula snapped, glaring at Marcus as if it were his fault that a band of travellers had decided to take up residence on her land. 'This is typical of what's wrong with this country. Give someone the right to roam and they end up living in your back garden.'

'It's rather a large back garden,' Marcus said quietly, no doubt thinking of his own small house with its tiny rectangle of lawn and a few petunias in the flowerbed and understanding why the travellers might have made a mistake.

Vanessa stared at him, wondering if he was being brave, or downright stupid, considering the circumstances. 'Didn't you hear anything last night?' she said.

'Only that blasted dog,' he muttered.

Bruno! Of course. No wonder he'd been so restless. That clanking noise must have been the chains they used to tether the horses, and the shuffling must have come from the... She paused in her thoughts, aware that her mother was watching her with an eagle eye.

'I don't suppose you noticed anything when you left Grey Lodge to come home?' Ursula said suspiciously.

'Me? No!' Vanessa shook her head. 'Not a thing. Um, why don't we call the police? Has anyone called the police?'

'Yes,' Marcus said. 'They're not interested.'

'Ah!'

'Ah indeed,' Ursula snapped. 'Come on.' She waved an irritated hand in the direction of Vanessa's car, as if expecting the door to spring open for her.

'Why? Where are we going?'

'To see my solicitor. And don't leave the house,' she called through the window.

'But mother!' Caroline groaned.

Marcus patted her fondly on the arm as they watched the car zoom off down the drive. 'Don't worry, darling,' he said. 'You've got the dog for company.'

'But what about you,' she said. 'Won't you be staying here with me?'

'You're joking aren't you,' he said, giving her a peck on the cheek. 'I've got to go to work. I'll see you tonight.'

'Marcus!' Caroline stamped her foot in frustration as he breezed past her with his briefcase and car keys. 'Marcus!'

How dare he leave her, and in a moment of crisis too?

She watched him drive away and realised that she too was being watched, by an interested audience of travellers on the other side of the fence.

With a small cry of alarm, she grabbed Bruno's collar and dragged him into the house, bolting the door firmly and securely behind her.

Chapter 5

The upshot of the travellers arriving at Grey Lodge was the extra security measures Ursula decided were needed at the stables.

'You can't tell me they've only come here to look for work,' she said, 'not with all those expensive properties in the village. They'll be out to see what they can steal – you mark my words.'

'Rubbish,' Sally said. 'Ella's often had travellers in the bottom paddock, and they've been no bother at all, and Richard Hudson's employed them on his fruit farm for years, and he's got no complaints against them.'

'Well, he wouldn't, would he,' Ursula muttered. 'They're cheap labour. No one else round here would work for the amount he pays.'

Sally struggled to hold her tongue. Ursula, in her opinion, was over-reacting. Despite there being not one shred of evidence against the travellers, she had made it quite clear that they would be her only suspects for any wrong doings or thefts in the area. If so much as a trowel went missing from her garden shed, she would know who was to blame.

The fact that her solicitor had told her it would take at least a fortnight to go through the process of obtaining a County Court Order to have them evicted from her land was partly the reason for her bad mood. That and the fact that she detested people who got the better of her, and this unruly group of gipsies seemed to have done just that. But she'd show them. She'd already arranged to have security lights installed all round Grey Lodge and a new burglar alarm fitted. Now she was planning to do the same at Hollyfield.

The foaling boxes had closed circuit television in them, which enabled Thomas or whoever were on duty to keep an eye on the mares without disturbing them. Now Ursula was considering extending it to cover the whole yard.

'Have you any idea how much that would cost?' Sally said, flicking her way through the filing cabinet until she found the relevant invoice. 'And that's only for the stud building,' she added, placing the sheet in front of her.

'Hmmm. Well, perhaps just the tack room,' Ursula decided. 'If they're going to pinch anything, it'll be saddles and stuff they can get rid of quickly.'

'Have you told Ella?'

Ursula sighed. Why did this blasted girl want Ella to know everything? 'No, I haven't told her,' she said. 'I don't want her to worry about something that might never happen. It's only a precaution,' she added.

'A pretty expensive one.'

'Fine. Right, well, I'll tell her. But in the meantime, get in touch with that company and see how quickly they can install some more cameras.'

Having paid out handsomely for the purchase of the new Western tack, Ursula had no desire to see it disappearing in the back of a van, to be sold off cheaply at a gipsy horse fair. The Western saddles, complete with blankets, bridles and everything else had been delivered to the tack shop while they were at the solicitor's office, and Vanessa would be bringing them up to Hollyfield that evening. Security was therefore of paramount importance.

It was the last thing on Vanessa's mind as she gaily unpacked the heavy leather saddles and colourful horse blankets from the crates that had been delivered earlier that day. Adam had signed for them with all the confidence of a person twice his age, and even tipped the driver. A fact that hadn't pleased Vanessa, but she hadn't the heart to complain. The boy had done brilliantly whilst she'd been away. He'd sold two pairs of riding boots, a bag of chaff and a feeding bowl.

'See!' Vanessa said. 'I knew I could rely on you.'

Adam shrugged as he peered into the largest crate. 'It's still not legal.'

'No. Well, it was an emergency.' Vanessa handed him the Western riding hat with a gleeful smile. 'Go on, try it on.'

The hat looked like a proper cowboy hat but had a hard lining inside which made it suitable for riding, particularly for those who weren't inclined to ride without proper head protection. For insurance reasons, Vanessa knew that all riders at the stables would be required to wear hats irrespective of whether it was a Western lesson or not, and this would be the obvious alternative to the standard skull cap. In fact, if the venture took off as her mother hoped it would do, she might order a few more in, to sell to customers.

'Suits you,' she said, holding up the fringed shirt in front of her.

'I like that,' Adam said approvingly.

'Tough,' Vanessa said. 'It's mine.' She tossed it onto the pile that included her new jeans and riding chaps. 'You couldn't put those out the back for me, could you?' she said. 'And then sort out some stuff for the new display?'

'Yeah, sure.'

The bell above the door jangled just as Adam disappeared into the stock room carrying a pile of goods. Vanessa was doubled over and reaching to the bottom of the crate for the pair of soft leather riding gloves she could see lodged in the corner.

'Won't be a minute!' she panted, groping through a mass of polystyrene packaging.

'Maybe I could help.' The softly spoken drawl came from somewhere just behind her. Vanessa jerked her head up, flustered and breathless, to see Hank peering down at her, an amused glint in his eye. 'Here,' he said, leaning past her. 'Let me.'

Since he seemed to be at least six feet four, he could reach the bottom of the crate with relative ease. 'Is this what you were looking for?' he said.

'Um, yes, er, thanks,' was all Vanessa could manage to say. The way he had brushed against her, coupled with the subtle hint of woody aftershave was sending her senses into total disarray.

'These are real nice gloves,' he said, examining them carefully before handing them over. 'Soft, but tough – just what you need for riding.'

'Mmm,' Vanessa agreed, wondering why it was that she could never think of anything witty or entertaining to say when it was most important that she say something. She hung on to the gloves as if they were a lifeline. 'Can I...er...help you?' she said, fervently hoping that her cheeks did not look as scarlet as they felt.

She was ordering herself to remain calm, to breath deep and count to ten. All the while she was telling herself that this man was just a customer, a client, like the dozens of others who visited her shop each day. Except that he was drop-dead gorgeous, and he was making her heart race like she'd run the marathon.

'I sure hope so,' he said. 'My name's Hank and I'm doing some work up at the stables for your mother.'

'Oh yes,' Vanessa said breathlessly. As if she didn't know.

'Well, she told me you'd got your delivery of Western tack.'

'Yes. Yes, it's right here.' Vanessa pointed to the half empty crates. 'I was unpacking them when you came in.'

'So, I saw.'

Vanessa flushed beetroot. Her bottom upended over a wooden crate was probably not the best view she wanted him to see.

'They look like real good saddles,' he added, saving her from further embarrassment by bending over to examine the simple hand tooling in the close-grained leather.

'They weren't cheap,' Vanessa said. She was discreetly admiring the slim fit of his jeans, and the way his white t-shirt hugged the contours of his firm chest and broad shoulders. His dark hair was cut short but had started to curl over at the nape of his neck.

'See the neat stitching here, and here.' He pointed, and Vanessa tore her gaze away from him and examined the intricate detail on the saddle.

'Uhuh.'

'That's a good indicator of quality.'

'So was the price.'

He glanced sideways across at her and gave her a wry smile.

Vanessa felt her heart flutter madly against her ribcage.

Jed was slightly bemused by the way the woman was staring at him like a star-struck teenager. It was quite bizarre considering he'd just met her. He gave her the quick once over. She was okay looking - a bit on the plump side, he supposed - but with a nice smile. And she had a dry sense of humour. He liked that in a woman.

'Do you ride, Miss...er?'

'Vanessa,' she said.

'Vanessa,' he repeated softly.

'Yes…well, actually, no. I mean, not for ages,' she blustered. 'The shop keeps me so busy. But I used to ride. I used to compete.'

'Really?'

'Oh yes,' she said. 'But that was years ago.'

He detected a hint of wistful regret in her tone. 'Do you miss it?'

Vanessa shook her head. 'I wasn't much good,' she admitted ruefully. 'And when you keep losing, it makes you wonder why you keep doing it. So, I gave it up in the end.'

'There's honesty for you,' he laughed. 'Me, I just ride for the sheer pleasure of it. Man and horse and the freedom to go wherever the fancy takes you.'

'In the States, maybe,' Vanessa said, 'but you've got to stick to the proper bridleways in this country else you'll have the landowners complaining.'

'Yeah, I guess,' he sighed, running his hands over the back of one of the saddles. 'Tell you what, why don't you give Western riding a go?'

'Me?'

Jed glanced round the shop and returned his gaze to her. His dark blue eyes gleamed with mischief. 'Well, I don't see anyone else in here.'

'I don't know,' she said. 'I don't think I'd be very good at it. I hadn't even thought about it.'

'Well, think about it now,' he said. 'I'll take you out if you want to give it a go?'

'You,' she gasped? 'Oh, I couldn't.'

'Why couldn't you?'

'I don't know. I mean,' she blinked dazedly up at him 'I mean I'd like to.' She paused. 'I would like to, but…' God, she'd like nothing more. Especially if he was going to show her what to do. Oh, what total, utter bliss, her and Hank, riding out together. But what if she made a fool of herself. What if she couldn't do it? Or, worse still, what if she fell off?

'No buts.' He slapped her lightly on the shoulder and she positively quivered at his touch. 'Let's do it.'

Vanessa swallowed hard. She couldn't believe this was happening to her. 'Um, when?'

'I'd say as soon as possible, before you change your mind.' He grinned and glanced at his watch. Vanessa feasted her eyes on his tanned arms and the glint of gold on his wrist. 'How about tonight?' he suggested. 'After you're finished here at – say – six o'clock?'

'Six o'clock,' she repeated dreamily.

'That'll give me the time to pick out a couple of suitable horses,' he added, picking up one of the saddles and tucking it under his arm as if it weighed next to nothing. 'Does that sound okay to you?'

Vanessa's head was bobbing up and down like that of a nodding dog in the back of a car. This was so unreal. Things like this didn't happen to her.

'Great. Well, I'll see you later.'

He touched his fingers to his forehead in a kind of half salute.

Vanessa thought she was going to swoon. She was actually feeling quite giddy. But her nephew's timely reappearance was enough to concentrate her mind and galvanise her into action. 'Adam, can you give Hank a hand,' she said, bustling him out of the door with an armful of horse blankets. 'He's taking the Western tack up to Hollyfield.'

'What, now?' Adam protested. 'But I thought you wanted me to help you sort out the display. I've got loads of stuff out of the storeroom.'

'It'll keep,' Vanessa said.

'Why, what are you going to be doing?'

'Something else,' she said hastily. Her hair and make-up, for starters. 'Oh, and Adam, you don't need to come back here,' she said. 'I'm going to be closing up early today.'

Her nephew looked at her suspiciously. 'Why?'

'Never you mind,' she said. But eagerness and excitement got the better of her. She thought she would burst if she didn't tell somebody. 'He's asked me to go Western riding with him,' she panted, waving a hand in Hank's direction. The tall American was loading the saddles into the back of the van.

Adam raised his eyes to the roof. 'Is that all,' he said, shaking his head. 'And here's me thinking it was something really exciting.'

Vanessa's mouth dropped open.

'See you later, Aunty Van.'

'Yes,' she sighed, somewhat deflated.

She should have told Caroline first. Caroline would have been impressed. Adam was too young to appreciate what she was going through. It was almost like a first date. She sat down, pondering for a moment. Maybe it was a first date. And with that happy thought in mind, she reached for the phone.

Caroline was not in the least bit impressed, not after the day she had had. A prospective evening with Hank the Yank meant nothing to her, compared to being barricaded into Grey Lodge with an incontinent dog and a hoard of itinerant brats destroying her peace and quiet.

'You have no idea what it's like,' she moaned, twitching back one of the blinds so she could keep an eye on the two boys who were kicking a football around. 'Marcus has gone off to work and left me here, and Mother won't let me go to work.'

'So, you're all on your own,' Vanessa said.

'Of course, I'm on my own. And I can't even sit in the garden, not with the racket those kids are making. I don't suppose you could come over and keep me company for a few hours.'

'How can I?' Vanessa said. 'I've got the shop to run.'

'Oh, but you've time to go off with this Hank bloke.'

'That's different.'

Caroline sniffed noisily on the other end of the phone. 'It's not fair. I was so looking forward to staying here, and now it's all been spoilt. I've a good mine to just pack up and go home.'

Vanessa was mortified. If her sister left Grey Lodge, she would have to move back in herself, and no way was she prepared to do that. The house stood on its own in several acres of land, and had a history stretching back to the eighteenth century, when the main block had been built. Several outhouses and greenhouses had been added later. When they had first moved in to the house, following Ursula's whirlwind marriage to Michael Lloyd Duncan, it had been like living in a stately home. It was only after his death that Vanessa had become aware of various undercurrents in the atmosphere of the place; cold spots, and unexplainable noises in the middle of the night. She might have a vivid imagination, but that was beside the point. She was convinced the place was haunted and nothing was going to convince her otherwise, but she wasn't going to tell her sister that, no way.

'Oh, all right,' she said. 'I'll pop over when I've finished riding. What time will Marcus be home?'

'Late,' Caroline sniffed. 'He's doing some work on a tax fraud.'

'Right, well, I'll come around as soon as I'm free. I'll bring a bottle of wine and we'll have a good old chat.' Anything to cheer her up, she reasoned.

'There's stacks in the cellar. Marcus thinks some of the bottles are valuable. Not that I'd know.'

Neither would Vanessa. She'd never set foot in the cellar and had no intention of doing so either.

'All right, well, I'll see you later.'

She replaced the receiver and glanced at her watch. Oh, to Hell with it. She might as well shut up shop now, for all the business she would take in a couple of hours. She needed time to get ready for her lesson with Hank. She hoped he was looking forward to it as much as she was.

Hank, in his alter ego as Jed Harrison, however, had other things on his mind. Seeing Giles Peterson arrive in his gleaming silver BMW at Hollyfield being one of them.

'What are you doing here?' he said, striding up from the stable block. He glanced quickly over his shoulder to see if he had been seen. Apart from a couple of livery owners grooming their horses, there was no one else in sight.

Giles Peterson ground the stub of his cigar into the gravel of the car park and brushed a smear of ash from the lapel of his suit. 'Thought I'd come and see how my investment was doing,' he said.

'What investment?' Jed snapped. 'You haven't got one, remember.'

'It's only a question of time.'

Giles stood and surveyed the landscape in front of him. 'I take it that's the stables,' he said. 'Stables, barn, indoor school.' He turned slowly. 'So that must be the stud block over there.'

'Yeah, yeah.' Jed nodded.

'And Midnight Prince is kept in one of those boxes, right?'

'Yes.'

'Good.' Giles clapped him on the shoulder. 'Let's go take a look at him.'

'Now hang on a minute,' Jed said. 'You can't just walk in there.'

'Why not? I might have a mare I want to send to stud. They don't know any different.'

'No, but...' He broke into a stride to keep up with him. 'It might make them suspicious.'

'Of what? You?' Giles smiled, but there was no humour in his eyes. 'The quicker we do this, Jed, the sooner I'm out of here. I've found another stallion,' he added, lowering his voice to a hushed whisper. 'Looks perfect. Only a trained eye could spot the difference. I'm having him shipped over from Ireland this week. We can make the swap before this one gets too settled. Know what I mean?'

Jed nodded grimly. It took time to get to know the different character traits of each individual horse. The longer Midnight Prince remained at Hollyfield, the more chance the stud grooms would get to know them. If he was exchanged early enough, they might not notice any difference.

'It doesn't make sense, though,' he said. 'Everyone knows what Midnight Prince is worth in stud fees alone. You're onto a loser by stealing him, because you'd never be able to let anyone know who he was.'

Giles shrugged. 'I'm looking at the whole picture, long term,' he said. 'The first yearlings won't be worth much, but you wait till they start winning. That, my boy,' he added, quickening his pace, 'is when the money will start rolling in.'

Jed couldn't understand the logic behind it, nor the man's intense desire to own this particular horse. The fact that a woman had thwarted him in his ploy to buy it might have something to do with it. After a bitter and expensive divorce Giles had sworn never to be upstaged by a woman again. Women, he had said, were meant to be kept in the kitchen and the bedroom and the sooner they knew their place in the world, the easier life would be.

Jed didn't agree with his line of reasoning, but he could see where he was coming from. Chrissie Peterson had bled him dry. It was only through shrewd business investments, and a cool head at the gambling tables that he had clawed his way back to the top. However, stealing a prize stallion seemed a risky way of doing business, even for someone who was used to bending the rules. There had to be more to this than met the eye.

'This way?'

Jed nodded. 'He's in the block on the right.' He was getting increasingly wary now. He didn't want to be seen with Giles, no matter how innocent it might appear. 'I'll leave you to it,' he said. 'I've got things to do.'

'Course you have.' Giles murmured, his eyes narrowing. 'That's why you're here. I'll be in touch,' he added, with the hint of a smile.

'Yeah. Can't wait,' Jed felt distinctly uneasy. He hadn't expected to see Giles again so soon. Nor was he convinced that he was helping him for the right reasons. He had gambling debts for sure, but he was getting them under control. The sale of his house had gone a long way to settling the bulk of them. Now all he had to do was keep his head above water. If he could do that and still manage to put money aside, he'd be in the clear in no time. He didn't want to be beholden to anyone, least of all Giles Peterson. Nor did he want to spend time languishing at her Majesty's pleasure, which was the probable outcome if this all went pear-shaped.

'Hank!'

He pulled himself up short, having barged straight into Tamsin who was coming out of the barn with an armful of bulging hay nets.

'Christ! I'm so sorry,' he said, stooping to pick up the ones that she'd dropped. 'I was miles away.'

'So, I gathered.'

'Are you okay?'

'Yes, I expect I'll live.'

'Here.' He took the hay nets from her. 'Let me carry those for you.'

'Thanks.' She rubbed her arm where she had collided with the barn door. 'What were you doing, anyway?'

'Oh, nothing much,' he said, falling into step beside her. He wondered if she had seen Giles go into the stud block, but as she didn't mention him, decided that she hadn't. 'I was thinking about home,' he said.

'You must miss it.'

'Yeah, I do.'

Tamsin stopped outside the first stable and took one of the nets from him. 'How much longer have you got here?' she asked, as she went to tie it up.

'A few more weeks, I guess.'

'And then you're going back to…Montana, that's right, isn't it?'

'Yep.' He handed her the next net. God, he was getting good at lying. Sometimes he was so convincing, he almost believed it himself.

'I've never been to the States,' Tamsin said.

'It's a pretty big place.'

'You don't say.'

Jed knew she was trying to draw him into conversation and at any other time, he would have been glad of the banter, but right now he was eager to be on his way. Giles Peterson, for all he knew, was still lurking round the stud, and he didn't want any associations to be made between them.

'Look, I better be going,' he said. 'I've got to saddle up a couple of horses. Are you sure you're okay?'

'I'm fine.' Tamsin said. 'No really, I'm fine.'

He left her tying up the rest of the hay nets and made his way to the tack room. He was looking forward to trying out the new saddles, if only because it would give him something to think about, other than the debt he owed Giles Peterson, and the way he wanted it repaid.

By the time Vanessa arrived on the yard, he had groomed and tacked up two of the horses that he had tried out with the stock saddle the day before. One, a golden coloured palomino, with a flaxen mane and tail, had the characteristics of a quarter horse when it came to agility and speed. The other was of a slightly chunkier build but had responded well to neck reining. Both were ideal for what he classed as a pleasure ride, a relaxed hack through the countryside.

Vanessa, he noted, looked up for the part. She was wearing pale denim jeans and fringed chaps. Her mousy hair had been drawn back into a ponytail, and she carried a riding hat under one arm.

'Hi there,' she called, hurrying over. 'I hope I'm not late.'

'Nope. I'm just about ready, here.' He tightened the cinch round the palomino's belly. 'You can have Lady,' he said, indicating the other horse with a tilt of his head. 'Do you need a hand getting on?'

'No, I'll be fine,' Vanessa lied. It had been months since she'd last ridden and her legs were feeling weak to start with, but she wasn't going to let Hank know that. A quick flick through one of her self-help books on 'How to find and keep the perfect man' before she left for the stables had bolstered her confidence. She could do this, she told herself firmly. All she had to do was relax.

The Western saddle was surprisingly comfortable to sit in and she felt secure in her seat from the start. Getting the hang of the reins was a different matter. Not only did Hank tell her to hold them in one hand, he insisted she use her left hand.

'And keep your right hand on your thigh,' he said. 'That way you've got a free hand for opening gates.'

'I'll let you do those,' she said.

'You'll be fine,' he assured her. 'Now then, want to try a few turns?'

In no time at all, he had her weaving backwards and forwards in large loops around the sand school, using her legs as aids and with only the lightest of touches on the reins.

'Hey, you're a natural,' he said.

'You mean the horse is.'

'Her rider's pretty good too.'

Vanessa blushed furiously. She wasn't used to getting compliments. Her mother had always been quick to find fault with her riding, and hardly ever used praise. Perhaps if she'd had more encouragement, she would have persevered. She could have been a show-jumper like Ella. Well, maybe not quite like Ella. Her stepsister, she conceded, was the one with real talent.

'Want to try a lope?' Hank said, jogging along beside her.

'A what?'

'A lope – a canter,' he added.

'Why not.'

Hank grinned. 'Okay, try for it on the bend.'

Vanessa was thrilled at how well Lady performed. It was almost as if she knew what to do. Despite the loose reins and the different way of riding, the horse moved smoothly from one transition to the next. What's more, she seemed to be enjoying herself. Her ears were pricked, and she seemed relaxed and responsive.

'I'd say you were ready for the open road,' Hank said. 'Shall we go for it?'

'Ready if you are,' Vanessa said.

Grinning, he leaned forwards in his saddle and unlatched the gate.

Vanessa thought she was going to burst with pride as she jogged past him and into the field. The stable girls had chosen that precise moment to fetch the horses in for the evening, and they stood and stared in surprise, as she rode past them, with Hank following close behind.

'That's not Vanessa with Hank, is it?' hissed one.

'It bloody well is, you know.'

'Oh my God!'

'She can do it, though, can't she,' said Gemma, a pretty girl with striking red hair. 'See how she's holding the reins.'

'She's actually quite good.'

'Yeah, but she's with Hank,' groaned Sara, in disbelief.

It was music to Vanessa's ears. She didn't know when she had ever felt so happy. She sneaked a glance at her companion, who was loping easily up the field alongside her. She didn't know why he had asked her to ride with him, but it gave her a warm feeling just thinking about it.

For two hours they hacked through the fields and woods, sometimes walking, but mainly jogging, the horses content to go side by side.

Hank didn't talk much at first. It was as if he was miles away, and Vanessa didn't want to gabble, which she always did when she was nervous, so she kept a companionable silence.

He liked that about her, liked the way she let him have his own space. She was a good riding partner. He watched her tackling one of the horse gates with a steely determination and found himself wondering what else she might be good at.

'Did it!' she said, swinging Lady through the opening.

Jed found himself smiling, despite himself. Her enthusiasm was infectious.

'This is great. I'm really getting the hang of it,' she said. 'Can I do the next gate as well?'

'You can do whatever you like, honey,' he said. 'But first, I'm going to beat you to the top of that rise.'

'That's what you think,' Vanessa said. She dug her heels in and Lady took off at a gallop, powering her way up the shallow hill. Hank was close on her heels, urging the palomino to greater speed, but what the horse had in agility, it lacked in stamina.

'Shit!' Jed said, as he felt his mount start to tire.

Vanessa's laughter echoed back to him as she reached the summit and pulled Lady up.

'Okay, okay, you win!' he said, ambling towards her.

Vanessa had never been first at anything in her life before. She was ecstatic with joy. She was happier than she would have been if she'd won the Championship trophy at the Annual Show, or the Pony Camp Cup (not that she'd ever won them, but she was sure she'd feel like this if she had.)

Jed was amazed at the transformation in her. He decided she was actually quite pretty when she wasn't looking so tense and worried. Poor woman, she looked as if she carried the weight of the world on her shoulders. If she could learn to relax more, he was sure she'd be a happier person all round.

'Guess I'd better buy you a drink, then,' he said ruefully.

'Me?' Vanessa choked, her eyes widening.

'Yeah, I reckon you deserve it.' He grinned as he reached the top of the rise and turned his horse's head around. 'The loser always pays in my book.'

'Thanks,' she said.

'It's my pleasure.' He gave her a warm smile that sent a rush of colour flooding to her cheeks. 'We'll head back now, and that'll give us time to get changed and cleaned up a bit. Then we can make a night of it. What do you say?'

What could she say? Vanessa was speechless. He was asking her out, actually asking *her* out. It was like a dream come true.

And then she remembered Caroline, and the promise she had made about calling round to keep her company. Well, she could forget that, she thought, staring longingly at the object of her greatest desire. But at the same time, she realised that she had to keep her sister happy. If she didn't, then Caroline and Marcus might leave Grey Lodge.

For one brief and horrible moment, Vanessa didn't know what she was going to do.

Chapter 6

'Thank God you're here,' Caroline said, as she edged the door open a fraction and peered at Vanessa over the safety chain. She shut the door again and began fumbling with the lock.

'She's your sister, right?' Hank whispered. He was standing so close behind her that she could feel the warmth of his breath on the back of her neck. It was doing all kinds of weird and wonderful things to her insides.

'Yes, look I'm really sorry. We won't stay long.'

'Hey, it's not a problem,' he said. 'As long as she doesn't mind me tagging along.'

As if she could, Vanessa thought, sneaking a sideways look of admiration at him. He was dressed in black jeans and a pale cream shirt, which only served to emphasise his tanned skin and ruggedly handsome features. How could Caroline possibly object?

The door banged open and Vanessa was instantly rewarded by the look of stunned surprise on her sister's face.

'This,' she said, stepping to one side so Caroline could be afforded the best possible view of him, 'is Hank.'

'Hank Raymond Jefferson,' he said, offering her his outstretched hand. 'Glad to meet you, Ma'am. I hope you don't mind me coming along with your sister like this?'

Caroline's mouth opened and closed like a fish that had just been landed.

'We were going out for a drink,' Vanessa explained, 'but I thought we'd call in and see if you were all right, first.'

'Well, I'm not all right,' Caroline hissed, practically yanking them through the door and shutting it firmly behind them. 'I'm sure there's someone in the house,' she whispered, casting a fearful gaze up the curving staircase behind her.

Vanessa felt a cold chill settle in the pit of her stomach. 'What do you mean, you think there's someone in the house?'

'I keep hearing footsteps,' she said. 'And Bruno won't settle. Well, I mean, he's settled now,' she added, giving a disdainful look at the now slumbering black Labrador that had whined and barked for the best part of the day. 'I'm sure it's one of those gipsy brats. They've been hanging round all day, trying to pinch vegetables and apples from the garden, I shouldn't wonder.'

Hank stood at the bottom of the stairs and rested his hand on the polished wood banisters as he stared upwards. 'Want me to look around?'

Vanessa felt her heart surge with pride as she considered how brave he was, how manly, how utterly gorgeous.

'Oh, well, yes, actually, if you're sure you don't mind,' Caroline said. 'The thing is, I don't know how they would have got in. I've locked all the doors and windows.'

'Depends how determined they were, Ma'am,' Hank said, taking the steps two at a time. Don't worry – if there's anyone still up there, I'll find them.'

'Hank, do be careful,' Vanessa said, her bottom lip quivering. The last thing she wanted was for someone to leap out of the shadows and attack him. Not now she'd got herself a date with him.

'I'll be fine,' he said. 'You go open the bottle of wine. I'll be back in two ticks.'

Vanessa was almost beside herself with excitement as she followed her sister into the kitchen. 'Well?' she whispered. 'What do you think?'

'Not bad,' Caroline mumbled, searching through the drawers for a bottle opener.

'Not bad!' Vanessa said. 'He's bloody gorgeous.'

'Yes, all right.' She snatched up the wine bottle and forced the opener into the cork. 'He is, hmm, how can I put this - better than your usual type.'

'I'll say,' Vanessa sighed. 'I mean I still can't believe he's here.' She perched herself on the edge of a pine stool and watched her sister dig out some wine glasses from a cupboard. 'I mean, one minute he's asking me to go riding with him, and the next, he's offering to buy me a drink.' She shook her head in disbelief. 'And he's got all the girls at the yard swooning over him, and it's me he's asked out.'

'Yes, it's very strange,' Caroline said.

Vanessa gave her a peeved look. All right, so she was the first to admit that she didn't have the stunning good looks of her stepsister Ella, nor the figure of her recently slimmed down sister, but she had made an effort tonight, and was feeling rather pleased with the result. A pair of well cut and expensive trousers, matched with a low-cut top that skimmed over her ample curves had given her a flattering profile, even if she said so herself. Her hair had been washed until it was squeaky-clean, and her freckles had been camouflaged under a dense covering of foundation. A free sample of Passion Rose lipstick from the front cover of a magazine she had found in the scullery had completed her make-up, along with a liberal squirt of one of her mother's expensive perfumes. She was, she decided, looking pretty good.

She took a large mouthful of chilled wine from her glass and then a second even larger one, to bolster her nerves. The faint thudding of footsteps above her head had both of them gazing upwards towards the kitchen ceiling.

'Wonder if he's found anything?' Caroline said.

'I doubt it,' Vanessa murmured. She didn't like to say that she'd been hearing noises on and off for months now. 'Are you sure it wasn't the central heating coming on?' she added. 'The pipes can be terribly noisy.'

'It's summer,' Caroline said scornfully.

'Well, the boiler, then?'

'I don't know, do I?' Caroline looked as if she were about to burst into tears. 'It would be different if Marcus was here and those gipsies weren't,' she sniffed. 'I wanted to sunbathe this afternoon, but I didn't dare go out – not on my own.'

'Why don't you suggest he takes a few days off work, then?' Vanessa said.

'He won't.'

'He might if you ask him. I mean, it's not as if you're going away anywhere this summer. You could have a party – a garden party,' she added, knowing that this would appeal to her sister's ideas of grandeur. 'You could invite some of Marcus' colleagues from work.'

Caroline sipped at her glass of wine and looked immediately brighter. 'We could, couldn't we,' she said, mulling over the idea. 'But not with those gipsies around,' she added, deflating rapidly.

'Stuff the gipsies,' Vanessa said. 'They'll be gone soon, anyway. Mother's getting a Court Order served on them. It'd give you something to look forward to,' she added, knowing how much her sister adored the thought of being the perfect hostess. 'You could have champagne and strawberries on the lawn.'

'And entertainment,' Caroline enthused. 'We could have musicians, a local band, or something.'

'That's the spirit.'

The sudden creaking of floorboards above her head had her wishing she hadn't said that.

Caroline's gaze followed hers upwards. 'He's taking a long time, isn't he?'

'I expect he's being very thorough.' Vanessa took another mouthful of wine. At least, she hoped that's what it was. She hoped he hadn't found anything.

Jed stared at the silver framed photograph on the dressing table beside the bed. What the heck was that doing there? He crossed the room in three strides and snatched up the frame. Unbelievable. It couldn't be, could it?

He swung round, searching the room – the main bedroom - if he wasn't mistaken. The floral prints on the wall showed a women's taste, all pastels and watercolours. A doorway led through to an en suite bathroom in shades of peach and cream. Jed poked his head into the shower cubicle. Empty, as he thought. He stepped back into the bedroom. A quick glance in the wardrobe revealed rows of skirts and dresses, and a shelf of hats. This was Ursula's room, he decided.

Vanessa had told him how they were staying at Hollyfield while her stepsister was abroad, and that her sister Caroline was house-sitting for them.

If that was the case, he wondered, what the hell was Ursula doing with a picture of Lewis Trevelyan, with his arm round a young woman, beside her bed?

'Hank? Oh Hank?' Vanessa's concerned voice echoed up the stairs.

'Yeah, hang on, I'll be down in a minute,' he called. He pulled out a couple of drawers and flicked through some papers. Ursula Lloyd Duncan – Lewis Trevelyan – what was the connection? He glanced at the photograph again. The girl was beautiful – no, stunning – a model, perhaps? A relative?

Maybe it was a snapshot taken on set somewhere? Look who I've met, that kind of thing.

'Hank? Are you okay? Have you found anything?'
'No,' he called.
'Shall I pour you a glass of wine?'
'Yeah, that'd be great.'

He stuffed the papers back into the drawer. They didn't tell him a thing. He picked up the frame again and stared at the photograph, as if it would reveal its answers to him just by looking at it. What the hell was the connection here?

Vanessa looked up and beamed as he strolled into the kitchen. She'd had the best part of a large glass of wine already and was feeling quite relaxed and happy.

'Everything's fine upstairs,' he said, reaching out for the drink she offered him. 'I checked all your windows, Ma'am,' he added, turning to face Caroline,' and they're all closed and locked. There's no sign of anyone forcing an entry, so I reckon you're okay.'

'But I definitely heard noises,' she said.

Jed shrugged. 'Could be anything – wood settling, a door blowing shut - who knows? It's a big and draughty old house. Bound to have a few creaks and groans.'

'Really?' Vanessa said.

'Oh yeah. All these old houses make noises, especially on hot, dry days like today, when the wood's drying out and the plasters contracting. Your best bet,' he added, 'is to play some music or switch the television on, and then you won't notice it.'

'Thank God for that,' Caroline sighed. 'You know, I was beginning to think I was hearing ghosts, or something.'

Vanessa gave a short, nervous laugh. 'Ghosts.'

'Silly, isn't it?'

'Hmm.' She drained her glass.

'It's a beautiful place,' Jed said, wandering over to the window and looking outside. 'That must be the gipsy camp over there, is it?'

'Unfortunately,' Caroline muttered. 'They turned up in the middle of the night. Look, they've got a bonfire going now.' She pointed to where the wisps of smoke were rising above the privet hedge. 'You'd think there'd be some law against it.'

'I don't expect they'll stay long,' he said.

It was small comfort to an already distressed and unhappy Caroline. She had thought that moving to Grey Lodge would be delightful, particularly over the summer months when the garden was a riot of colour. The vast sweeping lawns and secluded gardens would be a godsend, after the noise and troublesome neighbours at her home in Laverne Meadows. Last week an abandoned car had been left outside their front door and been smashed and trashed by the morning. An old mattress had been dumped in the alleyway and set on fire by local youths, who thought it amusing to toss their empty beer bottles into Marcus' small, but tasteful garden pond.

'Mother won't allow them to stay any longer than she has to,' Vanessa said, topping up the glasses, and wondering if she should open another bottle.

Caroline took the decision from her, by producing a bottle of chilled Chablis from the fridge. 'Marcus was saving this,' she said, 'but I think we deserve it.'

'Not for me, thanks,' Jed said, holding a hand over his glass. He wanted to keep a clear head. Seeing the picture of Lewis Trevelyan in the bedroom had been a bit of a shock to him. He and Lewis went way back. As a jobbing actor and stunt rider, their paths had crossed on many an occasion. It was less than two years since he had worked with him on the set of 'Divided,' doubling up for the main star in several action scenes. Swimming a horse across a flooded, raging river was one that sprang to mind – both him and the horse had nearly drowned. (That's what came of filming after a torrential storm had swept the valley the night before filming was scheduled to take place, he recalled ruefully.) What he didn't get was the link between Ursula and Lewis. Unless – he thought back, trying to remember something he'd heard – and then it hit him. Lewis Trevelyan had married a professional horsewoman. He gulped back the last of his wine. A rather uncomfortable thought was starting to stir in the back of his mind. Was Lewis somehow related to these people? He glanced over at Vanessa. 'So, um, you normally live here, do you?'

'Yes.' She sipped the new wine and nodded approvingly. 'But with Ella away in Paris I thought I'd be more useful helping mother if I stayed at Hollyfield.'

'And Ella's your sister, right?'

'Stepsister,' she said. 'I don't suppose you've heard of her, but she's quite big in the show-jumping world. She was on the short list for the Olympic team,' she added.

'She didn't qualify,' Caroline muttered, dipping her finger in her wine glass and trying to retrieve a bit of cork that was irritating her. 'She's given up competing now, anyway.' She scooped the offending bit of cork out and flicked it away with a pointed fingernail.

'Only because she wants to spend more time with her family,' Vanessa said.

'She's got kids?' (Kids invariably meant a husband, Jed thought).

'Two, a boy and a girl. You've met Adam' she added. 'He's the young lad who brought the tack up to the stables for you.'

'Oh yeah,' Jed said, picturing the tall, good looking young man. 'He helps Thomas out quite a bit.'

'That's right. He's staying here for the summer, and Rosie's gone to Paris with her parents. She's only ten.'

'Is that for a holiday, or something?' Jed asked. It was the "something" he was most interested in.

'Work,' Caroline said, reaching into the cupboard. 'Anyone want a bag of crisps or a few nibbles?'

Vanessa was about to say, "yes", until she saw Hank shaking his head. 'No thanks,' she sighed. She was starving. All that riding had given her an appetite. She had spent so long getting ready that she hadn't had time to eat. Consequently, the wine was going straight to her head and she was starting to feel quite dizzy.

'I thought you said she'd given up competing.'

'She has.' Caroline opened a bag of crisps and started to munch on them. 'It's Lewis that's working. That's her husband,' she explained, offering the bag around.

Vanessa thought a teeny-weeny handful wouldn't do her any harm. She must have burned a load of calories while she was out riding. She selected a few small crisps and felt her mouth water at the prospect of eating them.

Hank was showing more interest in what Caroline was saying, than on what his date was doing. Vanessa took another handful from the bag.

'He's a film producer,' Caroline was saying.

Jed breathed in deeply and tried to keep his features calm and impassive. 'You don't say. A film producer, huh.'

'Yes. Quite famous, actually. Isn't he, Vanessa?'

'Hmm, what? Oh yes. Lewis is,' she mumbled, through a mouthful of crisps and wine. 'He's always at some awards ceremony. We've met loads of stars through him. Well, one or two,' she corrected herself. 'They're always popping in at Hollyfield when he's at home. Simon De Silva learned to ride at the stables. You must have heard of him.'

'Yeah, yeah, I've heard of him,' Jed said. He'd been lined up to do a body double for him once, but the actor had insisted on doing his own stunts.

This information that was coming to light was shedding a whole new perspective on things. Jed liked Lewis Trevelyan. Hell, he'd worked with him often enough to know a decent bloke when he met one, and in his experience, there weren't many of them in the film business. If he really was married to the owner of Hollyfield Stud, then no way was he going to be ripping off her prize stallion from her. No way. Giles Peterson would have to find some other mug to do his dirty work for him. Except, he realised, that not many people knew how to handle a Thoroughbred stallion. They could kick and rear and bite just as soon as look at you if they had a mind to. This wasn't some lazy old riding school pony. Midnight Prince was one of the elite in the racing world. Okay, so he was getting on a bit, but he was still a pretty valuable prospect in breeding circles. (Valuable enough for Giles Peterson to break the law over.) He would need to think this through very carefully.

'How long are they staying in France?' he asked.

Caroline shrugged. 'A few weeks, I think.'

'Hmm,' Vanessa agreed, nodding her head. 'I can't see them coming back before the end of August.'

'Rosie will need to be home for school,' Caroline said. 'It'll be early September at the latest.'

That was some consolation. At least it gave him time to consider his next move. If he could negotiate a deal with the bank his problems would be solved once and for all. The trouble was his bank manager was proving to be an unwilling ally. The lack of a steady income didn't help. Nor was the fact that his only collateral was his house, and that had been sold to pay off his debts. No permanent address, and no income invariably meant no deal. But there were other ways of raising cash, Jed mused. If only he could think of them.

The sudden banging and rattling of the front door jerked everyone out of their (for some, alcohol induced) thoughts.

'Come on, open up! It's me.'

'Marcus!' Caroline gulped, jumping to her feet in alarm. 'I left the chain on the door. I'm coming, darling,' she called. 'Hang on a minute, I'm coming.'

Jed nudged Vanessa's arm. 'Time for us to go,' he murmured.

'Hmm, what? Oh yes, yes, of course.' Vanessa leapt down from her stool and wished she hadn't. Her legs felt quite wobbly. She should have known that drinking on an empty stomach was a bad idea.

'What's going on?' Marcus said, plonking his leather briefcase down on the polished wood of the hall floor. 'I couldn't open the bloody door.' His beady-eyed gaze took in his flustered looking wife, a glassy-eyed Vanessa, and a tall and handsome stranger.

'Nothing, darling,' Caroline soothed. 'I thought I heard noises, and Vanessa came round to keep me company until you got back.'

'Vanessa and?' he said pointedly.

'Hank,' the stranger said, stepping forward with an outstretched hand.

Marcus felt his damp fingers gripped in a firm, hard handshake that had him wondering if his bones were going to survive. He jerked his head in the direction of the garden. 'You're not one of those...'

'Gipsies?' Jed grinned. 'No, Sir. I work at the stables for Vanessa's mother.'

'Stepsister, you mean,' Marcus said.

Jed nodded. 'I guess so, though I haven't had the pleasure of meeting her yet.'

Marcus perused him like a cat eyeing up a cornered rat. 'I take it you're an American,' he said, 'judging by your accent.'

'He's from Montana,' Vanessa giggled. 'Cowboy country.'

'Really.' Marcus picked up his briefcase and made his way into the kitchen with it. 'You've got the necessary permission to work here, I suppose,' he added, almost as an afterthought.

Jed raised an eyebrow at Vanessa. 'Yes, Sir,' he said, grabbing hold of her arm. 'Come on, let's go,' he hissed.

Vanessa almost tripped over herself. 'Oops. Well, looks like we're off now,' she called to her sister, who had followed Marcus into the kitchen. 'Thanks for the wine.'

'Wine?' Marcus repeated. 'Caroline! Have you been drinking?'

'We did have a couple of glasses, darling.'

Jed pulled open the front door. 'Bye, now,' he called.

'Bye!'

'My Chablis!' Marcus bellowed. His indignant roar followed Vanessa and Hank down the drive as they headed back to the car. 'I can't believe it. They've drunk my bloody Chablis!'

'Pleasant chap,' Jed said, pushing his keys into the ignition of the van he had borrowed for the evening from Jimmy McPherson, one of the stud grooms.

Vanessa giggled as she flopped back against the headrest. 'He's horrible. In fact, he's a mean little gnome of a man. I'd rather stay single,' she sniggered, 'than face waking up with him every morning.'

'There's nothing wrong with being single,' Jed said.

Vanessa nodded her head vigorously. 'Nothing whatsoever.' Whom was she trying to kid? 'I like my own company.'

Jed grinned. 'Yeah, well, I kind of like your company too. So where shall we go to eat? I've heard the Red Fox is pretty good.'

'The Red Fox,' she sighed, basking in his compliment, 'sounds perfect to me.'

Sunlight streaming through the blinds stirred Vanessa into consciousness. She blinked sleepily and turned over in the bed, feeling her legs encountering something firm and warm beside her. 'Get off, Bruno,' she murmured, pushing the dog to one side. Except it wasn't the dog.

'Morning,' Hank said.

Vanessa's eyes shot open.

He was propped up on one elbow, peering down at her. Naked. Or at least, his chest was naked. Vanessa didn't like to think about the rest of him, lying half covered with the duvet. Was he – had they? She searched her brain for memories, however slight, but everything eluded her. A bank of fog lurked behind her temples. A thudding pain jarred into her eye sockets.

'M...morning,' she croaked, tugging the covers up to her chin. Oh my God! Oh my God! She was in bed with him. Her eyes darted round the room. His bed! Oh my God! Oh my God! She hadn't even got home.

'Coffee?' he suggested, flinging back the covers on his side of the bed. Vanessa's eyes darted out from under her eyelids – boxer shorts – he was wearing boxers.

'Uhuh,' she managed, trying desperately to keep her eyes averted from the sight of his broad shoulders and powerful looking limbs.

'I'll put the kettle on,' he said, reaching for his jeans, which were draped over a nearby chair.

Vanessa watched in shocked silence as he pulled them on and buckled his belt. Her mind was racing away like a runaway train. She slid her hands down her body and discovered, to her relief, that she was still wearing her clothes - everything but her shoes, she realised, which were sitting tidily together at the side of the bed.

'Milk and sugar?' he asked, pausing in the doorway.

'Black, thanks,' she said, blushing furiously. Oh my God! What must he think of her? She groaned as the pounding resumed behind her temples. What had she been drinking? There was the wine at Caroline's house – and then she'd had a couple of drinks at the Red Fox – and after that, she couldn't remember much at all.

'Shit!' she muttered, pushing the duvet to one side and attempting to sit up. Her head clumped against the sloping ceiling round the eaves. It was with a horrible feeling of 'déjà vu', that she realised she was in her old bedroom in the Groom's Cottage; the one Ella let the stable staff use when they were required to stay overnight, particularly in the foaling season.

She plucked at the fluff covering her smart new trousers and tried to straighten the creases in her top. Her mouth felt disgustingly sour and dry. She desperately needed a glass of water – several glasses of water.

The bathroom was across the landing. Vanessa groped for her shoes and squeezed her feet into them before making her way there and locking the door.

A glimpse at her reflection in the mirror above the hand basin told her all she needed to know. She looked awful. Her face was pale and sickly, and her eyes were bloodshot. Her hair was all tangled and hung like rats' tails.

With a groan, she splashed water on her face, and then drank from the cold tap, swilling the water round and round her mouth before spitting it down the plughole. A tube of half used mint toothpaste lay on the side of the basin. Vanessa squirted some of it onto her finger and rubbed it into her teeth and gums. Then she straightened up and tried to comb her fingers through her hair.

'Coffee's brewed,' Hank called.

'Coming.'

Vanessa clutched onto the banister for support as she eased herself down the stairs. Her legs were feeling wobbly and her head was throbbing. There was no way, she decided, that she could go to work.

Hank was standing by the kitchen table, stirring sugar into one of two mugs.

'Oh God' Vanessa groaned, slumping into the nearest chair and holding her head in her hands. 'Hank, I'm so sorry.' She was feeling horribly, painfully ashamed of herself.

'What for?' he said, sliding the mug across the table towards her. 'You had one too many to drink, but so what? It's not a crime. No one got hurt.'

'I must have made a right fool of myself.'

'Actually, you were quite amusing,' he said, which didn't make her feel any better. 'We've all been there, honey,' he said.

His voice was kind – much kinder than Vanessa felt she deserved. A lump rose in her throat, and she felt a tear pricking at her eyelids. She was sure she had ruined her chances by behaving like a drunken little slut. She was no better than the teenagers she had scorned and derided in the past – the girls who spilled out of the nightclubs in town with their skirts halfway up their backsides and their knickers on show – the ones who were so drunk they didn't care who saw them.

She sniffed and rubbed the back of her hand across her eyes.

'Here.' Hank handed her a wad of kitchen roll.

'Thanks.' She took it gratefully. The tears, once started, wouldn't stop. Vanessa felt so ashamed of herself she couldn't bring herself to look at him.

'Look,' he said, 'don't beat yourself up about it. You'll feel bad enough today, and I reckon that'll be punishment enough for you. I can't cure your hangover,' he added, 'but I can make you feel better.'

'How?' she sniffed.

'By saying we go out again another night.'

Vanessa peered up at him through a mist of tears, not sure if he was being serious with her or not. 'Do you mean that?'

'Yep. Course I do,' he said, his deep blue eyes gleaming warmly at her. 'It was fun – well, let's say it was fun till you started passing out on me.' He patted her tissue-clutching hand reassuringly as he spoke. 'I couldn't take you home in that state, so I brought you back here. Nothing happened,' he added.

Vanessa blinked. 'It didn't?'

Hank grinned. 'I kind of like my women conscious and willing.'

Vanessa felt like curling up and dying of embarrassment. Her cheeks flushed scarlet. 'I don't usually drink,' she said. 'Well, not much, anyway.'

'That's what I figured. It's a good job one of us kept a clear head. Go on, finish your coffee,' he said, giving her arm a squeeze as he strolled over to the door. 'I'd better get dressed. I've got to get ready for work.'

Work. Vanessa glanced at her watch. She didn't think she could face it. But if she didn't open, she might lose some valuable customers. She'd have to ask Adam to help. He could stay in the shop while she lay down and died in the back room. A migraine seemed the most sensible explanation.

She fumbled through her bag and found her mobile phone. A short text message would suffice for now, she decided. It was all she could do to focus on the letters.

'Need a lift?' Hank said, breezing back down the stairs in a denim shirt and faded jeans. A white t-shirt showed at his neck. 'I've still got the keys to Jimmy's van.'

Vanessa nodded weakly. She felt like death warmed up. Driving was way beyond her current capabilities.

If she'd been more aware of her surroundings, she might have noticed one of the stable girls strolling down to the yard as Hank helped her out of the cottage and into the van. She would have seen the expression of incredulity on her face and observed how she broke into a run towards the stable block.

But all Vanessa was conscious of was the fact that Hank had his arms round her, that he'd acted like a gentleman and that, despite her inexcusable behaviour, he wanted to take her out again.

Chapter 7

'Right, Charlotte, I think we'll try you on Flossie,' Tamsin said, leading her group of beginner riders into the sand school, where several helpers stood holding a line of waiting ponies. 'That's the small grey one over there.' She pointed with her riding whip. 'Laura will help you on.'

Kate gave her daughter an encouraging little wave and then took a seat on the wooden benches surrounding the arena with the rest of the parents, grandparents, and siblings who had come to watch the lesson.

She wished it were Ella who was standing there, entrusted with the care and safety of her only child. Ella had known Charlotte from birth and would have picked out a suitable pony for her. What if this Flossie was excitable, or frisky? (Kate, who had never ridden, had no idea what constituted a placid animal – they all seemed scary and dangerous to her). She wasn't convinced that she could believe Tamsin either; even though she had assured her that all the beginner's ponies were quiet and even-tempered. One of the little Shetlands was stamping its leg in a most disconcerting manner.

'Good luck, darling,' she mouthed, giving her daughter another little wave.

Charlotte was beaming the most wonderful smile as she was hoisted aboard the little grey pony. Kate wondered if her riding hat was perhaps a size too large for her. It looked huge on her small head.

The class consisted of six children between the ages of five and eight, each with their own helper walking alongside them. The helpers tended to be teenage girls with more experience of horses, though Kate felt sure that none of them were older than about twelve or thirteen.

'It's my daughter's first lesson,' she said, to the dark-haired woman in a wax jacket who was sitting beside her on the bench. 'I'm a bit nervous for her.'

'She'll be fine,' came the encouraging reply. 'Tamsin is very good with the young ones. My daughter, Molly, has been coming here for several weeks now.'

'Which one is she?' Kate asked, peering over at the group, who were all now mounted and in the process of being shown how to hold the reins.

'There – on the Dartmoor pony.'

Since Kate didn't know a Dartmoor pony from a donkey, this information didn't help her very much. 'That's Charlotte on the grey one,' she said.

'Oh, that's Flossie,' the woman said. 'Molly loves riding her. She's such a sweetie.'

Kate relaxed a little. That didn't sound too bad.

'I'm Paula,' she added. 'Paula Ward.'

'Kate Mayhew. Nice to meet you,' Kate said. 'I wouldn't be surprised if our girls know each other, if they're both at the village school.'

'Molly goes to St Mary's,' Paula said.

Since St Mary's was the expensive fee-paying school in the next town, Kate decided her new-found friend and her probably didn't have much in common after all.

'It's a wonderful little prep school – I could get you a prospectus if you're interested. I'm on the parent/teacher committee.'

'That's very kind of you,' Kate said, 'but my husband and I happen to like the village primary school and Charlotte's very happy there,' she added, emphasising the word "very".

The expression on Paula's face seemed to say, 'well, suit yourself, then.'

Kate smiled benignly and turned her attention back to the class. It was all rather boring, she decided, fidgeting uncomfortably in her seat. The children were slowly walking round the arena, supported by the teenage helpers, and didn't seem to be doing much else. Still, Charlotte was smiling, and that was the main thing. She glanced at her watch. With twenty minutes to go, she wondered if she should slip away and get a cup of coffee or something. She was sure she'd seen a vending machine somewhere.

'I'm going to get a drink,' she whispered to Paula. 'Do you want me to bring you one back?'

'No thanks.'

'Okay.' Kate squeezed past her and signalled to Charlotte where she was going, tapping her watch to let her know she'd be back in a few minutes. Her daughter nodded, giggling. She was having the time of her life.

Kate had never caught the "I love horses" bug, despite being best friends with Ella for most of her formative years. In her experience, the children whose parents let them ride when they were very young tended to go mad over horses and ponies once they became teenagers. Kate had never wanted to ride, not even as a youngster – not since a belligerent pony had chased her across a field when she was walking her grandmother's dog one day and frightened the life out of her. She could never understand how Ella was prepared to work so hard, and for such long hours, for such little reward, either. Rising before dawn to muck out smelly stables and trudging across muddy fields in the freezing wind and rain was not her idea of fun. No way.

Still, it had all been worthwhile, she mused, as she strolled back to the centre of the stable block, where she was certain she had seen a drinks dispenser. Ella's name was now among the top names in the show-jumping circuit, the stables were running at a healthy profit, and Hollyfield was establishing a name for itself as a stud and breeding centre. Thomas had made enough profit in the last yearlings' sale to enable Ella to buy her new stallion outright. It wasn't too bad, Kate thought, for a girl who had worked her socks off as a teenager for a pittance and a load of grief.

And the person who had been instrumental in handling Ella's difficult teenage years, was none other than the woman Kate saw heading straight towards her.

'Morning Mrs Lloyd Duncan,' she said.

Ursula stopped dead in her tracks. A faint flicker of recognition flitted over her face. It was that old school friend of Ella's - Kate something or other. She was hopeless at names. 'Morning,' she said. 'How nice to see you again. It's Kate, isn't it? I'm afraid if you've come to see Ella, she isn't here.'

'I know,' Kate said. 'She's in Paris. No, I've brought Charlotte up for a riding lesson.'

'Charlotte?'

'My daughter.'

'Goodness,' Ursula said. 'Is she that old?' The last thing she'd heard, Kate had been hiring a nanny to look after her baby while she went back to work.

'She's seven.'

'Seven,' Ursula echoed, shocked at how fast time seemed to be passing her by. 'It doesn't seem possible.'

'I think that myself, sometimes,' Kate said. The years between Charlotte's birth and the present had hurtled past in a blur of work, and nappies and school. 'But yes, she's seven now, and anxious to start riding, so here we are.'

'You've got her in Tamsin's class?'

Kate nodded. 'I would have preferred Ella really. It's just my luck she's gone away for the summer.'

'Oh, but Tamsin's very experienced,' Ursula assured her. 'She was here in my time, you know. I expect Ella's told you that she's left me in charge while she's away?'

'No. Really?' Kate said, feigning surprise.

Ursula nodded. 'Well, you can't blame her. I mean, I do know more about running these stables than most people. The stud, I told her, should be left in Thomas' capable hands, and she agreed with me there. He does such a good job, and he's got some wonderful staff, but the running of the school and the livery yard are down to me.'

'That's a big responsibility,' Kate said.

'And one that I'm more than happy to do.' Ursula, full of her own importance, was delighted to have found an audience. 'In fact, I've got some interesting ideas for attracting new clients and I know Ella's going to be thrilled when I tell her what I'm doing.'

'Which is what, exactly?'

Ursula beamed. 'Western riding. I don't know why Ella hasn't thought of it before. We've got an American working with us for the summer, and he's an expert at it. He's going to start taking classes very soon.' She flapped the piece of paper she was holding in front of Kate's face. 'I'd been planning a bit of publicity to advertise it and then I suddenly had a brainwave. Why don't we hold a barbecue and barn dance – a kind of Western event, and Hank can give the guests a Western riding display as part of the entertainment?'

Kate was finding it hard to keep a straight face. 'Sounds interesting.' (Or at least, she thought, Ella was bound to think so when she told her about it.)

'Don't you think it's a good idea?'

'I don't want to get involved,' Kate laughed, shaking her head. 'I know even less about Western riding than I do about normal riding.'

'Yes, but a barn dance – a party,' Ursula said. 'Don't you think it would bring in the locals?'

'Are you sure it's the locals you want to attract?'

'Hmm, well, there is that,' Ursula said, frowning. Some of the yobs in the village would not be welcome. She could imagine them yee-hahing and making a mockery of everything. Nor did she want those itinerant gipsies either. Perhaps she'd send out selective invitations. Yes, that's what she'd do, she decided. She'd make it an invitation only event – a taste of America.

'You'll come, won't you, Kate?' she said.

'Naturally. I've never been known to turn down an invite to a party. When are you planning on holding it?'

Ursula hadn't thought that far ahead. She opened the folder she was carrying and picked out her pocket diary. 'Saturday the fourteenth,' she decided, circling the date in black with a felt tipped pen. She wanted it as soon as possible, given the fact that Hank wouldn't be around for very long. Apart from the food and entertainments, there wasn't much to organise. The invitations could be printed off on the computer, and she could have them in the post by the following morning. Never one to rest on her laurels, Ursula was already planning the sequence of events in her head.

'Great,' Kate said. 'I'll make sure I keep that date free.'

'A barn dance!' Ella said in disbelief when Kate phoned to tell her about it later that same day. 'Ursula's organising a barn dance.'

'That's what she said.'

'And Western riding classes.'

'Yes,' Kate said. 'With this American she's got working for her.'

'That must be Hank,' Ella said. 'Honestly, I don't believe that woman. No wonder she didn't want to talk to me. What else has been going on that I ought to know about?'

'Well, I don't mean to gossip,' Kate said, wandering through into the kitchen and closing the door so that Charlotte wouldn't hear what she was saying. 'But I did hear a rumour about Vanessa and that American.'

It had all happened by accident, she recalled. She had been waiting for Charlotte to finish her riding lesson and had gone to buy a drink from the machine in the yard. Two of the stable girls had been rinsing hay nets under the tap nearby and had been talking loud enough for her to hear them.

'They said that Vanessa had spent the night with that Hank guy.'

'No!' Ella gasped.

'Yes,' Kate confirmed. 'And they weren't best pleased about it either. I haven't seen him yet, but I gather he's some kind of hunk by the way they were talking. One of them said she'd seen Vanessa draped all over him, and that they'd come out of the Groom's Cottage together, first thing in the morning.'

'That doesn't necessarily mean anything,' Ella said. And knowing Vanessa's past track record with men, it probably didn't.

'Well, they'd been seen riding together the day before. Gone for hours, according to one of the girls, and they'd been pretty close when they got back. Gemma – is it Gemma?' she added. 'The one with striking red hair?'

'Yes.'

'Right. Well, she said she'd heard Vanessa asking him what time he was picking her up.'

'Blimey,' Ella said, who couldn't quite believe the fact that her stepsister might have found herself a boyfriend at last. 'I can't wait to see this Hank.'

Kate laughed. 'You're not the only one. I'm taking Charlotte back tomorrow for a private lesson with Tamsin. She really enjoyed herself today, and I thought it might help her to catch up with the rest of the class. So, don't worry – I'll be keeping my eyes peeled for him. How's Lewis getting on?' she added, wandering back through into the lounge where Charlotte was lying on the settee watching cartoons on the television.

'Fine. They've sorted out several locations and he's got a meeting with a French film company to see if they can get some mutual sponsorship lined up.'

'Which means you're not seeing much of him.'

'Not really, 'Ella sighed. If she was honest with herself, this holiday in Paris wasn't turning out how she had expected it to. Lewis seemed to spend most of his days in meetings or visiting prospective sites for filming. Apart from the odd meal together, most of the time she found that she and Rosie were left on their own. Once the initial euphoria of exploring the city had worn off (and in the heat of summer, it had worn off pretty quickly), there wasn't much else for them to do. She would be glad when they moved into Marcel's apartment - a move that was scheduled to take place in the next couple of days. Staying in a luxury hotel was all well and good, but it started to pall after a while - particularly with a young child in tow.

'Have you thought anymore about coming out here?' she asked.

Kate laughed. 'I've thought about nothing else. No, seriously, what would you say if Charlotte and I came over next weekend, and we took the girls to Euro Disney? Graham is quite happy for me to go, oddly enough,' she added. 'I think he wants a bit of peace and quiet round the house. Plus, he did mutter something about playing golf on Saturday.'

'I'd love it if you could,' Ella said, who was feeling almost as bored and lonely as Rosie. After such a hectic lifestyle, she was finding her self-imposed relaxation and luxury a bit of a bind. 'Will you fly out?'

'God, yes. You're not getting me on a train that goes under the sea. Do you want me to go ahead and book some flights?'

'Yes, and I'll see if Lewis can arrange a car to pick you up from the airport.'

'Excellent,' Kate said. 'Thanks, Ella. I'm really looking forward to this. Charlotte will be thrilled when I tell her.'

'So will Rosie,' Ella agreed.

'I'll be in touch.'

'Bye.'

Ella replaced the receiver, her thoughts churning. It was almost seven o'clock, and Lewis had promised to be back at the hotel for dinner. As usual, he was running late. At this rate, they would end up having a meal sent to their room so that Rosie could go to bed.

She was currently having a luxurious bubble bath in the sunken, marble suited bathroom, and wisps of steam were billowing out from under the door. Ella looked in on her and smiled at the mountain of fluffy white bubbles surrounding her. 'That looks like fun,' she said.

'It is,' Rosie giggled as she pressed the whirlpool button and a froth of foam bubbled up from the depths of the water. 'Can we have one of these at home, Mummy?'

'I doubt it.' Ella smiled. 'That was Kate on the phone. She said Charlotte had started having lessons at Hollyfield.'

Rosie wiped a smudge of foam from the side of her face with the back of her hand. 'Who did she ride?'

'I didn't ask.'

'Mum!' Rosie groaned. 'I wish I'd been there,' she added.

Ella sat down on the edge of the bath and looked fondly down at her daughter. She was growing up fast. This was her final year at primary school, and then she'd be off to senior school with Adam. It didn't seem possible.

'How would you like it if Charlotte and Kate came over here for a few days?' she said. 'Then Charlotte can tell you all about it.'

'Yeah!' Rosie said eagerly. 'When?'

'At the weekend,' Ella said with a smile. 'Kate wants us to go to Euro Disney'

'Oh Mum!' Rosie's face lit up with excitement. 'That'll be brilliant. Poor Adam,' she added, 'He won't know what he's missing.'

'I expect we'll make it up to him some other way,' Ella said, who was almost as excited as her daughter. She couldn't wait for Kate to arrive. It would be good to have some company at last, because one thing was for sure - no way was she facing Mickey Mouse and his entourage on her own.

'You don't mind, do you?' she asked Lewis later, once Rosie had gone to bed.

They were lounging on the huge, cushioned sofa, having polished off the best part of a bottle of wine and a delicious tomato and pepper chicken dish that had been sent up from the kitchens courtesy of the exorbitantly expensive room service.

'I mean, Rosie's bored without any of her little friends to play with, and to be honest, we're not seeing as much of you as we thought we would.'

'I know,' Lewis sighed. 'It's my fault. I'd no idea Matthew would pull out at the last minute. Cheryl's gone into labour,' he added. 'I couldn't say no.'

'Of course not,' Ella agreed. Matthew was one of the founder members of Blackwater Films, and one of Lewis' closest friends. He'd only been married a couple of years, and this was his first child.

Lewis put his arm round her shoulder and pulled her closer. 'I'll ring Marcel tomorrow and see if I can pick up the keys for the apartment. You'll be happier once you're out of this hotel,' he murmured, nuzzling her neck.

'Hmm,' she nodded. 'All this luxury takes some getting used to. However, there are some advantages,' she murmured, running her fingers down his chest. 'The king size four poster bed takes some beating.' With a suggestive smile, she started to prise open the buttons of his shirt.

'Mrs Trevelyan, are you trying to take advantage of me?'

'Guess so,' she said.

'In that case,' He grinned. 'Feel free.'

Back in England, Ursula had plenty of things to concern her. Worrying about what her stepdaughter was up to in Paris was not one of them. She had enough to contend with trying to track down Vanessa, whose failure to appear behind the counter of the tack shop that morning had sent rumours circulating like wildfire around the stable yard.

The fact that Hank was also conspicuous by his absence was adding some credence to the story that they'd last been seen driving off together in Jimmy McPherson's white van.

'What tittle tattle is this,' Ursula said, rounding on the poor unfortunate Gemma, who had been relating the tale to Sara, unaware that the older woman was lurking in the background.

Gemma blushed profusely. 'Well, she's not in the shop,' she said. 'Tommy Young's just come back from there. He says Adam's running things.'

'Don't be ridiculous,' Ursula snapped. 'The boy's only thirteen. He can't be there on his own.'

Gemma gave her an infuriating little smirk, which had Ursula stomping back to the house determined to get to the truth of the matter.

'What do you mean, she's not able to come to the phone?' she demanded, on hearing Adam's voice on the other end of the line. 'Is she there?'

Adam peered through into the storeroom, where his aunt was lying sleeping on a bed of stable rugs and padded jackets. She was snoring loudly and peacefully. 'Um, yes,' he said.

'Well put her on the phone. I need to speak to her.'

'She's busy,' Adam said. 'I'll get her to call you back.'

'Adam. Adam!'

Ursula stared in disbelief at the receiver. He'd cut her off. Either that or the line had gone dead. She pressed the button several times and then re-dialled, but succeeded in only getting the engaged tone. How strange.

Adam, meanwhile, had wandered into the storeroom and poked Vanessa gently with the toe of his trainer. He was starting to get a bit worried about her. She had been conked out for hours.

'Aunty Van. Hello, Aunty Van, are you awake?'

'Ugh!' Vanessa groaned. 'Leave me alone.'

'I think you ought to get up,' he said. 'Gran wants to speak to you.'

'Oh my God, she's not here, is she?' Vanessa said, panicking. She raised herself up on her elbows and blinked like a frightened owl. Maybe her mother had seen the unmade bed and realised she hadn't come home that night. Not that it was any of her business, she told herself firmly, but she would make it hers.

'No,' Adam said. 'She was on the phone. I told her you'd call back. Are you feeling any better?' he asked, with such genuine concern in his voice that Vanessa felt quite touched.

'Not really,' she sighed. 'But I suppose I'd better ring her. Thanks for looking after things for me, Adam. I don't know what I'd have done without you.'

'That's okay,' he said, wandering back into the shop where he was busy re-organising a display of gifts and fancy goods for the discerning horse owner.

Vanessa hauled herself into a vertical position and wondered when the queasy feeling in her stomach would wear off. Probably about the same time as the thumping in her head, she figured, as she groped for the phone.

'Mother,' she said. 'You rang?'

She listened with half an ear as Ursula gave her a rambling account of her plans for the riding school, but her attention pricked up when she suddenly brought in Hanks' name.

'I thought he could give a Western riding display at the barn dance,' she said.

'What barn dance?' Vanessa asked, wondering if she'd missed the thread of the conversation somewhere.

'On the fourteenth,' Ursula groaned, and Vanessa knew that she had. 'Gemma said you'd been trying out one of the saddles with him and I was wondering how you'd got on?'

With the saddle, or with Hank, Vanessa mused. 'All right,' she said, hoping that covered both eventualities.

'Excellent. I've got some good news too,' she said. 'Lucy Woods has broken her arm.'

Vanessa frowned. How was that good news?

Ursula enlightened her. 'She's put her horse in full livery with us, and it's a genuine American Quarter horse. Can you believe that for a stroke of good luck? Six weeks he's going to be here. I can hardly believe it. We can use him in the display and everything.'

'Have you told Hank?'

'Not yet,' Ursula said. 'I can't find him. I was wondering if you knew where he was?'

'Me?' Vanessa croaked.

'Gemma said she saw you leave in the van with him this morning?'

Gemma would, Vanessa thought furiously. 'He, um, he gave me a lift to the shop.' she said airily.

'Oh. And you've no idea where he was going?'

'No.'

'Pity. Oh well, if you see him, you can let him know.'

'I will,' she said. 'Bye.'

Odd, Vanessa thought, as she hung up the phone. Hank had told her he was going back to work. So, if he wasn't there, where had he gone?

A message on his mobile had diverted Jed from his normal daily routine. Instead of heading back to the stables after dropping Vanessa off, he had been obliged to take a sixty-mile detour.

Giles Peterson was waiting for him in the bookies where they had first made their acquaintance several years before. Giles had owned the place then. Now, he also owned a string of casinos and nightclubs and had his fingers poked in several lucrative pies.

Fortune had been kind to Giles. Jed wished he could say the same thing about himself. As a self-confessed gambler, he had been hooked from the start, betting first on horses, and then the roulette wheel. Poker, black jack, you name it. He'd done them all before he realised that it was a mug's game. But by then it was too late. Faced with crippling debts and no way to pay them, he had sold his house and turned to Giles for a loan - a loan that the self-made businessman had been more than happy to provide, with conditions attached, naturally. Being at his immediate beck and call appeared to be one of them.

'He's in the back,' said the young man on the counter, jerking his head at the door behind him. 'He's expecting you.'

'Thanks,' Jed said, walking on through.

Giles was smoking his customary fat cigar and leafing through a bulky portfolio when he strolled into the room.

'You wanted to see me?' Jed said.

'Hmm, yes. Sit down.' He buzzed on the intercom. 'Clare, can you bring two coffees in here, please.'

Jed pulled up a chair and reluctantly sat down on it. He was wondering, not for the first time, why he had ever got himself involved with such an unsavoury character as Giles Peterson. The man was a leech - sucking the goodness out of everyone he met. But he knew the answer as sure as eggs were eggs. It was purely a question of money, or, in his case, the lack of it.

'Got a good tip for the two thirty at Doncaster,' Giles murmured. He didn't look up from his portfolio. 'That's if you're interested, of course.'

Jed sighed. 'I don't expect you brought me here just to tell me that.'

'No.' Giles puffed at his cigar and exhaled a cloud of pungent smoke into the room. 'But if you've got a few bob spare, you wouldn't go far wrong if you placed it on Moneypenny.'

'If I had a few bob spare,' Jed said, 'I expect you'd have your hands on it, with interest.'

'Maybe, maybe,' Giles chortled. The folds of fat beneath his jaw line bounced up and down as he spoke. 'Ah, thank you Clare,' he said to the young woman who brought in a tray with two cups of steaming coffee on it. 'Sugar?'

Jed shook his head.

'Sweet enough, eh?' Giles laughed at his own joke as he ladled three heaped spoonsful into his own cup. 'Now then,' he said, lowering his voice, 'how's the role play going?'

'Okay, I guess. They obviously think I'm genuine. The old dear in charge has got me organising a Western riding class.'

'Good, good. 'Giles took a mouthful of coffee and smacked his lips. 'Sweet and strong, just how I like it. So,' he continued, 'there'll be no questions asked when you supposedly shoot off back to the States.'

'Probably not.'

'What will you say? That its a family crisis, a bereavement, perhaps?'

'I'll think of something,' he muttered. He was used to ad-libbing.

'We don't want them to get suspicious.'

'They won't,' Jed said. 'I'm telling you they think I'm a real Montana cowboy. Heck, they've got me believing it half the time myself.'

Giles nodded admiringly. 'Oscar material - I've always said it. You've got the accent as well.'

'I've lived in the States for long enough,' Jed said crisply. He wasn't taking any pleasure from the role he was playing. It was a means to an end as far as he was concerned. Lying and deceiving people didn't come naturally to him, particularly as he was starting to like some of the people he had to deal with. 'So, what's the deal, Giles? Is this swap going ahead, or not?'

'Yes, yes, all in good time, my boy. O'Brien's having the stallion shipped over in the next day or so. We'll install him at a stud in Norfolk. I've got connections there. That's far enough away, don't you think?'

Jed shrugged. 'It's a couple of hours drive, I guess.'

'So, it can all be done under cover of darkness.'

'When?'

Giles blew a stream of smoke rings into the air. 'That's up to you,' he said. 'You choose the time and the date. All I'm asking is that you see it through. I want that horse,' he added, 'and I aim to get him, understand. Midnight Prince,' he paused a moment as if savouring the thought. 'Midnight Prince, is going to be mine.'

Chapter 8

'Steady! Steady boy!' Thomas hung on to Midnight Prince's reins as Jimmy McPherson hopped up onto the black stallion's back. 'He's a bit of a handful this morning,' he said.' You'd best take it easy.'

'A bit like yesterday, then,' Jimmy said. He was one of the few riders skilled enough to exercise the stallion, having spent many years as a jockey until a growth spurt had ruled out his chances of riding in top competitions.

The black horse pranced sideways across the yard, snorting and tossing its head.

'It can smell the mares,' Thomas said. 'You'd better take him over to the east paddock. He can have a good run up there.

Jimmy nodded as he tightened his helmet. 'Wish me luck.'

He would need it, Thomas thought, as he stepped to one side and watched them move off the yard. He was a fine-looking beast, sure enough, but he wouldn't want to be the one sitting on his back. The days when he would have jumped up on anything with four legs, a mane and a tail were long gone.

Thomas made his way back to the stud office where he had a pile of paperwork to deal with. He kept strict records of everything from mares' covering charts, nominations forms, details of veterinary and farrier visits, covering certificates, registration, and invoicing. In this way he ensured the efficient running of the stud.
Keeping everything in order meant that if ever he was absent, for any reason, other members of staff could see at a glance what needed doing, and when.

He was thinking of taking a few days off in the near future. Maisie had been on at him for weeks about visiting her sister down in Dorset. The trouble was, there was always something that needed doing. He glanced at the mares' record charts. Only two mares were left to foal, with one due in the next day or so if he had read the signs right, and the other by the end of the week. Both had swollen udders and Gemini was starting to show milk. Maybe he could take some time off after that. Jimmy was perfectly capable of looking after the stallions and they didn't have many visiting horses booked in. Most breeders wanted their mares covered in early spring, the earlier the better, when it came to Thoroughbred breeding.

He took a red pen and circled the middle of August on the calendar. That would be about right. The foals should have been born by then. Normally, he would have asked Ella and she would have confirmed if the dates were suitable or not. As she wasn't available, he would have to speak to Sally, because there was no way he was going to ask Ursula. The woman only had to look at him, and he felt his blood boil. He had distant memories of her that he would never forget.

'You're like a bull elephant,' Maisie told him.

'Aye, well, some things are best remembered and not forgotten,' he said. 'That old crow only does what she thinks is right, whether it is, or it isn't. Take this Western riding lark,' he scoffed. 'She gets one young American to work for her, and thinks she's got the makings of a new business venture under her wing.'

'Well, you can't say she isn't trying.'

'Oh, she's trying all right,' Thomas muttered.

'Then tell Ella. Give her a ring,' Maisie suggested.

'It's none of my business. If she keeps her nose out of the running of the stud, I'll be happy, and that's all there is to it.'

Ursula, however, was never one to keep her nose out of anything. On hearing from Sally Dickson that Thomas was planning to take a few days leave, she decided to pay him a visit, and get confirmation from the man himself.

'It's highly inconvenient,' she said, following him round the stud office like a terrier hounding its prey. 'You know Ella won't be back by then, and I'm trying to arrange a barn dance for the fourteenth.'

'Which affects me, how?' he said, twiddling a pen between his roughened fingers.

Ursula looked taken aback. 'Well, because there'll be lots of people here. They might want to look around.'

'So, let them.'

'Thomas, I do think you're being unreasonable.'

'Really.' He stuck the pen behind his ear and turned his attention to the paperwork on his desk.

If Ursula had been a small child, she might have stamped her foot in frustration. As it was, she managed a pretty sulky glare at him. The man was old and insufferable, she thought, and the sooner Ella got rid of him and passed his job on to someone younger and fitter, the better.

'Fine!' she snapped. 'Well, I expect we'll cope.'

'Good,' Thomas said.

The door banged loudly as Ursula slammed it shut behind her.

Shaking his head, Thomas managed a rueful smile.

Meanwhile, back at Grey Lodge, Ursula's daughter, Caroline, was conducting a room-by-room search, dragging a disgruntled Bruno by the collar as her unwilling accomplice. The strains of Pavarotti belting out of the stereo had not masked the sinister thuds and creaking noises she kept hearing. Someone, or something, she decided, was in one of the rooms upstairs.

'Hello?' she said, somewhat tentatively as she reached the landing at the top of the stairs, because if anyone had replied she would have died on the spot. 'Is anyone there?'

The silence seemed to settle round her like a smothering mantle. She tilted her head to one side and strained to listen. Bruno flopped onto his belly and laid his head on his paws.

'Get up,' she hissed, yanking his collar.

The thudding was coming from the end of the corridor, where a narrow staircase led up to the attic rooms. Caroline swallowed nervously. Her throat felt dry and hoarse. She knew that in days gone by those rooms had been used as servant's quarters. What if the ghost of a wretched scullery maid or hard done by kitchen hand was roaming the corridors?

'Hello?' she croaked.

Pavarotti was approaching the climax of his performance. The orchestra had reached a crescendo. The rapturous applause of the audience deafened all but the faintest of thuds and squeaks.

Caroline reached the narrow staircase and peered upwards at the closed wooden door at the top. There was no way she could get the cumbersome bulk of the elderly

Labrador up the steep stairs. 'Stay there,' she hissed, positioning him at the bottom step as she reached for the rail.

Bruno, who had never been the most obedient of dogs, turned and ambled back along the corridor, intent on finding a more comfortable resting place, such as the sofa or an armchair downstairs.

Caroline didn't notice. She was too pre-occupied with rushing up the stairs and flinging the door open before she lost her nerve.

The dim length of the empty attic stretched out in front of her. Cobwebs hung from the rafters and dust shimmered in the rays of sunshine beaming in through the dormer windows.

She could see from one end of the room to the other and apart from the odd box and a couple of unwanted chairs, the place was empty. She stepped up into the attic and made her way over to one of the windows. Now, the thudding seemed to be coming from somewhere beneath the floor. Peering out of the window, she finally discovered the source of the noise. An old oak tree with huge branches had grown close to the house, and one of the branches touched the side of the wall each time there was a gust of wind. The thudding and creaking, was the noise of the wood scraping against the brickwork.

Caroline, who had been holding her breath for what seemed like forever, breathed out slowly and steadily. How stupid could she be? Frightened of an oak tree - how silly. She leaned forwards and rubbed the grime from the window with the back of her hand. The view was quite magnificent from such a height. The fields stretched in all directions, marred only by the colourful assortment of vans and trucks parked on the field to the right of the house, and the strings of gaily coloured washing suspended from the nearest trees. In the furthest distance she could see the roof of the black barn at Hollyfield, and the trees surrounding the cross-country course. Small dots moving across the fields were horses - oh, and she could see the pigs over at Barrowby Farm.

So engrossed was she in the panorama spread out before her, that she didn't hear Bruno barking, nor did she realise that somebody else was in the house.

Vanessa had taken the chance of her lunch break, when she closed the tack shop for an hour, to call a taxi to take her up to Grey Lodge. She needed to have words with her sister before her mother caught up with her, if only to give herself an alibi for the night before. Since Caroline had refused to answer any of her phone calls, and since she knew she had to be somewhere in the house, the only option open to her was to get a taxi to Grey Lodge.

'If I'm not back in an hour,' she told Adam, 'would you mind opening up again for me?'

'I suppose so,' Adam said. 'Only I had planned on riding Blackthorn this afternoon.'

'Please,' Vanessa said. 'I'll bring you back a burger and a bag of chips.'

'Okay,' he said. 'But don't be too late.'

The cost of the taxi was extortionate. Vanessa stared at the driver in disbelief as he pulled up outside Grey Lodge and told her the fare. 'It's only two miles,' she said

'Should've walked then, shouldn't you.'

Vanessa held out her hand for the change. No way was he getting a tip. The driver dropped the coppers into her outstretched palm with a sullen scowl on his face.

'Thank you,' she said.

'Pleasure.'

With her head still aching, and her stomach marginally less queasy, Vanessa hurried to the front door and inserted her key into the lock. Bruno was delighted to see a familiar face, and thumped his tail madly, upsetting the small hall table as he did so.

'You daft dog,' she said, stroking his silky black head. 'What have you done with Caroline?'

She wandered through into the kitchen, then the drawing room, the lounge, the study and the dining room. 'Yoo-hoo!' she called. 'It's only me.'

Silence answered her. Vanessa felt the first cold prickle of fear. She left her bag on the kitchen table and stood at the base of the stairs. 'Caroline?'

A faint thudding, creaking noise came from somewhere above her. 'Are you up there?' she said. 'Caroline!'

Vanessa had a bad feeling about this. She caught hold of Bruno's collar. The dog gave her a look, which implied 'not again', and planted itself squarely on its backside. No amount of persuasion could get it to budge.

Bruno's obvious reluctance to go upstairs could only mean one thing as far as Vanessa was concerned. Something had happened to Caroline. Oh God - as if she didn't feel bad enough. Vanessa caught hold of the banisters and gingerly edged her way up to the first-floor landing. The floorboards creaked loudly, making her jump. She was jittery enough to start with, but she got a lot worse when she heard footsteps clumping across the floor above her head. Her eyes were on stalks as she stared at the narrow staircase up to the attic. 'Caroline?' she croaked, her heart thumping, 'is that you?'

It was debatable who got the greatest fright - Vanessa, on seeing an apparition appearing at the top of the attic stairs, sheathed in sunlight from the dormer windows - or Caroline, seeing a hunched and wild-eyed figure cowering on the landing.

The resultant screeches of terror had Bruno bounding up the stairs like a dog half his age, whereupon he started to bark and howl until both sisters, still barely recovered from the shock, ordered him to 'Shut up!'

'Why didn't you answer the phone?' Vanessa demanded, as they made their way back downstairs.

'I didn't hear the bloody phone,' Caroline snapped. 'I was listening to a CD. You know - listen to some music - that's what your American friend said. "It'll disguise the noises, so you won't hear them," he said.'

'That's why I'm here.'

'About the noises?' Caroline said. 'I know what's causing them now.'

'No, about Hank,' Vanessa said in exasperation. 'What do you mean, you know what's causing them?'

'It's the branches from that old oak tree rapping on the wall,' Caroline said, picking up the kettle and sticking it under the tap. 'You want to get mother to have someone prune it back a bit. In fact, she could ask the gipsies. They ought to be doing something for their keep.'

'Yes, yes, okay,' Vanessa said. 'I'll tell her. But listen, I need to get you to cover for me. If she asks, will you say I stayed here last night.'

Caroline turned from ladling a spoonful of coffee into the mugs, her face a picture of disbelief. 'You want me to lie for you? Why?' she said. 'Where were you last night? Oh.' The penny finally dropped. 'Vanessa!'

'What?'

'You were with him, weren't you? That Hank. You lucky bloody cow!'

'Nothing happened,' Vanessa groaned, though she was beginning to wish it had done. 'If you must know, I had too much to drink and passed out.'

'Oh,' Caroline said. 'Oh dear.'

'Don't lecture me,' she snapped. 'I don't think I can stand it.'

'I wasn't going to lecture you.' Caroline said, with a small smirk. 'I was just thinking, oh dear, hasn't this happened to you once before?'

'Shut up,' Vanessa said. 'I don't need reminding. It's all your fault, anyway, plying us with that expensive wine.'

'Ah yes, the Chablis,' Caroline sighed. 'Marcus was so annoyed.'

'Yes, well, you can tell him I won't be touching the stuff again, thank you very much. I've never felt so ill.'

'Hmm - you do look a bit sickly. I doubt it was the Chablis, though. Good wine doesn't give you a hangover.'

'Oh, you think,' Vanessa snapped. 'What's this I'm feeling then?'

'Sorry,' Caroline said, as she handed her a mug of coffee. 'There's no need to bite my head off.'

'I wasn't,' Vanessa muttered. 'I just don't feel well.' She took a small sip of coffee. It was strong and hot and burned a path all the way down to her churning stomach. Perhaps water might have been the more sensible option, she thought, pushing it to one side. 'So, do me a favour, and don't tell mother. If she asks, will you tell her I slept here?'

'If she asks,' Caroline said. 'Though to be honest, I doubt she'll have noticed. You know what she's like at the moment, what with all the worry about the gipsies, and Ella being away.' She stirred a spoonful of sugar into her own cup. 'So,' she added, 'Are you going to be seeing him again?'

'I think so,' Vanessa said.

'Only think?'

'All right then, yes,' she said recalling his words to her about going out again another night. 'But I don't know when. We haven't arranged anything yet.'

Caroline gave her a sympathetic little smile, which spoke volumes.

'You'll see,' Vanessa snapped, snatching up her bag. She was annoyed that her sister seemed to assume she had been dumped. 'I've got to go. I've left Adam at the shop.'

She was outside the front door before she realised that she didn't have a car at Grey Lodge, nor had she asked the taxi driver to wait. Sod it, she thought, setting off at a brisk pace down the long and curving drive. She would have to walk. The fresh air would do her some good.

Adam wasn't best pleased to see her roll up over half an hour late and minus the promised burger and chips.

'I'm starving,' he grumbled, following her into the storeroom, where she was prising off her shoes and wiggling her toes.

'I know, and I'm sorry,' she said. 'Ah, that's better. If I'd known I was going to be walking I'd have put my other boots on. Take a tenner out of the till,' she added, 'and nip down to the fish and chip shop.'

'They'll be shut,' he muttered.

'Adam, I'm really sorry. What more can I say? Look, take the money anyway,' she said, trying to appease him.

He pulled a face. 'A twenty would be more useful.'

'All right, take twenty pounds,' she said. She knew when she was beaten. She needed to keep on the good side of Adam. He was useful to have around the place and didn't seem to mind all the fetching and carrying that she found such a burden.

'Thanks Aunty Van,' he said, his face brightening. 'Is it okay if I shoot off now? I want to go riding.'

'Yes, off you go,' she said, prising her feet back into her too tight shoes. She would have blisters come the evening. 'And thanks, Adam, thanks for everything you've done. I do appreciate it.'

Goodness knows what she would have done if he hadn't been able to come in that morning. The problem with running a small one-person business like hers was the difficulty in getting cover for sickness or holidays. Normally her mother would have been on hand to help, but she was fully occupied with the running of the stables.

In Vanessa's opinion she was taking on far too much. Why couldn't she let things be until Ella came home? According to Sally Dickson, all the schedules had been changed so that lessons could be given seven days a week instead of the usual six. No wonder the stable girls were complaining. Instead of putting all the horses out for one day, and consequently having an easier time of it themselves, they were required to be on hand to bring them in and tack them up as usual. Any profit being made from the extra lessons was going on staff wages, so, as far as Vanessa could see, it seemed a bit of a pointless exercise.

Not to Ursula, it wasn't. She had drawn up a list and slotted both staff and horses into various timetables for the whole week. Each horse and every member of staff was given a day off on a rolling rota, so what was marked down one week, would be different the next and so on. It wasn't a popular move, and particularly with the staff who did other things on their days off.

Sarah attended the ladies swimming group on a Monday morning. Now it looked as if she'd only be able to go once every three weeks.

'She's put me in for the instructional hacks,' she grumbled, peering at the list that Ursula had conveniently stapled to the wall of the tack room. 'Look - this Monday and next. I swear she's done it on purpose.'

'Yes, and I'm getting my highlights done,' Maxine said. 'I've had the appointment booked for ages. It's at that posh place in town. You know how hard it is to get a booking with them.'

'I'm not doing it,' Gemma said. 'I'll go sick, if need be. Ella wouldn't agree to it, so I don't see why we should.'

'Yes, but Ella's not here.'

'I've a good mind to phone her,' Sarah said. 'I'm sure I've got her mobile number. It'll still work in France, won't it?'

'Only if she has it switched on,' Maxine said.

They leaned over Sarah's shoulder as she scrolled down the phone book on her mobile. 'There it is,' she said. 'What do you think? Shall I give her a ring?'

'Yes,' came the resounding chorus.

Ursula thought, naively, that the girls were rejoicing at their new duty schedules, since they all seemed to be gathering around the notice board staring at them when they all cheered.

'I must say,' she said, breezing into the tack room with a jubilant smile on her face. 'You're all taking the changes rather well. I was expecting at least one of you to complain. But if you're all happy about it, that's wonderful.'

'We're not,' Gemma said bluntly.

Ursula's eyes narrowed. A mean little expression crept over her face. 'What appears to be the problem?' she said.

'How's about, "no consultation" for starters?'

'I didn't think it was necessary,' Ursula said coldly. 'I took a management decision based on the grounds of greater efficiency and output.'

'Bollocks,' Gemma said.

'I beg your pardon.'

'Sarah, phone Ella. Go on. Let's see if she approves of all this.'

Ursula looked incensed. She took a step towards the petrified Sarah, who was holding the mobile as if it were red hot in her hands.

'I have spoken to Ella,' she said. 'So, there's really no need for you to bother her with the petty details.'

'Ella knows about this?' Sarah choked. She couldn't believe it. Ella was the one who had always insisted on a regular rest day for both the staff and the horses.

'Naturally,' Ursula lied. 'But go on, phone her if you must.'

Gemma nudged her arm and motioned her to go ahead, but Sarah was frightened of Ursula. She switched off her phone and slipped it inside her jacket pocket.

Smugly satisfied, Ursula stepped over to the saddle racks, and poked a finger at one of the stirrup leathers. 'This tack needs a good clean. See to it,' she snapped, before turning and striding back across the yard.

Maxine made a mock salute that had Gemma in fits. 'Give me that phone,' she laughed, holding her hand out. 'I'll call Ella.'

'You can't!' Sarah gasped, but she fished her mobile phone out of her pocket just the same.

'Who can't?' Gemma said, opening the cover. 'Watch me.'

Chapter 9

Adam dug his heels in and leaned forwards over Blackthorn's neck as he launched himself over the brush hedge half way round the cross-country course. The horse's hooves pounded down onto the soft ground and he felt a rush of adrenalin as they headed for the double log spread.

At thirteen he was more than competent to tackle a cross-country course that would have fazed many adult riders. He had been practically raised in the saddle, and not many jumps or situations worried him. Out of all the horses stabled at Hollyfield, Blackthorn was his favourite. The chestnut bay was a cross between an Irish Draught and a Thoroughbred, so had the benefit of both speed and stamina.

'Come on, boy,' he urged, feeling the wind whistling past his ears as they sailed over the coffin jump and galloped up the long stretch into the woods.

The air was pleasantly warm amongst the shelter of the trees, and it felt good to be out of the burning glare of the sun. Adam pulled Blackthorn up and decided to let him amble for a while to cool off. The constant hum and buzz of insects and the chirping of birds surrounded him as they walked along the shaded track.

The course had been well maintained with sand and wood chippings to provide a decent riding surface. Regular competitions were ridden there over the summer, and it was imperative that the ground was kept in good order. At high speed no one wanted to risk a horse stumbling down a rabbit hole or falling over a broken branch that hadn't been pulled clear.

So Adam wasn't in the least bit surprised to see Hank appear in the distance, though he was a bit puzzled to see him crouching down by the perimeter fence. He looked as if he was hiding something; though Adam couldn't for the life of him, think what it was.

Some inner instinct warned him that perhaps this wasn't the time to shout a greeting. In fact, it was probably better if Hank didn't know he was watching him. Adam turned Blackthorn into the cover of some bushes and kept a curious eye on the American. He was covering up a hole, by the look of things - shovelling earth and leaves across the area with the side of his boot and dragging a few branches over the spot. Marking it, Adam decided - but what for, and why?

He stroked Blackthorn's neck, willing him to remain still and silent. The horse was breathing rapidly and seemed grateful for the opportunity to take a break.

Hank had finished hiding whatever it was he was hiding and was now standing talking into a mobile phone.

Adam strained to listen but couldn't hear anything of the conversation. Whoever Hank was talking to, it was obviously someone he didn't want overheard.

At that moment, Blackthorn tossed his head at an irritating fly and snorted down his nostrils, and Adam's cover was blown. He would have to bluff it out, he decided, as he watched Hank turn.

'Hi!' he called, kicking Blackthorn into a trot towards him (Hank had pocketed his phone and was standing staring at him.) 'I thought that was you. We've been round the cross country,' he added, jogging to a standstill. He loosened Blackthorn's reins and leaned forwards to pat his neck. 'He's a bit hot. Mind you, so am I.' He straightened up in the saddle. 'Been checking for rabbit holes, have you?'

'Yeah, that's right.' Jed nodded. 'They're a bit of a nuisance at the moment.'

'Tell me about it,' Adam sighed. 'I hear that's how Lucy Woods broke her arm. The horse was okay, but she fell off. Gran was saying that Arizona's a purebred American quarter horse. Have you ridden him yet?'

'No.' Jed shook his head. 'No, I've just got back. I had to go out this morning. I thought you were helping Vanessa in the shop?'

'Yeah, I was.'

'How is she?'

'Better than she was first thing,' Adam said. 'She had a really bad migraine. It was so bad that she had to go and lie down. I was left running the shop,' he added, with a touch of self-importance. 'It was no big deal, and now she's let me have the afternoon off, so I can exercise Blackthorn.'

'That's good,' Jed said, taking a small step sideways.' Well, don't let me stop you. I'd better get on, here, anyway.'

'Yeah. See you,' Adam said. He rode back onto the track and ambled slowly through the shade, glancing behind him every so often to see if he could see what Hank was doing. The American looked to be doing what he said he was doing - filling in rabbit holes and cleaning up the course. But Adam wasn't sure that was all he was up to. He made a mental note of the place - it was past the coffin jump and up through the woods, on the right-hand side by the fence.

Hank had buried something there - he was sure of it. Curiosity and a fertile teenage imagination had Adam assured of one thing - he was going to go back later, to check it out for himself.

Jed wondered if Adam had seen anything. It had been sod's law that the boy had chosen that precise moment to come through the woods. The schedules had shown that no one was doing the cross country until later in the day. Hence the reason he had offered to check out and repair the track.

He didn't want to be caught with the map Giles had given him of the directions to the Norwich stud at North Wall Farm, nor the cash he had been handed for transport expenses ("Cash only, my boy. We don't want any deals traced back to me"). Getting rid of them had been his first prerogative. Finding a safe hiding place had been his second. No way could he risk leaving them in the cottage, where the diligent but efficient cleaning lady, Rita, might discover find them. He had to find somewhere to hide the tin that was outside - somewhere that no one else would think of looking. The woods were ideal. The road passed the perimeter fence close to where he had buried it. He wouldn't even have to come across the course to retrieve it but could pull up on the verge and hop over the fence.

Jed crossed to the tangle of undergrowth and wondered if he should move the tin. It wouldn't do any harm, he decided, pulling the branches to one side. Better safe than sorry. The kid hadn't behaved as if anything was amiss, but that was no guarantee he hadn't spotted him.

He dug out the small, rectangular cigar tin, and placed it to one side as he recovered the hole and piled up the branches so that it looked as it had done a few short moments ago. Where to put it now, was the next thing?

A short walk down the path stood an ancient oak tree that had been felled by lightening. Where the main branch had sheared away from the trunk was a gaping hole. Birds had nested in the convenient dark hollow and an old nest remained. Jed lifted it out and pushed the tin into the space it had vacated, gently pressing the nest back down on top of it.

Satisfied, he hurried back to the path and counted his steps to the fence. As long as he could find the correct tree, he thought, he'd be fine.

Which was exactly what Adam was thinking, as he ran back to where he'd left Blackthorn tethered, hopped up on his back, and headed back to the stables.

The trouble with hangovers, Vanessa discovered, was that they tended to last for the best part of the day. She had gone through the range of feelings from distinctly nauseous and dizzy with a thumping head, to feeling tired and dehydrated. She had a raging thirst that a full bottle of water and two cans of coke had not touched, and all she wanted to do now was go home and soak in a hot bath before retiring to bed.

The woman and child in the tack shop were driving her nuts, if only because they couldn't agree on what hat, coat, boots or even gloves they should buy.

Vanessa retreated behind the counter, having decided that her sales pitch was only confusing the situation. She would leave them to their own devices, while she sought comfort in a can of fizzy orange and a couple of headache tablets.

'Is this jacket waterproof?'

'Shower proof,' Vanessa mumbled, through a mouthful of orange and tablets. Obviously, her presence was required after all.

'Oh. What does that mean?'

'Well, it'll keep you dry in a shower, but probably not in a downpour.'

'That's no good. Harriet - Harriet, try this one.' The woman pulled an expensive wax jacket from the rail.

'Yuck. I don't like green.'

'Have you got this in any other colour?'

Vanessa gulped back the last bitter dregs of tablet and shook her head. She had an extra large one in brown, but no way would it have fitted the little girl fiddling with Adam's model pony display.

'What about this purple one?' suggested the mother, brandishing a padded Puffa jacket at her daughter.

'It's all right,' the girl said.

'Well try it on, then. Come on. Hurry up. We haven't got all day.'

Vanessa sneaked a glance at her watch. It was half past five. She should have been cashing up by now.

The jangle of the bell made her jump. She was just about to announce that the shop was closing when Hank pushed the door open.

'Hi,' he said. 'Thought I'd catch you here.'

Vanessa was, quite literally, transformed. All thoughts of nausea, headaches, bath and an early night disappeared in a flash.

'Hi,' she said, wishing that her cheeks would stop flushing each time she saw or spoke to him.

'How are you feeling?' he whispered, stepping round to her side of the counter. 'Adam said you were a bit better.'

'I'm fine,' she said, sincerely hoping that she looked it. 'When did you see Adam?'

'This afternoon. He was riding the cross country.'

'On his own?'

Jed nodded. 'Yes, I think so.'

'Excuse me. It looks a bit big,' complained the woman, plucking at the sides of the padded jacket.

Vanessa gave Jed a despairing look. 'It's the smallest size I've got,' she said.

'Looks real swell to me, Ma'am,' he said, giving the woman the benefit of one of his most charming smiles. 'Kids that age need plenty of growing room. I promise you that'll fit her real fine by the winter.'

'Well, I suppose she won't be wearing it much over the summer.'

'And it's a bargain price,' Jed said. 'Be twice that come the autumn.'

Vanessa was astounded at his confident sales patter. She couldn't have done better herself.

'What about you, little lady,' Jed said, crouching down in front of the child. 'What do you think? Do you like the colour? It's pretty cool, huh?'

The girl nodded shyly. 'I like it,' she said.

'Well, there you go,' Jed chuckled, straightening up. He winked at Vanessa as the woman reached into her purse for a credit card.

With the transaction duly completed and both child and mother satisfied with their purchase, Vanessa rushed to let them out, so she could lock the door behind them.

'I could do with you in the shop more often,' she said, as she emptied the till and began to count the day's takings. She was bound to make a mistake, she thought. It was hard to concentrate with him standing watching her.

'Now that'd be a real pleasure,' he said.

'Stop teasing me.'

He grinned. 'Okay, I draw the line at shop work, but it'd be good to spend some more time with you.'

Vanessa's hands shook as she piled up the coins. 'What, even after last night?' she said.

'Especially after last night.' He laughed. 'You've no idea how frustrating it was to share a bed with you, and not be able to do anything apart from watch you sleep.'

Vanessa's cheeks flushed scarlet. 'I'm so sorry.'

'Not half as sorry as I was, I'm telling you.' He chuckled. 'Come on, bag that lot up, and let's get going.'

'Where?'

He shrugged. 'Anywhere you like. We could go for something to eat, a drink. Ok, maybe we'll skip the drink,' he said teasingly. 'We could go for a walk, a ride, anything you want to do.'

Vanessa scooped the money into the bag and popped it into the safe. When she turned back, he was sitting on the counter, swinging his long, denim clad legs in front of him, and watching her with an incredibly sexy and half slanting smile.

'Why me?' she said quietly. She couldn't believe this was happening to her. Men like Hank weren't interested in someone like her. They went for beautiful young women like

Gemma, for instance, with her glossy red hair and figure to die for, or Sarah, or even Ella, who was stunning despite being the mother of two children, one of who was a teenager. They didn't go for the frumpy, freckled one, who lived with her mother and worked on her own.

He jumped down from the counter and grabbed hold of her hand. 'Why not you,' he said. 'We had a good time yesterday, didn't we?'

'Yes,' she sighed. It had been wonderful - or at least, what she could remember of it had been.

'So, let's do it again,' he said, squeezing her fingers. Vanessa felt like her hand was being zapped by an electric fence.

'Okay,' she said. 'But first, I need to go to Hollyfield and freshen up a bit.' Having slept in the things she was wearing she felt in dire need of a wash and a change of clothing.

'No problem,' he said. 'It'll give me a chance to talk to your mother about the Western riding class.'

That was the plan, anyway. But sometimes the best-laid plans had a habit of not working out, and this was no exception.

Vanessa had barely set foot inside the front door, when an agitated Ursula ushered her out again.

'Quick. You've got to get over to Grey Lodge,' she said, stuffing the keys to the Range Rover into her hand and bundling her out of the door.

'What? Why?' Vanessa choked; side stepping smartly to avoid colliding with Hank, who was trying to follow her into the house.

'Marcus and Caroline are going out,' she said. 'Hurry up. Oh.' She forced a smile onto her face. 'Hank.'

'Evening Ma'am.'

'I didn't see you there. Were you wanting to speak to me?'

'Yep,' he said, 'but it can wait.'

Ursula's jaw dropped as she watched him turn and follow Vanessa. 'Well, I never,' she said. He was getting into the car with her. The rumours on the yard had some truth in them after all. Still, she thought, he was a nice enough young man. It was just a pity it wouldn't last.

120

'Bother!' Vanessa muttered as she started up the ignition.

'Hey, don't worry about it,' Jed said. 'I'm easy - a night in, or a night out - I don't mind. We can order a takeaway.'

'Yes, but it's not the same,' she said. She had been hoping they could go somewhere more public - somewhere that people might see her with him.

'There'll be other nights,' he said, patting her knee as he spoke. Vanessa nearly drove the car into a ditch. 'If we survive this one,' he added dryly.

'Sorry.'

Caroline and Marcus were waiting impatiently in the doorway for them, having been instructed by Ursula not to leave the house, on pain of death, until Vanessa arrived.

'Where have you been?' Marcus snapped, straightening the front of his smartly tailored suit. 'We're late enough as it is.'

Vanessa banged the driver's door shut with a thud. 'I've been at work,' she said. 'And I haven't had time to get washed or changed. Nor have I had anything to eat. Why didn't you tell me you were going out?' she demanded, rounding on Caroline. Her sister was looking reasonably attractive in a knee length skirt and floral blouse. A string of pearls nestled round her throat.

'I forgot,' Caroline said sheepishly.

'You forgot?'

'Come on,' Marcus snapped, yanking his wife forwards by the hand. It was then that he noticed Hank watching them with interest from the front passenger seat of the Range Rover. 'And lay off the wine,' he added, fumbling for his car keys.

'Don't worry,' Vanessa said. 'I intend to.'

Bruno, at least, was pleased to see them. With a frantic wagging of his tail, he followed them into the lounge and flopped down onto the plush carpet. Marcus had kept him confined to the kitchen and hallway, since he kept leaving little accidents around the place, so he was making the most of being allowed to lie on something soft and comfortable.

'What shall I order?' Jed asked, flicking through the phone book. 'Indian or Chinese?'

'Anything,' Vanessa said, turning on a few lamps to give the room a warmer ambience. With the central light on it looked stark and unwelcoming. 'There,' she said. 'That's better.' She drew the curtains to shut out the prying eyes of the travellers in the next field, though unless they had binoculars, it was doubtful whether they would have been able to see in.

'Chinese,' he suggested. 'I'll order a few different dishes. I don't know about you, but I'm starving.'

Vanessa hadn't managed to eat anything all day, though she had drunk enough fluids to sink the Titanic. Now, however, she was starting to feel peckish. She was also feeling a tad grubby.

'I'll pop up and have a quick shower while we're waiting,' she said. 'You don't mind, do you, only I need to get out of these clothes?'

'No, you do what you like,' he said. 'I'm easy. I'll watch a bit of TV.'

Vanessa galloped up the stairs two at a time, desperate to be away from Hank for as short a period as possible. She could hardly believe that he was here - alone - with her. She stood under the hot shower, lathering soap all over and humming happily to herself as she did so. A quick rub down with the towel, a generous squirt of perfume and she felt almost human again. What to wear was her next problem. Her most flattering pair of trousers had been slept in, and her best clothes had been carted over to Hollyfield in a suitcase. All that remained was stuff she wouldn't be seen dead in. There was a reasonable looking white blouse, though. She could team it with a pair of jeans and have it hanging over the waistband. Perhaps with the collar turned up, she thought, holding it in front of herself and modelling it before the mirror.

'You could, of course, stick with the towel,' Jed said.

Vanessa jerked her head round in surprise. He was lounging in the doorway, watching her with interest, a faintly amused smile tugging at his lips.

'Hank!' she groaned. 'Go away. I'm not ready.'

'You look pretty good to me,' he said.

Vanessa could feel goose bumps popping up all over, and it wasn't because of the cold either. It was the look she could see in the depths of his deep blue eyes - the look that said he wanted her - really wanted her.

'The...um Chinese should be here any minute,' she said.

'Yeah. I expect so - though they did say half an hour.' He stepped into the room and Vanessa felt her heart give a sudden drum roll against her rib cage. It was hammering away so loud she felt certain he must hear it.

'Half an hour, huh?' she said.

'Hmm.' He reached out and lifted a strand of hair from her damp cheek. 'Still,' he murmured, 'I'm sure we can think of something to do to help pass the time?'

Vanessa had not had much in the way of sexual experiences with men. A drunken coupling with Duggie Jamieson behind the cow barn at the Young Farmer's Ball had not been a particularly memorable occasion. Nor had the brief holiday fling with Pedro in Barcelona. Alcohol had played a big part each time, but now she was stone cold sober - hung over, perhaps, but still stone cold sober. And surprisingly enough, she was feeling rampant - rampant, wanton, and utterly desirable.

With a wicked smile, she let the towel drop to the floor.

'Something like this?' she murmured.

Jed grinned. 'For starters.'

The shrill ringing of the doorbell stirred Vanessa from her state of blissful dreaminess. She was draped in a tangled sheet, her head resting on Hank's shoulder. One of his arms lay possessively across her middle.

'That's the door,' she murmured.

'So, it is.'

The bell rang a second time, this time for longer.

Jed groaned and lifted his head from the pillow. 'Guess I'd better answer it,' he said, sitting up and reaching for his jeans. 'Don't move,' he added.

Vanessa had no intention of doing any such thing. She stretched out languorously, like a cat in front of an open fire. She would never sleep in this bed again without remembering the last few glorious, and utterly fulfilling moments. Even thinking about them made her shiver with pleasure. Hank had been everything and more than she had expected of a man who was obviously experienced with women.

She wondered if he had ever been married. Or worse, if he still had a wife? It was an awful thing to realise that she knew next to nothing about him, but it hadn't stopped her leaping into bed with him. If she was honest with herself, she had wanted him as much as he had wanted her.

So, what happens now, she thought?

'Dinner is served, milady.'

Jed pushed the door open with his foot and came striding into the bedroom carrying a silver tray heaped with little foil dishes, cutlery, plates, two crystal glasses and a bottle of wine. 'I thought we'd have it up here,' he added. 'It's much cosier.'

He laid the tray on the end of the bed and began prising off the cardboard lids. The aroma of the varied assortment of Chinese dishes was making Vanessa's mouth water.

'No wine for me,' she said, leaning forwards with the sheet tucked like a toga round her shoulders and middle. 'I've got to drive us back, remember.'

'A little won't do you any harm,' Jed said, removing the cork in one easy, fluid motion. 'Call it a hair of the dog.' He dribbled a few mouthfuls into her glass, and then chinked it with his own. 'To us,' he said.

Vanessa blushed. 'To us.'

The meal was delicious - the best food she had ever tasted. Or perhaps it was because the company was so good that she was enjoying it so much. Hank was an amusing and entertaining companion. He was easy-going and made her laugh - a lot. But he never said a lot about himself. In fact, he seemed quite guarded when she asked him about his past.

'You don't want to know,' he groaned.

The trouble was, she did - very much. She had told him all about her life. How her father had died, and she'd been brought up by a succession of stepfathers - all now deceased. How they had once lived at Hollyfield, and now lived at Grey Lodge - even how lonely she had felt when Caroline married Marcus and left home.

'And we did nothing but argue when we all lived together,' she said. 'Have you got any brothers or sisters, Hank?'

'A sister,' he replied, reaching for the wine bottle. 'Shall I top your glass up?'

He was changing the subject again, and Vanessa didn't know whether to feel hurt or peeved. What was he trying to hide? They all had skeletons in their cupboards, but she couldn't imagine him having anything so terrible that he didn't want to talk about it. He was such fun - so easy-going and friendly. How could a man like that have anything to hide?

Jed drained his glass and poured himself a refill. He was feeling relaxed and contented. Vanessa was a good tonic for taking his mind off his problems. She had a funny and self-deprecating dry wit that made him laugh. She knew she wasn't anything out of the ordinary in the beauty stakes, but she didn't seem to care. What you saw was what you got, freckles and curves and all. Jed could see the inner attractiveness of the woman that few others had even glanced at. She might come over as awkward and outspoken, but underneath she was timid and naïve, and utterly delightful. He really liked her.

'Do you want that last spare rib?' he said, offering her the foil dish.

'No, thanks. I'm stuffed,' she said, flopping back on the pillows. 'That was gorgeous.'

Jed grinned. 'So are you, honey.'

'Oh, stop it,' she said. 'You know that's not true.'

'Beauty,' he said, 'is in the eye of the beholder.'

'I suggest you get your eyes tested then,' she giggled, darting away from him as he made a grab for the corner of her sheet. 'Hank, stop it! I'll catch my death of cold.'

'Come here, then, and I'll warm you up.'

'You already have done,' she laughed, as she headed for the door. 'I'm going for a shower.'

'Need any help?'

Vanessa smiled. 'I think I can turn the tap on by myself, thanks.'

'I'm good at scrubbing backs.'

'Oh, come on, then,' she giggled. It was turning into a day for novel experiences, so sharing a hot shower with Hank might as well be one of them. Whatever else might happen, she reflected, she wasn't going to forget the last few hours in a hurry.

Chapter 10

It was after midnight by the time Caroline and Marcus returned from the annual tax inspectors' dinner, by which time Jed and Vanessa were comfortably ensconced on the large and squashy sofa in the lounge.

'Had a good night?' Vanessa asked sleepily. She had almost dropped off. Her eyelids felt heavy and tired.

'Splendid, thank you,' Marcus said, swaying unsteadily at the foot of the stairs. His tie was undone, and his jacket swung open.

Caroline raised her eyes to the ceiling. 'He did,' she said.

'Do I smell food from the Orient?' Marcus looked as if he was drooling.

'We had a Chinese, mate,' Jed said. 'Sorry, there's nothing left.'

'I had a Chinese once.'

'Marcus!' Caroline snapped. 'Go to bed.'

'Hmm. All right, dear,' he mumbled. 'Off to bed. Good idea.' He swung for a moment on the end of the banisters. 'Now then…up the stairs, off we go. One step, two steps…'

'Give me strength!' Caroline muttered. 'You know, there's only so much back-clapping and false flattery I can take, but Marcus has revelled in it all night - and I think he believed it too, and now look at the state of him.'

Vanessa rejoiced at the thought of the hangover her much disliked brother-in-law was going to suffer the following morning. 'Tell him to drink lots of cold water,' she said.

Caroline put on her prim and proper "Ursula" face. 'I think I'll let him suffer,' she said. 'It'll do him good.'

'Then I suggest you leave him with a bucket,' Jed said, standing up and stretching wearily.

'If he throws up, he cleans up.'

'Depending on how sober he is at the time,' Jed said. He winked at Vanessa.' Come on, honey, let's go.'

Honey? Caroline followed them to the door. He'd called her sister "honey". That was a term of endearment. People didn't speak to Vanessa like that. Well, not usually.

127

She tried to draw Vanessa a look, but her sister was having none of it.

'Night,' she called as she skipped out to the Range Rover and flicked open the doors.

'Um, night!' Caroline called, giving them a small wave. How strange, she thought. Vanessa had seemed so unlike her usual self tonight. She wondered if she was coming down with something.

'You're nothing like your sister,' Jed said, as they sped down the narrow lanes leading to Hollyfield.

'Aren't I?' Vanessa, said, glancing sideways at him. All her life people had been comparing her to Caroline. It was the first time anyone had said they were different.

'You know you're not,' he said. 'Mind you, living with that Marcus, I can see where she gets it from.'

'Mother says they're well suited.'

'I expect she's right,' he laughed.

Vanessa swung the powerful car up the drive towards Hollyfield. The house was in darkness save for a light left on over the porch, and one in the stable yard.

'Coming in for a coffee?' she suggested, switching off the ignition. She didn't want the night to end. Making love with Hank had been the most wonderful and liberating experience of her life for her and she was rather hoping he felt the same.

'Best not,' he said, causing her hopes and dreams to come tumbling down like a pack of falling cards. 'I've got an early start in the morning.' He leaned over the gear stick and kissed her, and she felt her spirits lift a little. 'I'll see you tomorrow, though, and that's a promise.'

'I'll look forward to it,' she said.

'You and me both.' He swung open the door, but he didn't make any move to get out. Vanessa wondered if he'd changed his mind.

He hadn't. 'Who's that?' he said.

'Where?'

He pointed a finger in the direction of the house. 'Over there. I think it's Adam.'

'Adam!' Vanessa followed the line of his gaze, her thoughts racing. She was sure he must be mistaken. It wouldn't be Adam at this time of night. It was more than likely to be one of the gipsies. She peered into the darkness. Bloody hell - it was Adam. He was walking down the side of the house carrying a torch in one hand, and he had Ella's black and white collie, Jessie on the lead beside him.

'Bit late for dog walking, isn't it?' Jed said.

'I'll say.'

Vanessa jumped down from the driver's seat. 'Adam!' she shouted. 'What on earth are you doing?'

'Shit,' he muttered, yanking on Jessie's lead. Where the heck had they come from? He'd waited hours for Gran to go to bed. He'd lain fully clothed under his duvet for the best part of the evening whilst she had roamed round the house making phone calls to people, something about a party, though goodness knows why she had chosen that night to organise it all. And then, just as he had thought it was safe to go out, his aunt had turned up with Hank in tow. He hadn't seen the lights of the Range Rover sweep up the drive, nor had he expected anyone to be there. How was he going to get out of this one? It was half past twelve at night.

'Where do you think you're going?' Vanessa said.

'Um...' He shifted from one foot to the other, trying to think of an excuse. The faint flickering of a light from the stud office gave him a brilliant and fool-proof plan. 'The...um foaling boxes.'

'At this time?'

He nodded. 'Thomas is expecting Gemini to foal tonight. I didn't want to miss anything.' It wasn't a lie, he reasoned, the birth was imminent.

'Oh.' Vanessa glanced at Jed. 'I've never seen a mare giving birth before.' Vanessa liked to see the foals all spindly legged and frolicking in the paddocks with their mothers. She wasn't sure that the actual blood and gore of the birth process was something she wanted to see. Nor did she think that it was particularly suitable for an adolescent schoolboy to witness, either.

'He said I could watch.'

'That's as maybe,' Vanessa said,' but I don't think he'd want you to bring Jess along. It's hardly the right place for a dog.'

Adam couldn't argue with that, so he remained silent, not knowing what else to say. It was a shrewd move.

Vanessa decided she had embarrassed him. He was obviously scared to be alone in the dark but wouldn't admit it to anyone. She could understand that. She didn't much like the idea herself.

'Oh, go on,' she said, in her most reassuring tone. 'Put Jessie back in the house, and we'll come with you.'

Oddly enough, he didn't look pleased with that suggestion, either.

'It's okay, Aunty Van. You don't need to.'

'I know,' she said. 'But I don't want you wandering about here on your own.'

There was no way out of it. Adam realised he was going to have to go along with her and hope to goodness Gemini was about to drop her foal.

As luck would have it that was exactly what the mare was about to do.

Since most births took place in the middle of the night, Thomas had set up a list of watchers to keep an eye on the foaling box via closed circuit television whenever one was imminent. It was his turn to sit up in the relative comfort of the stud office that night, and it was there that Vanessa and Jed found him, sitting watching the small black and white screen with avid interest.

'Now then, folks,' he said, rising from his chair. 'What can I do for you at this ungodly hour?'

Vanessa pushed Adam in front of her. 'He wants to watch,' she said.

'Does he now.' Thomas turned the screen towards him. 'Well, in that case, my boy, you've come at just the right time. See how she's pawing the ground and swishing her tail? She'll be going down again any moment.'

Vanessa felt Hank's hand settle on her shoulder as he came to stand behind her. 'You want to watch this,' he murmured, nuzzling against her ear.

'I don't think I do,' she replied.

The mare flopped onto her side. She looked to be in some discomfort. Vanessa wondered how Thomas could remain so calm. He was sitting back in his chair, sipping a cup of coffee from a flask he had brought with him, and looking completely unperturbed.

'Shouldn't you be doing something?' she said.

'Not at this stage.'

'The mare's best left to her own devices,' Jed whispered. 'If you disturb her now, she might change her mind about giving birth.'

'She can do that?' Vanessa said in surprise.

'If she's a mind to,' Thomas agreed. He leaned towards the screen and touched it with his finger. 'See that, Adam? It won't be long now.'

Vanessa watched the events unfolding on the screen with one eye shut and the other only half open. She was squeamish at the best of times and this was not her idea of fun. But once the mare started her contractions in earnest, she was as transfixed as everyone else in the room. It was the most amazing thing she had ever seen in her life. The emergence of the foal from a slippery slimy bundle into a gangling little heap of waving legs and bewildered looking face was breath taking. The mare lifted her head and turned to inspect the new arrival, nuzzling and licking its little face.

Vanessa burst into tears. It was the most magical thing she had ever seen.

'Told you,' Jed said, giving her a hug.

Adam tried to show enthusiasm, but his heart wasn't in it. He was more concerned about when he would be able to get to the woods. If he left it until the morning it might be too late. But the way his aunt was snuffling into Hank's sleeve suggested that they weren't going anywhere fast.

He tried to stifle an exaggerated yawn.

Vanessa pulled herself together with admirable self-control. 'Goodness' she said. 'Is that really the time? We'd better get you to bed Adam.'

'I'll stay and help Thomas,' Jed said. 'Unless you want me to walk you back?'

Vanessa shook her head. She felt slightly miffed that he had turned down an invitation for coffee with her, but not, it seems, the opportunity to help with a new-born foal. 'I thought you said you had an early start in the morning?'

'You can't get much earlier than this,' he said.

'Come on, Aunty Van,' Adam said wearily. 'I'm shattered.' He yawned again, as if to emphasise the point.

'Oh, all right, come on.' She pushed the door open.

Thomas had gone into the foaling box and was doing whatever it was that needed doing with surgical gloves and disinfectant. Vanessa realised, begrudgingly, that he would probably appreciate Hanks offer of help.

But assisting the elderly stud manager was not the priority on Jed's mind. He waited until Adam and Vanessa had gone before peering at the closed-circuit television screen. Thomas was fully occupied in the stable. Jed crossed the room to the grey filing cabinet next to the desk. With one eye on the screen, and the other on the folders in front of him, he eventually found what he was looking for - Midnight Prince's registration papers and identification documents.

He had no intention of stealing them but misplacing them was a necessity. He didn't want anyone looking too closely at the details of the stallion. He found a folder in the back of the cabinet with the name 'Brandy' on the front, and deftly inserted the papers into it. Then he stuffed it back in its place but forced it down so that the other folders obscured it from sight. Unless someone was exceptionally thorough, the papers wouldn't be found for a long time.

Jed straightened up and glanced at the screen. Thomas was busy disinfecting the stump on the tiny foal.

He took a deep breath, closed the filing cabinet, and decided it was time he offered him some assistance.

Adam jerked awake at the first sound of the alarm clock, and stuffed it under his pillow, hoping no one had heard it. He lay still under the covers, listening intently. A faint glimmer of pre-dawn light shone through the gap in the curtains. Satisfied that all was quiet, he flung back the duvet and scrambled out of bed, still wearing the clothes he had gone to sleep in.

Padding barefoot down to the kitchen, he reached for his trainers. He would take Jessie with him, he decided, if only because it was a short time before dawn, and anyone seeing him would think he was taking the dog for an early morning walk, though five o'clock, he conceded, was perhaps a bit too early.

Boy and dog sprinted the short distance across the lawn to the first field, where he could use the hedge as a barrier to anyone happening to look out of the windows.

The grass was wet and slippery with dew. Adam wished he had put on his boots. His feet were soaked.

At the end of the field, he scrambled over the post and rail fence and ran to the first part of the cross-country course. It took him less than twenty minutes to reach the woods on foot. It was decidedly spooky in the darkness of the trees, and he was glad of the dog for company. Jessie, meanwhile, was having a wonderful time, frightening the rabbits in the undergrowth, and even managing to scare a young deer, before Adam called her back and clipped on her lead. 'And quit barking,' he hissed, frightened that someone might hear them.

The broken trunk of the oak tree loomed out of the shadows. Adam's heart was thumping like mad as he hurried towards it and slipped Jessie's lead over the end of a branch. He was barely tall enough to reach the hollow in the trunk of the tree, but reach it he did, standing on tiptoe until he could feel the empty bird's nest with his fingers. He eased it to one side and swallowed hard as he felt the shiny metal of the tin. What on earth was it? A cigar box, he realised, as he pulled it out and turned it over in his hands. His fingers were shaking as he prised open the lid. 'Jesus Christ!' he gasped. He'd never seen so much money. There had to be - he flicked through the notes - hundreds of pounds. A thousand pounds, maybe, in used notes, bound together with an elastic band. What the hell was Hank doing with all this money?

He picked up the folded piece of paper that lay under the notes. It was some sort of map - directions, by the look of it, to a place called North Hall Farm. He memorised the name and stuffed the paper back in the tin. The third item he found was a yellow post-it note, with a number on it; a phone number perhaps? He recited the sequence in his head and hoped he'd remember it.

Now he was seriously worried. He placed all the items back in the tin, closed it and stuffed it back under the empty bird's nest. Then he scuffed a few leaves over the area to hide his footprints and released Jessie from where she had been sitting watching him, panting, with her long pink tongue hanging out.

'Come on, girl,' he muttered, breaking into a run down the shaded track. 'It's time we were getting home.'

Vanessa found that Saturdays in the tack shop tended to be the busiest day of the week. In fact, it was the only day that she absolutely relied on Adam's help, but he had failed to turn up that morning as promised. A phone call to her mother had informed her that he was having a long lie in after the exciting events of the previous evening.

'He saw Gemini's foal being born,' Ursula said.

'I know,' Vanessa snapped. 'I was there with him.'

It really was too bad. If anyone deserved a long lie it should be her. It had been after two before she had crawled into bed that night, only to have her alarm go off at eight as she was in the middle of a blissful dream. Hank had featured strongly in it, along with the gipsies, who had been dancing some kind of fandango on the lawn at Grey Lodge. He could be a gipsy, she thought dreamily, with his dark hair and flashing blue eyes. A delicious little shiver ran down her spine as she remembered the events of the night before - the tenderness of his caress, the firmness of his touch - she was getting all hot and bothered just thinking about it.

'Morning.'

Vanessa snapped herself out of her reminiscences at the sound of her sister's cheerful greeting.

'What are you doing here?' she said, her eyes narrowing suspiciously as she watched her waltz through the door. She was wearing dark blue jeans and a pale pink blouse that didn't do a lot for her ruddy complexion. A knowing smile was cemented firmly on her face.

Vanessa viewed her with suspicion. Caroline didn't normally come to the tack shop. The fact that she had done meant that she was after something.

'I was just passing,' she said.

'Passing on the way to where? And what have you done with Marcus?'

'Oh, him!' Caroline sighed. 'He's sleeping off the worst hangover you've ever seen. I can't remember how many times he threw up. I've left him to it. Grape and grain, I did warn him, but he wouldn't listen?'

'Does he ever,' Vanessa said.

Caroline ignored her sarcastic aside. 'Anyway, I thought I'd take the chance to get out, seeing as how I've been confined to the house all week.'

'And you thought you'd come here.'

'Why not?' She picked up a china ornament of a Shetland pony and turned it over to look at the price. With her eyebrows raised she glanced back at Vanessa. 'Do you sell many of these?'

'Yes, as it happens.'

'Bit expensive, aren't they.'

'Not particularly,' Vanessa said, taking it from her and putting it back on the display. 'What do you want, Caroline?'

Her sister looked slightly put out. 'Well if you must know,' she said, 'I've been a bit worried about you.'

'About me?'

'Yes,' she said. 'I couldn't help noticing how much you seem to like this American chap.'

'Hank,' Vanessa said. 'His name's Hank.'

'I hope you realise how totally unsuitable he is for you.'

Vanessa thought she could detect a hint of jealousy in Caroline's tone. 'Why is he unsuitable?'

'Because he's a drifter,' she said. 'And I don't want to see you getting hurt.'

As if you care, Vanessa thought peevishly.

'Mother says he's only here for the summer,' she continued. 'And I know what you're like. You'll fall head over heels for him, and then he'll dump you. I can see it happening already. You were hanging onto him like a leech last night.'

'I was not,' Vanessa said hotly.

The bell above the door jangled, and she gave her sister a warning glare as two teenage girls wandered into the shop, closely followed by a middle-aged man and a small child.

'Can I help you?' she asked.

'No, we're just looking, thanks,' replied one of the girls.

Caroline sidled up to Vanessa. 'That's why you were so keen to go line-dancing,' she hissed. 'You thought it might impress him. It's like this Western riding business as well. Honestly, Vanessa, you're so naïve. If you keep throwing yourself at him, he'll take advantage of you and then leave. That's what men like him do.'

'Oh, and you'd know that, would you?'

'Everyone knows it,' Caroline said, 'except perhaps you.'

Vanessa felt deeply hurt. How could her sister say such spiteful things? It wasn't as if she was a complete novice when it came to relationships. She had been out with a few men over the years. (Admittedly, none of them had lasted.) But Hank was different. She had admired him from a distance, but he had made the first approach. She had already decided that he was way out of her league, and no one could have been more surprised than she was when he asked her out.

She forced a smile onto her lips as the man came to the counter and handed her a tiny pair of jodhpurs and a bag of horse treats.

'I'll take these, thanks,' he said.

The little girl stood on her toes to peer over the edge of the counter. She had big, baby blue eyes and a halo of golden curls poking out from beneath a floppy sun hat. 'They're for Bramble,' she said, pointing at the bag of treats.

'Lucky Bramble,' Vanessa said, popping them into a bag and handing them over. She was the first to admit that she'd never been a great fan of small children, but this little girl was so cute that she felt quite taken with her. It must have been seeing Gemini give birth, she decided. It was making her feel broody.

Not so Caroline, who was peering down her nose at the child as if she might be harbouring some deadly disease.

'Thanks,' the man said, pocketing his change. 'Come on, poppet.'

'Bye.' The little girl gave Vanessa a wave.

'Bye.' Vanessa waved back. 'What?' she said, catching sight of her sister's horrified expression. 'She was such a sweetie.'

'Now I'm really worried,' Caroline muttered.

'Oh, go away.'

Vanessa stomped into the storeroom to fetch a bag of feed for one of her regular customers. Humping heavy sacks around was normally Adam's job on a Saturday, and she was sorely missing his presence. She stooped to pick up the bag of pasture mix.

'Here, let me get that for you.'

She jerked her head up in surprise. 'Hank!' So great was her shock that she nearly dropped the sack. He was dressed in faded jeans and a black t-shirt that showed every firm and rippling muscle on his chest and forearms. A thin gold chain hung round his neck. 'What are you doing here?' she croaked, as images of him naked in bed with her flashed to the fore.

'Hopefully, seeing you,' he said, levering the sack out of her arms. He carried it as if it weighed no more than a bag of sugar. 'Where do you want it?'

'By the door,' she said. 'They're coming to collect it later.' She followed him into the shop, where Caroline was picking her way through a rack of cards and trying to appear as if she was studying them intently.

Vanessa ignored her. 'How's the foal doing?'

'Yeah, good.' He nodded, grinning. 'That was quite some night, wasn't it?'

'Unbelievable,' Vanessa agreed, and she didn't just mean about the foal. Jed smiled and squeezed her hand - an action that caused Caroline to purse her lips in annoyance.

Vanessa noticed it, even if Jed didn't. 'Weren't you going somewhere?' she said pointedly.

'What? Oh, yes.' Her sister snatched up a birthday card and slapped it on the counter. 'I'll have this one.'

Jed sidled up behind her. 'How's your husband this morning?' he asked, with an amused glint in his eyes.

'Much as you'd expect,' Caroline said, fumbling in her purse for some change.

She didn't look at him as she stuffed the card into her handbag, though she was patently aware of his presence. It was making her feel strangely hot and flustered. She glanced up at Vanessa. 'Remember what I said,' she warned. 'I'll talk to you later.'

Jed raised a quizzical eyebrow as Caroline sailed past him. 'What was that all about?'

'Oh, nothing,' Vanessa sighed.

'I thought I detected a bit of an atmosphere.'

'No really, it's nothing. Well, just her, nit-picking about things.'

'About me, I suspect,' he said, with a knowing smile. 'Don't worry. I can take it. She's not my type either.' He lounged back against the counter and folded his arms across his chest. 'So,' he said, 'have you got any plans for tonight?'

'I'm not sure,' she replied, reaching for the blue bound desk diary on the counter as she spoke. She knew full well that most of the pages were empty, but Hank didn't know that. 'I'll need to check my diary.'

'Okay. Well, if you're free we could go into town,' he suggested. 'That's if you want to, of course.'

'Hmm.' She made a show of flicking through the pages, since she didn't want him to know how keen she was. She was playing it cool, just like it said in chapter three of her self-help book. 'Yes, I'm free,' she said, closing the diary and glancing up at him with a warm smile. 'And I'd like it if we could go into town.' Somewhere public - somewhere she could show him off to all and sundry. She wasn't going to say no to that.

'Good.' He straightened up, grinning. 'I'll pick you up about eight.'

Chapter 11

'Right, Charlotte, I think we could try a little trot, now,' Tamsin said. She was surprised at how well her small learner was doing. The child had natural balance and a complete lack of fear for one so young. It was nice to get them started at this age. Sometimes the older girls tensed up or were frightened of taking a tumble. Little Charlotte was taking it all in her stride.

'It's going to feel a bit bumpy at first, so hold on to the front of the saddle,' she added. 'Sarah, can you make Flossie trot on for a few paces.'

Kate sat on the bench watching the progress of her daughter's private riding lesson. (It was costing her an arm and a leg, but she had assured Graham it would be money well spent.) Tamsin, as Ella said, was a lovely young woman who seemed to know how to get the best from her pupils. Charlotte was bobbing up and down on the pony's back and enjoying every minute of it.

'Hold tight, darling,' she mouthed as they jogged past.

'Good. Well done,' Tamsin called. 'We'll walk another circle, and then try that again.'

Kate, as a proud parent, was snapping away with her camera. She wanted to take some photographs of Charlotte so that she could show them to Ella when they went to Paris. Ella, she knew, would be thrilled to see them.

'And trot on - that's it.'

As Charlotte reached the far corner of the arena, Kate noticed a man in jeans and a denim shirt leading a chestnut horse to the gate. The horse was tacked up in the most amazing Western saddle, with a coloured blanket on its back.

This just had to be Hank, Kate decided, reaching for her camera again. It was the third time she'd come up to the stables, and not managed to see the American. Now, with her camera, it was too good an opportunity to miss.

'I'll be about ten minutes,' Tamsin called to him. 'You can come in a warm up, if you like.'

'You sure?'

'Yes. We'll keep down this end.'

Kate watched, impressed, as Hank vaulted up onto the horse and rode it into the arena. He looked every inch the Western cowboy, (despite the fact he was wearing a normal riding hat). The horse strolled along with its head hanging low as he put it through a range of moves - stopping, turning, going backwards and then forwards, and all with the minimum use of the reins.

Kate snapped away with her camera. If this was the man Vanessa was rumoured to be seeing, she was one lucky girl. He was bloody gorgeous. His dark hair curled under the rim of his hat and a gold earring glinted in one ear. He had the look of a gipsy about him, she thought, studying his long, tanned arms beneath his rolled-up shirtsleeves, and he had the most amazing physique. She hadn't seen muscles like that for a long time. (She made a mental note to enrol Graham at the gym. He could do with losing a few pounds and toning up a bit.)

'Mummy? Are you watching me?'

'Hmm - what - yes, of course darling.' Kate tore her eyes away from the veritable feast of virile manhood in front of her and watched her daughter bouncing along on the little grey pony. 'I'm watching,' she called.

Five minutes later, and her eyes were straying in Hank's direction again. It was hard not to. For the first time ever, she found herself wondering if she should take up riding - preferably Western riding. The thought didn't last for long. God, no. Her, sit on a horse. She shuddered at the thought. Not even with someone as gorgeous as him to help her. She was better just daydreaming about it.

'Finished, Mummy,' Charlotte said. She was sitting on the pony just yards from the rail, wondering why her mother hadn't got up to meet her.

'Hmm - oh, good.' Kate picked up her bag and slung it over her shoulder. Charlotte liked to take the pony back to its stable and help un-tack it. Kate was more than happy to join her, as long as she didn't have to do anything.

'She did really well today,' Tamsin said, coming over to the gate. She turned to Hank and called, 'It's all yours.'

'Thanks,' he said, urging his horse into a gentle, loping stride around the arena.

'Who's he?' Kate whispered, though she knew she didn't have to ask.'

'His name is Hank Raymond Jefferson,' Tamsin told her. 'He's our new Western riding instructor. Fit, isn't he,' she added with a knowing smile. 'We've already got people asking when we're taking bookings for lessons. Are you tempted?'

'I'll say,' Kate said. 'Sadly, I don't think my husband would be too impressed.'

'Hmm, funny that.' Tamsin lifted the reins over Flossie's head and took control as they plodded towards the stable yard. 'Most of the requests have come from women.'

Kate kept a respectful distance from the pony's teeth and legs on the short walk back to the stables. She wasn't in the least bit surprised. What was amazing her was the fact that he was allegedly going out with Vanessa. Unless the woman had changed dramatically since Kate had last seen her, (and, in her opinion, nothing short of an extreme makeover would do) she couldn't imagine them together at all.

'I gather he's the main entertainment at the Barn Dance Ursula's organised for the fourteenth,' she said.

'So, I've been told.' Tamsin helped Charlotte dismount and handed her the reins while she undid the pony's girth. 'He's doing a riding demonstration. I'd love to know what Ella makes of it all,' she added. 'There you go Charlotte. Put this in the tack room, and then you can give Flossie a brush over.'

Kate watched her daughter walking away with the pony's saddle as if she were an experienced little helper. 'She loves it up here,' she said.

'They all do at that age - correction, most of them do.' Tamsin unfastened the bridle and pulled it over the pony's head. She clipped on a head collar. 'Can you hold her a moment while I fetch a hay-net?'

Kate looked appalled. 'I don't think so.'

'She won't hurt you.'

'So, you keep saying,' she muttered, taking a step backwards. The pony may be small, but she didn't intend to take any chances.

Sarah caught hold of the lead rope. 'It's okay, Tamsin. I'll do it.'

'Thanks.'

'Yes, thanks,' Kate said. 'I'm sorry, but I'm not a horsey person.'

'That's okay.'

Charlotte came wandering back from the tack room clutching a box with brushes and grooming equipment in it. Kate was full of admiration at the way her small daughter seemed so at ease with the pony. It could have been a lion as far as she was concerned and equally as dangerous. No way was she getting any closer. A tentative pat on the mane and that was it.

'You ought to have a go at riding,' Tamsin said, coming back with a dripping hay net and fastening it to a ring in the wall. 'I'm sure Ella would teach you.'

'She's already offered but I said no.'

'You might like it,' she persisted.

'I think not,' Kate said, glancing at her watch. She ought to be making tracks, but she was loath to drag Charlotte away when she was enjoying herself.

'She won't be much longer,' Tamsin said, sensing her uneasiness. 'It helps build their confidence if they can do things with the ponies other than ride them.'

It wasn't doing much for hers, Kate thought.

A clip clopping of hooves drew her attention away from the tranquil scene in front of her (of Flossie munching hay and Charlotte grooming her) and concentrated it on the loan horseman jogging out across the yard.

Hank Raymond Jefferson, she mused, taking one last picture while the opportunity presented itself.

She could hardly wait to show Ella these photographs. No woman, not even a happily married one, could fail to be impressed by them.

'What time do you call this?' Vanessa grumbled, as Adam made his appearance in the tack shop shortly after mid-day. She had been rushed off her feet all morning and was longing for the chance to sit down with a cup of coffee and something to eat. She hadn't even had five minutes to put the kettle on.

'Sorry,' he said, draping his denim jacket over a hook on the door. 'I slept in.'

'Lucky for some.'

Adam scowled. He wasn't in the best of moods, and he resented his aunt for picking on him. She ought to be grateful he'd turned up at all. Lack of sleep didn't help, but he was more concerned about the money he'd found and what he was going to do about it. He couldn't tell her he'd been spying on her precious boyfriend. Nor could he tell her what he'd discovered. But something told him it wasn't right. Hank was involved in some kind of shady deal - the question was what sort of deal?'

'Now what are you doing?' Vanessa asked, as she came back from the storeroom with a steaming cup of coffee to find him pouring over the phone book.

'Nothing,' he said, slamming it shut.

Vanessa raised an eyebrow at him.

'Just checking on a number,' he said. He'd been trying to find North Hall Farm, but it wasn't easy since he didn't know the name of the owner, and it wasn't listed under farms.

'Well, if you're quite finished,' she said. 'Perhaps you could bring some of those sacks of pasture mix through and a couple of bags of chaff. We've had a run on orders today. Don't ask me why.'

The physical exertion of the task kept Adam occupied, which was good, but it didn't stop him thinking. He knew he had to do something, but he wasn't sure what. He could confront Hank, but he was wary of going that route. The guy seemed okay, but he didn't know what he might be like if crossed. He could tell his aunt, but she might not believe him. (And why should she? He had no proof.) Telling his Gran was probably not a good idea either. She was the one who had taken the American on. No, he'd have to sort this one out for himself. Firstly, by finding out if money was missing from the stables, and secondly, by finding out exactly where North Hall Farm was.

Sally Dickson did the cashing up on a Friday afternoon, he recalled, and she banked the weeks' takings before she went home. If any money had been missing - and one thousand pounds was a considerable amount - he was convinced his Gran would have said something. Which meant that the money Hank had hidden in the woods was unlikely to have come from the business. So where had it come from?

Adam's imagination went into overdrive. Had there been a local robbery he didn't know about, a raid at the village post office, or someone pilfering the till in the nearby pub? Was it something to do with the gipsies camped out at Grey Lodge? They tended to do cash deals - his Gran had said so. ("That's how they can afford to drive round in those bloody great four by fours. I'll get Marcus onto them, though. They must owe a fortune in tax").

'Adam!'

'Uh! What?'

His aunt was glaring at him with an exasperated expression on her face. 'Navy tendon boots,' she said, jerking her head in the direction of the storeroom. 'He won't be a moment,' she added, smiling for the benefit of her waiting customer - an attractive looking woman with skin-tight jodhpurs and long dark hair that poked out the back of her green baseball cap.

Adam snatched down his jacket from the hook. He had to get out of here. He couldn't think straight.

'Adam?'

'Sorry, Aunty Van, I feel a bit sick,' he said, making a dash for the door.

The young woman stepped hurriedly to one side. 'Oh dear,' she said. 'Do you think he's going to be all right?'

'I don't know,' said, following her nephew's headlong dash with a worried frown. 'He seemed fine earlier on. Um - navy tendon boots,' she added. 'Right. I'll just get them for you.'

Vanessa was as surprised as her customer at Adam's sudden and unexpected departure. She had sensed something was upsetting him but had put it down to lack of sleep and teenage moodiness. She hoped he wasn't ill. Even more so, she hoped it wasn't catching.

144

Back at the stables, Ursula was watching Hank ride Lucy Woods' horse, Arizona, in the sand school. The chestnut gelding was a joy to behold. The transitions were performed with a seemingly effortless harmony between horse and rider, yet even Ursula knew that it took tremendous skill to achieve such perfection.

'Oh well done, Hank,' she said, applauding him. She'd never seen such sure and accurate leg-yields. 'Bravo.'

Jed grinned as he jogged over to the rail. 'He makes it seem easy. But yeah, he's done well today.' He patted the horse firmly on the neck. 'I'm going to take him out for a short hack. Call it his reward if you like.'

'Splendid,' Ursula beamed. 'He's going to be the star of the show.' She stepped forward to open the gate for him. 'How about the other horses? Are any of them ready to give Western lessons yet?' She was anxious to advertise them as soon as possible.

'Give me a few more days,' Jed said. 'They're getting there, but it won't happen overnight. Lady might be okay, but I can't guarantee that Jasper's up for it yet. He's still a bit strong at the lope. Some horses are like that when you give them their heads.'

Ursula could appreciate that. She had memories of a hunter that Caroline had once owned. The moment contact on the bit was lost, the horse would charge off like a runaway steam train, and no amount of hauling or heaving would bring it back under control until it had tired itself out. Needless to say, her daughter hadn't kept it long, but she had heard it had gone on to do exceptionally well at point-to-point events.

'Well keep me informed,' she said.

'Will do.'

Ursula watched Hank ride down the track and then up the side of the hedge to the bridleway. With his long, fringed chaps and authentic Western saddle, he looked like he had stepped out of a cowboy film set. Ella would be pleased when she saw how well she was handling things, she mused. And with that happy thought in mind, she set off for the stable yard so see what else she could do.

Adam sat hunched over the computer in his bedroom, scrolling through the lists of possible sites. He had found dozens of matches for 'North Hall Farm' from as far afield as Kentucky in the States to Adelaide in Australia. But it was the one in Norfolk that was attracting his attention.

'North Hall Farm and Stud has seventy-five acres of paddocks, thirty boxes for visiting mares and two foaling boxes,' he read.

In other words, it was the same sort of set-up as Hollyfield, apart from the fact it didn't have a riding school and a livery yard on site.

Adam scrolled further down the screen. He found a picture of the main farm building and stable block surrounded in sturdy double post and rail fencing, with several pictures of foals with their mothers, and two of the stallions on offer for the coming season. He also found directions on how to get there.

This was it! He leaned back in his chair and grinned at the screen. This was the place on the map - off the A120 - of course! But it didn't mean anything unless he could find out why Hank had the details of the farm - and why he was so keen to keep that information hidden. It stood to reason that nobody hid things in the middle of the woods unless they were distinctly dodgy or illegal. The money was the key factor here, Adam decided. But where had it come from. Had he stolen it? And then a horrible thought occurred top him. Maybe he'd stolen it from North Hall Farm and was planning to do the same thing here.

He frowned. He needed to find out. A further search of Internet sites relating to newspaper reports of thefts in that area yielded nothing. The village shop had been robbed by ram raiders who'd taken the till (empty) and several cash boxes but that had been before Christmas. There was nothing recent. Then he tried keywords, linking up 'North Hall Farm' with 'one thousand pounds' - still nothing.

It was driving him nuts. He had to know where Hank had got that money from, but this was getting him nowhere? If all else failed, he decided, switching off the computer and reaching for his jacket, he might well pluck up the courage and ask him.

The bridleway skirted the edge of the paddocks and up over a small rise to the woods, before dipping down to the distant estuary and nature reserve. Jed rode slowly, enjoying the warmth of the sun on his face and bare arms, and the saltiness of the breeze as it wafted in from the sea. Apart from the occasional dog walker, he saw no one. It was just how he liked it - peace, and solitude, with nothing but his horse for company. It gave him time to think, and boy, did he have a lot to think about.

When Giles had come up with the suggestion of swapping the stallions and settling his debts for the favour it had seemed like the answer to his prayers. He'd get the chance to work with horses, which was what he did best, and he'd get paid into the bargain. Plus, he'd be debt free for the rest of his life, because he had no intention of going back down the gambling slope again. A clean slate - that's what he was being offered. And he'd jumped at it. Only now, things were getting complicated. Not only did the horse belong to the wife of Lewis Trevelyan - a man he respected, admired, and bloody well liked, but he'd got himself involved with his sister-in-law.

And suddenly, things weren't so crystal clear as they'd once been.

The thought of all that money was bothering him as well. He'd taken it to pay for the hire of a horsebox, but he couldn't ignore the fact that the temptation to put it on a different kind of horse was still with him. Once a gambler, always a gambler, it seemed. He hated himself for feeling that way, but accepting it was halfway to overcoming it. But it still didn't change things.

Giles Peterson wanted Midnight Prince. The man was obsessed with the stallion, ever since he'd won a packet on him as a rank outsider at Newmarket several years ago. In fact, he'd credited the horse as being the main reason he'd succeeded in life where others, Jed included, had failed. He could, he said, recognise quality when he saw it, and that horse oozed quality.

Which was all well and good, but Jed reckoned that owning him would give Giles about as much pleasure as those who stole Old Master paintings. He wouldn't be able to declare his ownership, apart from to a select few who could be relied upon to keep their mouths shut. Any foals sired by the stallion could not be properly registered - or at least, not as being the offspring of one of the country's leading racehorses, and it would be years before he could recoup his money on the track.

Meanwhile, the Trevelyan's would be left with a stallion that might look as good but would never sire such high-quality foals as Midnight Prince would have done. Their reputation would be ruined - more so, if it was discovered they were passing off another stallion as the award-winning Midnight Prince - and charging the corresponding stud fees.

So, who wins in all this, Jed thought, as he urged the horse into a steady lope along the track through the trees? Not him, not Giles, and certainly not the Trevelyan's.

The crack of a shotgun going off startled both horse and rider. Arizona shied nervously and put in a tremendous buck before bolting for the woods. Jed, who had been riding on a loose rein, struggled to regain control whilst trying to keep his seat. This time, the crack came unmistakeably to his right. In the fleeting second before the searing pain in his side registered, he saw the blurred shape of a man crouching in the undergrowth and then everything started to swirl crazily around him. Jed knew he was falling, and there wasn't a thing he could do to stop himself.

Chapter 12

Vanessa luxuriated in a hot, foaming bath as she pondered over what to wear. Hank hadn't said where he was taking her. If they were going to a nightclub she'd need to dress up, but if they were having a drink in one of the town centre pubs she needn't be too dressy. Smart, but casual. On the other hand, she didn't think Hank did smart. She'd only ever seen him in jeans, be they denim or black ones.

She prodded the tap with her big toe and a welcoming gush of hot water cascaded into the bath. She'd need to do her nails, she mused, wiggling her toes - and shave her legs. She might have time to apply some fake tan. Then again, perhaps not. The last time she'd done it in a hurry she'd looked like a streaky carrot, and the smell had been vile. No, she'd skip that. There was nothing wrong in being pale and interesting. But what on earth was she going to wear?

A short time later the entire contents of two suitcases lay spread out on the bed in front of her. Dress, or skirt, she mused, holding one, and then the other in front of her. No - too boring, and too floral. Trousers - black, or brown - black went with most things, and she could wear her new strappy sandals with them (and hope she didn't break her ankle - the heels were rather high). Blouse, shirt, t-shirt - no (too clingy) - what about - she picked out a sky-blue blouse with a paisley print - this one. Vanessa held it in front of her. Not bad - not bad at all. Thankfully, it fitted her and didn't gape at the buttonholes, and it would go well with the black trousers. There - she'd decided. Humming softly to herself, she began her transformation.

The finished effect was remarkably pleasing.

She had pinned up her hair and allowed a few artistic curls to hang loose and frame her face. Then she had applied some make-up by copying a picture in a beauty magazine, which would give her a fresh and natural, sun-kissed look (allegedly).

She pouted her lips at her reflection in the mirror. Even if she said so herself, she thought she was looking pretty good.

She wandered down the stairs and into the living room, where Adam was sprawled on the floor in front of the television, flipping through the pages of a computer magazine.

'Do you have to make the place look so untidy,' Vanessa murmured, shoving him with her foot. 'Hank will be here in a minute.'

'So, what,' Adam said. 'It's my house.' He made no attempt to move from his prone position halfway across the lounge carpet.

Vanessa felt mildly irritated. 'You'd do it if your mother was here.'

'Well, she's not, is she?'

'Adam, get up!' Ursula waltzed into the room with a glass of what smelled strongly of gin and tonic in her hand. 'Vanessa's is expecting a guest.'

'What guest?' Adam muttered, raising himself to a cross-legged position. 'It's only Hank from the stables.'

'He's still a guest,' Ursula informed him. 'What time is he picking you up?' she added, glancing at her daughter. She was amazed at how nice Vanessa was looking. She had a certain radiance about her, and in that dainty blouse and trousers, she was looking quite pretty.

'He said he'd call about eight.'

'It's after that now,' Adam said, reaching for the remote control of the television. 'See - the footballs already started.'

'So?' Vanessa snapped, looking at her watch. 'He said "about" eight. That could be any time between now and when he arrives.'

'Whatever.' Adam flopped into the nearest armchair and dangled his legs over the side. A faint whiff of sweaty trainers mingled with the smell of Ursula's gin and tonic.

Vanessa hoped Hank wouldn't want to hang around, if he turned up at all, that is. She crossed to the window and parted the blinds. It was still light outside, but the sun was low in the sky. She peered across the lawns to the stable yard and wondered if she should stroll down to meet him. He was probably in the cottage getting changed.

'Oddly enough,' Ursula murmured, coming to stand behind her and breathing sickly sweet alcoholic fumes over her. 'I haven't seen Hank since he took Arizona out for a hack this afternoon.'

'What?' Vanessa said. 'You mean you don't know if he's back?'

'Oh, I'm sure he's back.'

'How do you know that?' Adam said.

Both women turned to stare at him.

'How can you be sure he's back if you never saw him?' he said, swinging his feet to the floor. 'He could have kept on riding, and you'd never know he was gone. Arizona's worth a lot of money, you know. Plenty of people would be interested in buying a horse like that.'

'Adam, what are you talking about?' Ursula said. 'Hank hasn't gone anywhere.' She raised her eyes at Vanessa. 'He only went on a hack. The boy's got a vivid imagination. Stop worrying your aunt. You can see she's getting upset.'

'She's probably got good reason to be.'

'What?' Ursula's voice rose an octave. 'Adam! Wait, where are you going?'

'The stables,' he called, as he headed for the door. Vanessa hesitated for less than an instant. As the back door closed, she was right behind him.

'Wait!' Ursula called. 'I'm sure there's nothing wrong.' She took a nervous gulp of her drink. Oh dear. She drained the glass. Oh dear, oh dear.

A few seconds later, and she was stuffing her feet into a pair of too large Wellington boots and reaching for her keys.

'See!' Adam banged open the empty stable door. A large hay net hung from a ring on the wall, and the water buckets were filled to the top. The straw bed had been laid in readiness. But there was no sign of Arizona.

'Oh my God!' Vanessa groaned. 'What if he's had an accident?'

Adam gave her a doubtful look. 'Or ridden off into the sunset with a valuable Quarter horse.'

'Don't be so stupid,' she snapped. 'We had a date.'

'So?'

'Mother!' Vanessa said, turning on Ursula, who was squelching her way towards them in giant sized boots, which had been the nearest things to hand. 'When did you last see him?'

'Is he not back, then?'

'No of course he's not back. The stable's empty.'

'Oh,' Ursula frowned. 'Well, it must have been about half past four. Let me see. I came back to the house. No, I'd gone to the stable block first, and then after…'

'Where was he going?' Adam said, snatching up the nearest head collar.

'What?'

Ursula looked a trifle confused.

'Where was Hank going? I'm going to look for him,' he added. 'And I need to know which direction he took.'

'He was heading out to the bridleway,' she recalled. 'The one that leads down to the nature reserve.'

'That's a start, anyway,' Adam said, as he ran into the next stable, where Blackthorn was munching his way through his evening supply of hay. 'Come on, boy.' He slipped the head collar over the horse's head.

Vanessa was on the verge of tears. 'You think he's had an accident, don't you?'

'I don't know what to think.'

'That's it,' she groaned. 'I'm coming with you.'

Adam gave her a cursory glance. 'You're hardly dressed for riding, Aunty Van. Anyway, I'll be quicker on my own.'

She stared down at her high-heeled shoes and realised that he did have a point. But she was feeling so helpless. There must be something she could do.

'Why don't you phone the police?' Adam suggested. 'See if there's been any reports of an accident.'

'The police!' Ursula choked, hurrying back across the yard. (She had been making herself useful by fetching the saddle and bridle from the tack room.) 'Good grief, you can't phone the police. We don't know what's happened yet. He might just have gone for a long ride and forgotten the time.' She dumped the saddle on a non-too pleased Blackthorn, who laid his ears back and tossed his head at her. 'Besides, if he'd been involved in an accident, they would have notified us. No, I think he's either got lost, or not realised how late it is.'

Vanessa wasn't so sure. How could he have forgotten he was meeting her? He was the one who had suggested they go out in the first place. No, she was convinced he was lying injured in a ditch somewhere, and it was up to them, or at least Adam, to find him.

'You will take care, won't you,' she said, as she watched him swing up into the saddle. 'Have you got your mobile?'

'Course.' He patted the pocket of his jeans.

'All right, well, ring if you find anything. In fact, ring if you don't,' she added. She didn't think she could bear the strain of waiting and not knowing.

Adam fastened his riding hat and checked his girth. 'Okay, the nature reserve, you say?'

Ursula nodded.

'Right. See you.'

It was still daylight as Adam headed out onto the bridleway and urged Blackthorn into a canter. He could see fresh hoof-prints in the sandy soil and knew that someone had ridden that way. Whether it was Hank or not, was another matter. He wasn't expecting to find him. He had the sneaking suspicion that both horse and rider had done a bunk. The money he had found in the woods could easily have come from the sale of a stolen horse - a horse from North Hall Farm, perhaps. He had never thought to look up 'horse theft' when he was doing his Internet search.

Arizona would command a good price at auction, of that he was quite sure. The horse was well schooled and well bred, plus it looked the part. Demand was high for horses of a certain calibre, and Arizona fitted the bill perfectly.

So no, he wasn't expecting to find Hank. And perhaps, because he wasn't expecting to find him, he didn't look as closely at the track as he might have done. As far as Adam was concerned, Hank had stolen the horse, done a runner and gone.

Up at Grey Lodge, Caroline was busying herself with the preparations for a romantic dinner for two. She had laid the table in the dining room with the best silver cutlery she could find. The beef and red wine casserole was simmering away nicely in the oven, filling the kitchen with a mouth-watering aroma, and the potatoes were done to perfection; brown and crunchy, just how Marcus liked them.

She lit the candles on the table and uncorked a bottle of wine. There, she thought, standing back to admire her handiwork. Everything looked lovely. Now all she needed was someone to share it with.

Marcus had taken Bruno for a walk round the orchard. Having spent the best part of the day in bed, he felt in dire need of some fresh air. The throbbing in his head had eased, but he was still feeling distinctly queasy. Caroline's promise of a candle lit dinner for two was not holding much appeal for him. Dry toast and an early night seemed much more preferable. However, he could see the effort she was making, and decided he had to appease her. He had made a bit of a fool of himself the night before. It was regrettable, but true, and he wasn't proud of the fact.

'Come on, dog,' he muttered, as he turned and headed back through the rows of apple trees. 'Bruno, come here.'

The Labrador was deaf at the best of times, and selectively deaf at others. This was one of those times. It was snuffling and sniffing at a rabbit hole it had found and was blatantly ignoring him.

Marcus stomped over to the dog and clipped on his lead. As he straightened up, he heard a chomping noise. What the devil? Marcus peered over the top of the privet hedge and found himself staring at a large chestnut horse that was grazing quite happily on the grass verge. Those bloody gipsies. They were supposed to keep their damn animals tethered up.

'Oi!' he shouted, attracting the attention of one of the men who was chopping wood by one of the vans. 'Get this horse away from my orchard.'

'It's nothing to do with me, mate,' came the reply.

'I am not your mate!' Marcus yelled. 'And if you don't do something about it, I'm calling the police.'

The man shrugged and came ambling over, swinging his axe as he walked. He looked to be about forty, with dark, curly hair and piercing brown eyes. A right ruffian, if ever he'd seen one. Marcus took a nervous step backwards. He was glad of the hedge between them.

'And keep it tethered with the others,' he snapped, waving at the trio of coloured cobs in the distance.

The man stooped to pick up the horse's trailing reins. 'If you say so.'

'I do,' Marcus muttered. 'Bloody cheek. You'll be out of here soon,' he added. 'You mark my words. The wheels are in motion.'

'Oh really.' The man's amused grin revealed a distinct lack of front teeth. His blunt nose looked as if a sledgehammer had battered it some years previously.

Marcus decided now was not the time to prolong the argument. 'You'll see,' he said, yanking Bruno's lead. The elderly Labrador lurched into the back of his legs.

'I expect we will,' came the amused reply.

Marcus went marching back to the house, oblivious to the activity that was going on in the camp behind him.

'What was all that about?' This from a woman who was hanging out washing on a makeshift clothes line between two trees.

'Search me,' the man said. He hoisted the saddle off the horse's back and placed it on the top rail of the fence. 'He told me to tether it with the others, so that's what I'm doing.'

'Why would he do that?' the woman said, glancing back at the huge old mansion house. Marcus had reached the front door and was standing watching them from a safe distance, his hands planted firmly on his hips.

'How should I know?' the man said, shrugging. He undid the bridle and looped a tethering line around the horse's neck. 'There you are, my beauty,' he said, 'Go meet your new field mates.' He gave the horse a slap on the rump, and then turned back to Marcus and gave him the thumbs up.

Marcus shook his head with disdain and marched into the house. That had sorted him out. Sometimes these people just needed to be told. He sniffed the air approvingly. Something smelt good. Thankfully, his appetite seemed to have returned as well.

'What time's supper, darling?' he called. 'I'm starving.'

Vanessa was distraught. There were no two ways about it. She couldn't stop crying. Something had happened to Hank. She knew it, she just knew it.

'I think we should phone the hospital,' she sobbed.

'Don't be silly.' Ursula poured her a stiff drink and made herself a large one as well. 'We'll have to wait till Adam comes home first. You never know, he might have found him.'

'If he had he would have phoned,' she said, pacing to the window. She couldn't stand all this waiting. It was getting dark outside. 'I'm going to go look for him,' she decided, drying her eyes. 'I can't hang about here any longer.'

She changed quickly into a pair of jeans and a sweatshirt, stuffed her feet into a pair of boots and ran down to the stables. There was no sign of Adam, or Hank for that matter. In fact, there was no sign of anyone.

Vanessa took a torch from the tack room, and decided to walk out towards the bridleway, so she could see Adam when he returned. The stupid boy should have phoned her by now. She'd told him to stay in touch.

Ursula watched the light wavering along the path from her vantage point by the lounge window. She was starting to feel a trifle concerned. Although she had great faith in Hank, she had to admit, that she knew next to nothing about him. What if he had stolen the horse, as Adam suspected? What on earth would Ella say? (Or Lucy Woods for that matter. Arizona was a much loved and valuable horse.) And what if Hank had gone for good? She'd invested all that money in Western tack, she'd arranged her 'taste of America' barn dance and riding demo, and it would all be for nothing. And as for her loss of credibility - well, she didn't want to think about that. Ursula gulped back her gin. She was starting to feel rather sorry for herself.

It wasn't the best moment for Ella to phone, either.

Ursula could have been forgiven for thinking it was Adam on the line, but her initial greeting of, 'Adam! Thank God. What's happening?' didn't do a lot for Ella's peace of mind.

'Ursula,' she said. 'It's me. What's going on? Where's Adam?'

'Um...um....' Ursula back-pedalled quickly. 'He's out,' she said. 'Darling, how lovely to hear from you,' she lied. 'How's Paris?'

'Stuff Paris,' Ella said crisply. 'You thought I was Adam on the phone. Why? Where's he gone?'

'Ah...well,' Ursula thought frantically. 'He's...um...he's gone for a ride.'

'At this time?'

'Yes - um, Vanessa's gone too. I did say it was a bit late, but you know what these young ones are like, and, um, Vanessa has been at work all day,' she burbled. 'It's a lovely evening here. What's it like where you are?'

'Raining,' Ella said.

'And how's Rosie?'

'Fine. Look, Ursula, I know you're up to something.'

'Me?'

'Yes, you,' Ella snapped. 'I've had a complaint from one of the girls. What's all that about?'

'I haven't the slightest idea,' Ursula said airily. 'I mean, it might be the new duty lists. I did make a few changes here and there.'

'A few changes,' Ella repeated, with more than a hint of sarcasm.

'Well, all right, I've adjusted the rotas so that we can give lessons seven days a week. There is a demand for it,' she added. 'I wouldn't have done it if I hadn't thought it was a good move.'

'Naturally.'

'And I've been thinking of adding Western riding classes to the timetable,' she said. She might as well admit it, now that she knew one of the gossiping young stable girls had done the dirty on her. (Though if Hank didn't come back, that could be a bit of a non-starter) 'It's all about keeping ones' eyes and ears open for new ideas.'

'Yes, and then running them by me,' Ella said. 'I trusted you, Ursula. God knows why. Lewis seemed to think it would be a good idea. Now I'm not so sure.'

'Darling, you can trust me,' Ursula assured her. 'Honestly, everything's fine here. I promise you.' (God help her if it wasn't, she thought, peering anxiously out of the window.) 'Gemini had her foal - a filly - it's ever so sweet.

Adam was there at the birth,' she added. 'And we've got one more foal due, and then Thomas is going to Dorset for a few days. You've really got nothing to worry about, Ella.'

'Well,' Ella sounded dubious. 'I hope so.'

'I'll get Adam to ring you, shall I? As soon as he gets back.'

'We're about to go out for dinner.' There was a pause on the line, and Ursula could hear her talking in a muffled voice. 'No, get him to ring me tomorrow,' she said. 'You've got the number for Marcel's apartment, haven't you? We've moved in there now.'

Ursula flicked through the phone book. 'Yes - yes, it's here.' She repeated it to Ella. 'I'll get him to call you back. Any particular time?'

'Early evening's best.'

'Right. I'll pass on the message. Bye Ella.'

Ursula replaced the receiver with a small shudder. Good grief, that was all she needed; Ella on the warpath. And why hadn't Adam phoned? That's what she wanted to know? Where was he, for goodness sake? It was nearly ten o'clock.

Adam was in the thick of the woods, trying in vain to track down the old oak tree in the pitch dark. He hadn't thought to bring a torch with him, and with a distinct lack of moonlight to help it was like searching for a needle in a haystack.

Blackthorn crunched his hooves over fallen twigs and branches and dried up leaves as Adam lead him through the undergrowth. He had decided it was safer to walk than to ride, since he couldn't see if a low branch was looming up on him or not. Since he hadn't found any trace of Hank and Arizona on the bridleway, his next thought had been to search the woods for the hidden tin of money. If the cash was gone, then the odds on the American not coming back to Hollyfield were, in his opinion, pretty high. But he was having problems proving it, because he couldn't find the right tree.

He wasn't the only one having problems.

Vanessa knew it was irrational, but she had an overwhelming fear of the dark. Ever since she'd been a small child, she'd needed a night light beside her bed before she could go to sleep. As an adult, she'd made do with the landing light, and her bedroom door left slightly ajar. A place that bore no fear for her during daylight hours could become positively terrifying once shadows started forming.

She flashed the torch up and down the bridleway, conscious of the fact that the hedge was casting the track in a dark and gloomy shadow.

'Adam?' she called, her voice quivering slightly. 'Adam!'

The silence surrounding her was making the hairs on the back of her neck stand on end. A loan owl swooped and screeched overhead, causing her to almost wet herself. 'Adam!' she shouted. 'Where are you?'

The groan was so soft it was almost inaudible. But Vanessa heard it. A cold chill froze the blood in her veins. 'Who's there?' she croaked, sweeping round with the beam of light from her torch.

Oh God! She sank to her knees, not quite believing what she was seeing. It was Hank. He was lying on his side by the hedge, a strange, sort of glassy-eyed stare on his face. 'What is it? What's wrong?' she sobbed, catching hold of his arm. 'Did you fall? Are you drunk? What is it?'

He clutched a hand to his side, and when he pulled it away, she saw the dark smear of blood on his fingers. 'I've been shot,' he gasped.

'Shot!'

Vanessa let out a cry of anguish. 'Oh God, Hank, what do I do?' She flapped helplessly.' Can you walk? Can you get up?'

'No.' He exhaled weakly. He'd got this far - he wasn't sure how - but he knew he couldn't go any further

'Oh no. Oh Hank! Oh God!'

'Get help,' he groaned.

'No, I can't. I can't leave you.' She ripped off her sweatshirt and laid it over his chest. His hands felt so cold. He felt cold. Oh God, he was going to die if she didn't do something.

She fumbled for her mobile phone. The shock was making her fingers feel clumsy and useless and she kept dropping it. Oh God, why couldn't she do it.

'Don't die, Hank,' she pleaded. 'Please don't die. Ambulance!' she shrieked, as her call was connected. 'I need an ambulance. Someone's been shot. Hurry. Please hurry.'

Jed watched her through blurred eyes as she made the first of several frantic phone calls. She was petrified, like he'd never seen anyone so scared before. But she was doing it. She was getting him help and the thought was a comforting one. He felt his head start to swim. He really was feeling quite woozy; warm, drowsy and very very sleepy...

'Stop it! Wake up! Hank, look at me. Talk to me,' she begged. Her face was next to his so that her hair fell on his cheeks. She was shaking his shoulders, pleading with him. She smelt nice, real nice.

'Hank!' she sobbed. 'Talk to me!'

He sighed. 'I'm tired, honey.'

'No, you're not.' She kissed him. Her cheeks were wet with tears. He felt so cold, so still. 'You're not tired. Talk to me, Hank. Tell me about home - anything. Come on, you've got to stay awake.'

'You'll let me sleep if I talk,' he mumbled.

'Course I will.'

'That's good.' His eyelids drooped.

Vanessa slapped him. 'Hank!'

'Okay, okay.' He sighed. 'Vanessa, honey, you are one feisty lady.'

'I'm also very determined,' she said. No way was she going to have him die on her. She tucked the sweatshirt tighter around him and tried to ignore the widening spread of blood down the front of his denim shirt. 'Now keep talking.'

He managed a weak smile. 'Yes, Ma'am.'

He couldn't remember what he told her. It was garbled rubbish, most of it - a bit about his folks, and his school days. And his dog - he told her about his dog, and every time he stopped talking, she kept asking him more and more questions, till finally, the lights started coming towards him, and she was jumping up and waving the torch and shouting 'Here! He's over here!' and he knew, even before he lapsed into unconsciousness, that she had saved his life, and he didn't deserve it.

Chapter 13

Rumours spread like wildfire around the village that Sunday morning. The fact that there'd been a shooting was gossip enough, but to have a valuable horse go missing - well, it was unheard of in such a small and rural community.

'They'd been lying in wait for him, right enough,' observed one local and elderly gentleman. 'Ambushed him on the track, so I heard.'

'Now that's rubbish William Brown, and you know it,' scolded Maisie Wilcocks, as she laid out the first of the days Sunday newspapers. 'The police aren't saying what's happened. See - an accidental shooting, it says here.'

'Poachers, I reckon,' Edward Patrick said, picking up a copy of the News of the World and handing over some coins. 'Stands to reason, it being a shotgun wound and all.'

'Well, I don't know,' William muttered, shaking his head. 'I can't see poachers being interested in the horse, and you can't deny that it's gone missing.'

'True, but my Thomas reckoned it must have taken off in fright. It could be wandering loose anywhere between here and the river,' Maisie said.

'You'd think it would have found its way home.'

'If it knew its way home,' she said. 'Thomas said it had only just arrived at the stables. The owner lives over Burningstone way. She had to put her horse on full livery at Hollyfield when she broke her arm in a fall.'

'She'll not be best pleased it's gone missing, then.'

'I don't think she knows,' Maisie said. 'I think they're trying to keep it hushed up until they find out what happened, but the American chap's not saying much - he's been in surgery most of the night.'

'Shame,' Edward, muttered, pocketing his change. 'Still, with the place swarming with police, I'm sure they'll find it soon enough.'

That's more or less what Thomas had said when he'd brought Maisie an early morning cup of tea. Like most of the staff, he'd been out since dawn searching for the chestnut gelding - ever since Ursula had awakened him with the dreadful news.

It seemed strange, therefore, that the horse hadn't turned up.

'I'll take a packet of your toffee bonbons, please,' William said. 'Next week is it, you're off to Dorset?'

'Hopefully. But with all this going on, who knows when we'll get away.'

'Oh, it'll be sorted by then. You'll see. Bye for now. You too, Edward.'

Maisie frowned as she rang the money up in the till. She hoped he was right. She was looking forward to seeing her sister again, and she knew Thomas needed a break from work. He'd been at the stables for several long shifts recently, what with the foals arriving, and then the new stallion to settle in. Though he'd never complain about doing the job that he loved, she felt it was time he gave himself a little rest. The trouble was, until this horse was found, she doubted that anyone would be getting much rest.

Ursula hadn't slept a wink. She'd been attempting to console a tearful and anxious Vanessa for the best part of the night and had been down at the stables since first light, trying to co-ordinate the search for Arizona. (A task that was hampered by the fact that half the bridleway had been cordoned off with police tape in the search for clues regarding the gunman's identity.)

Local farmers and people from the village had been out with dogs. Everyone, it seemed was eager to help. But still the horse had not been found.

Ursula had taken to driving the Range Rover down the lanes, in the vain hope that she might spot something from the road. After two hours of zigzagging back and forwards, she was ready to give up. The horse, she decided, had been stolen. She couldn't think of a single place left to look. As she reached the junction that led off to Grey Lodge, she just happened to glance up the drive, with the vague idea of calling in on Caroline, when she saw what appeared to be the chestnut gelding.

She fumbled for her glasses and perched them on the end of her nose. She couldn't believe what she was seeing. The horse was being ridden by one of the scruffy young children from the gipsy camp - complete with all its Western tack and saddle - her rather expensive saddle.

Right! Ursula snatched up her mobile phone. She'd got them now.

The police arrived in a matter of minutes, screeching up the lane in a blur of blue flashing lights and sirens.

Ursula wound down her window. 'Over there, officer,' she said, wagging her finger. 'You'll catch them red-handed. And I aim to prosecute them for theft,' she added. 'You can tell them I said so.'

She followed the cavalcade up the winding drive and drew to a halt beside the imposing grandeur of Grey Lodge.

Caroline and Marcus, having been woken from their Sunday morning lie-in by the blaring of sirens, had stumbled downstairs and reached the front door at about the same time as Ursula.

'What the devil's going on?' Marcus said, tying the belt of his dressing gown firmly around his middle and stepping out onto the porch in his slippers.

'Oh, hello, mother,' Caroline said, peeping round his shoulder and yawning sleepily. 'I take it you've got the Court Order?'

'Better than that,' Ursula announced. 'I'm prosecuting them for theft.'

'Theft, eh,' Marcus said, beaming. 'Well, I can't say it surprises me. They look a pretty light-fingered lot. Mind you, they haven't come anywhere near here, have they darling?'

'No. We've made sure of it,' Caroline said smugly. 'There's always been someone in the house at all times, and we've kept everything locked up. Have they been down to Hollyfield?' she added. 'Has something gone missing from Ella's house?'

'In a manner of speaking,' Ursula said. 'They stole a horse.'

'A horse?' Marcus swallowed nervously. He stared over the lawns to the distant field, where the police were gathering. They were talking to a group of men, one of whom was gesticulating wildly. Suddenly, the man stepped forwards and pointed straight at Marcus. Oh shit! He backed rapidly into the hallway. He was starting to have a bad feeling about this.

'In fact,' Ursula said, following him into the house, 'I wouldn't be at all surprised if it was one of those ruffians who shot Hank.'

'What?' Caroline gasped, clutching at her sleeve. 'Hank's been shot.'

Ursula stared at her in surprise. 'You mean you hadn't heard?'

'Why would we?'

'I thought - oh well, never mind.' She shook her head. 'Yes, it happened yesterday afternoon. Vanessa found him.'

'Is he all right?' Caroline choked. She couldn't believe it. Not Hank - why she'd only seen him the day before. 'Marcus, did you hear what mother said? Hank's been shot.'

'Hmm - oh, yes, dreadful…. dreadful.' He parted the blinds and glanced outside. Bloody hell - the police were heading towards the house with that rogue in tow. He hurriedly let the blinds drop back into place. 'I…I think I'll go and get dressed.'

'Marcus!' Caroline groaned. What was up with him this morning? He was like a cat on hot coals. It must have been that rich red wine sauce on the beef. She might have known it would upset him. She glared daggers at his back as he hurried up the stairs. He could have tried to be a bit less insensitive, though.

'Is Hank all right?' she said. 'He's not dead, is he?'

'No, no.' Ursula shook her head. 'He's lost a lot of blood, though. If Vanessa hadn't found him when she did, they said he would have died.'

'Oh my God, and they think the gipsies did it?'

'No, I think the gipsies did it,' Ursula said bluntly. 'I wouldn't put anything past that lot. I think they saw Hank riding the horse, and decided it was the only way they could get it.'

'By shooting him.' Caroline shuddered. 'How awful.' This was turning into a nightmare. Not for one minute had she envisaged living with a band of murdering thieving gipsies on her doorstep. Well, the sooner the police cleared them off the land the better. She, for one, wouldn't sleep easy in her bed until they'd all gone.

Just as she was thinking that perhaps she might join Marcus in putting some clothes on, a thunderous banging on the front door nearly gave her a heart attack.

'I'll get it,' Ursula said calmly. 'It's probably the police.'

It was indeed, the police. Two officers stood on the doorstep, accompanied by one of the men from the gipsy encampment. (A toothless and most unsavoury looking person, Ursula thought.)

'Mrs Lloyd Duncan?' asked the younger of the two, although they both looked to her as if they should still be in senior school.

'Yes.'

'Could we have a word with your husband?'

'Hardly,' Ursula said. 'He's been dead for five years.'

The two policemen exchanged awkward glances. 'I see. Well, perhaps if we could speak to the other…er…gentleman in the house?'

'That's him!' the dark-haired ruffian shouted, as he pointed an accusing finger at Marcus, who had chosen that moment to descend the stairs. 'That's the pillock that told me to tie the horse up with the others.'

All eyes swivelled towards the unfortunate Marcus.

'Is that correct, Sir?' asked one of the officers.

Marcus hesitated. 'Well, in a manner of speaking, you see…'

'Did you, or did you not, tell this man to take that horse?' He pointed out the front door, to where a female officer was standing holding the reins of the big chestnut gelding, 'and tie it up with his other horses?'

Marcus didn't like the man's tone. He didn't like it one bit. He opened his mouth to protest, but he didn't get very far.

'Just answer yes, or no,' the officer snapped.

'Well, yes, but….'

'In that case,' the policeman said, with the hint of a smirk on his lips, 'perhaps you wouldn't mind coming down to the station to answer a few questions.'

'Now look here, officer. I think there's been a bit of a misunderstanding.'

'I'll say,' the gipsy muttered, giving him a cold stare. 'Pillock.'

'Marcus?' Caroline whined.' What's going on?'

'To be honest, darling, I haven't a bloody clue,' he said. 'How was I to know it wasn't their horse. I saw it grazing loose on the grass verge last night and I told them to remove it.'

'You saw it?' Ursula choked. 'You saw Arizona last night, and you didn't think to let us know? Do you know how many hours we've been looking for that horse?'

'Well, he took it away,' he snapped, waving an irritated hand at the smirking and somewhat smelly rogue in front of him. 'He didn't exactly argue with me and say it wasn't his.'

'If you'd like to come this way, Sir.' The younger police officer held open the front door.

'This is ridiculous,' Marcus snapped. 'You're making a very big mistake.'

'We'll be the judge of that, Sir. In the meantime, we'd like you to assist us with our enquiries.'

'What!' Marcus's face was going a ripe shade of beetroot. 'What do you mean, with your enquiries?'

'We've got attempted murder, theft, aiding and abetting a theft...'

'What!'

Caroline thought Marcus was about to have a seizure. 'Officer,' she said. 'I think there's been a genuine mistake, here. My husband wouldn't have anything to do with horse stealing. He doesn't even like horses,' she added.

'In that case, he'll have nothing to worry about. Come on, you two. Let's go.'

'Mother!' Caroline pleaded, as she watched her husband being bundled into the back of the police car with the belligerent looking gipsy. 'Can't you do something?'

'I doubt it,' Ursula said. 'Besides, I dare say they'll let him go soon enough.' She turned back from the door and perused her daughter thoughtfully. 'Which will give you just about enough time to ride over to Hollyfield with Arizona.'

'Me?' she spluttered. 'You want me to ride him?'

'Well, I'm hardly going to get on him at my age,' Ursula said. 'No, you can do it. I'm sure you'll manage. As I recall,' she added, 'you used to be quite good.'

For the next few days Vanessa divided her time between the tack shop and Hank's hospital bedside, persuading Adam and one of his older school chums to run the shop for her in her absence.

Jed had been fortunate that the shot had missed his vital organs, entering his side below his rib cage, skimming the edge of his liver and embedding itself in muscle and sinew. Despite the amount of blood he had lost, and the subsequent surgery to remove the shotgun pellet, he was expected to make a full recovery.

Vanessa, however, was not convinced as she watched him drift in and out of unconsciousness. She was mortified by the thought that if she hadn't found him, he might have died. She squeezed his fingers reassuringly, but he had been sedated and showed little sign of waking.

'It's okay, Hank, I'm here,' she murmured.

A nurse in a dark blue overall and trousers came into the ward and checked his chart, then lifted his wrist and took his pulse.

'How's he doing?' Vanessa asked.

'Fine.' The nurse smiled kindly down at her. 'Don't look so worried. He'll be home before you know it. Sleep is the best thing for him now. His body has had one heck of a shock.'

'I ought to contact his parents,' Vanessa sighed. She'd been thinking about that for the past few days. 'They live in the States. In Montana,' she added. The trouble was, she didn't have a clue how to get hold of them. He'd never been very forthcoming about his family. Not until he'd been semi-conscious and she'd had to force him to keep talking in case he fell into a coma. Then he'd talked about his dad, Mitchell, and his mother Vera. Mitchell and Vera Jefferson. How many of them could there be in Montana, she wondered?

'I didn't realise he was American,' the nurse said.

'He's only here for the summer.'

'Oh, I see. Shame this had to happen to him.' She smiled. 'I suppose he's used to guns if he comes from the United States.'

'I suppose,' Vanessa agreed. She didn't know. She'd never asked him.

The details of his next of kin would be on his passport. If she could find it amongst his personal belongings, she would be able to get in touch with his folks, if only to let them know that he was all right. Hank wouldn't mind her doing that, she thought. It was the least she could do.

But finding his passport was not as easy as she thought it would be. A search of his room in the Groom's cottage had revealed nothing - no personal papers, no documents, no credit cards, nothing. His wallet had contained cash - no driver's licence or bankcards - just cash.

Vanessa rifled through all the drawers, searched his wardrobe, and even the backpack on top of the wardrobe, but found nothing. It was most odd.

Her mother wasn't much help in that direction either. She couldn't remember whether she'd seen his passport or not, and the fact that she'd taken him on as a casual worker, she hadn't bothered to check his references.

'But he did give you some, didn't he?' Vanessa said.

'Oh yes. He had a couple of letters from his previous employers.'

'In the States?'

'I think so.' Ursula hadn't looked that closely. Nor could she remember what she'd done with them. 'You'll need to check with Sally, but I don't know what you're worrying about. He's going to be all right, isn't he?'

Vanessa nodded.

'Well, then. He can let his parents know for himself. He's hardly a child, you know.'

That was beside the point, Vanessa thought crossly. It was the principle of the thing. The man might have died. (Perish the thought). They would have needed to get in touch with somebody then.

Adam listened to all that was going on with increasing sense of unease. He had been meaning to speak to his aunt about his find in the woods for quite some time. A discreet check during daylight hours had revealed that the cigar tin, complete with cash, was still hidden in the trunk of the lightning hit oak tree. He had been wondering whether to fetch it back to the house. Now, with all these undercurrents of uncertainty going on, he decided that the time was ripe to retrieve it. But he wanted to get his aunt on her own, so he could tell her about it first.

'I don't feel like riding,' she said, when he suggested going out for an early evening hack together.

'Please, Aunty Van. We could use the Western tack. Hank wouldn't want all his hard work with the horses to go to waste. You can show me how to do neck reining.'

'I've only done it once,' she said. She was flopped on the sofa in front of the television, and the thought of riding could not have been furthest from her mind. Moping and feeling sorry for herself came much higher on her agenda.

'Oh, go on, Aunty Van,' he pleaded.

'Yes, go on,' Ursula said. 'It'll do you good. And besides,' she added, 'if Hank isn't fit enough to do the Western riding demonstration on the fourteenth, then someone else will have to do it. You're the only one with any experience.'

'I'm not doing any stupid riding demonstration.'

'I'll do it,' Adam said eagerly. 'But you'll have to give me a few tips.'

'If I must,' she groaned, swinging her feet to the floor. 'Come on, then. I can see I'm not going to get any peace.'

Once the horses were tacked up, Vanessa felt a tad more enthusiastic. She had chosen Arizona for herself, and Jasper for Adam. The dark bay needed a bit more schooling, and her nephew, she felt sure, was more than capable of doing it.

'We'll start in the sand school,' she said, swinging up into the saddle. 'I think I can remember what Hank told me to do. Arizona will know, even if I don't,' she added.

The chestnut gelding was a joy to ride. He was so well trained he could have spun on a sixpence, and Vanessa was delighted to see Adam putting Jasper through the same movements with the minimum of effort.

'This is great!' Adam shouted. 'Look - no hands.'

Vanessa found herself enjoying the spectacle of his youthful exuberance. 'Try a few leg yields,' she said, 'and then do a couple of serpentines at a jog. No rising, mind. You've got to learn to sit to the pace.'

After half an hour's intensive schooling, Adam started agitating to go out for a hack. 'It won't be dark for ages yet,' he said, 'and there's something I want to show you.'

'What?'

'It's a secret.'

'Adam,' Vanessa groaned. She was tired, and she'd had enough for one day. 'Tell me what it is, and then I'll decide if I want to see it.'

'You won't believe me.'

'Try me,' she said.

Adam looked worried. He glanced back at the house, and then up towards the trees. 'I don't want anyone to hear,' he said, his voice hushed. Vanessa urged her horse to step closer to his. 'I've found something,' he continued. 'I think you need to see it. It's in the woods.'

Oh great - just what she needed. Another moonlight jaunt. 'Adam, I am not trekking up to the woods at this time of day. It'll be getting dark soon.'

'Aunty Van,' He caught hold of her reins with one hand. 'I found a load of money, and I mean loads,' he whispered. 'There must be a thousand pounds or more.'

'What?'

'It's true,' he said. 'It's hidden in the old oak tree. You know, the one that got struck by lightning a couple of years ago.'

Vanessa gave him a look that beggared belief. 'Adam, what are you talking about?'

'Hank put it there,' he hissed. Now he had her full and rapt attention. 'I saw him hiding something, and I went back to look. It's a box full of money, Aunty Van, and it's still there.'

'You're joking.'

The look on his face told her he wasn't. 'Show me,' she said.

It took them less than ten minutes to reach the thicket of trees on the cross- country track. Adam retraced the path he'd taken several times over the past few days, checking and rechecking to make sure he wasn't seeing things. He jumped down from Jasper and tethered him to a nearby branch.

'It's over there,' he said, pointing to the blackened oak.

Vanessa dismounted and followed him to the tree. The branch had sheared away from the trunk, leaving a burnt and gaping hole that was currently filled with an old bird's nest.

Adam stretched up and groped about in the hole, pushing the nest to one side. 'Got it,' he said, as his fingers closed on the shiny metal tin.

Vanessa's heart was thudding loudly against her rib cage as she peered over her nephew's shoulder and watched him prise open the lid.

'What do you reckon?' he said, lifting out the bundle of notes and flicking through them. 'A thousand quid - Maybe more.'

'Jesus,' Vanessa choked, her thoughts reeling. What was Hank doing with all this money, and why had he hidden it? She snatched the tin from Adam and tipped out the rest of the contents.

'It's a map,' Adam said, as she unfolded the piece of paper. 'A map for North Hall Farm in Norfolk,' he added. 'I looked it up on the Internet. The other bit is a number, a phone number, I reckon.'

Vanessa sank to her knees on the leafy ground. She was completely dumbfounded. She didn't know what to think.

Adam stuffed the money back into the tin. 'I've been wanting to tell you for days,' he said. 'What are we going to do, Aunty Van?'

'I don't know,' she said. 'Put it back, I suppose.'

'What if it's stolen?'

'Hank wouldn't steal,' she said.

'No?' Adam looked doubtful.

'I'm sure he wouldn't. He's not that kind of person.'

'And you'd know that for certain, would you?' His voice was scathing. 'Come on, Aunty Van. You've got to admit, there's something wrong about this.'

'Yes, I know,' she said, hauling herself up and brushing the dried leaves from her trousers. But for the life of her, she couldn't think what it was. 'Put it back,' she said. 'Until I've thought this through.'

'Sure?'

She nodded. 'It was him you saw, wasn't it?' A faint hope that Adam might have been mistaken was immediately crushed.

'Of course, it was,' he said, reaching up to replace the bird's nest on top of the tin. 'I even spoke to him.'

Vanessa looked horrified. 'He doesn't know…?'

'No.' Adam shook his head. 'I came back later, after he'd gone. He was acting strange, and that's what made me double back on him.'

Deflated, and with her last hope shattered, Vanessa turned and walked back to the horses. She was as bewildered as her nephew, and twice as troubled. Had Hank lied to her? Had it all been one big act? Her thoughts lingered on those few, precious, moments when she had felt closer to him than to any other living person. His passion had been genuine. She knew that much. He couldn't have pretended such emotion. No one could. But was he really a con man and a thief, as Adam suspected? And short of asking him outright, how on earth could she find out? God knows, she thought, as she swung up into the saddle and picked up the reins.

'I've got an idea,' Adam said, after several long and silent minutes had passed, with neither of them knowing quite what to say to each other. 'We could check out this North Hall Farm.'

'I thought you said you'd already done that.'

'I looked it up on the Internet,' he said, riding his horse alongside her. 'It's a stud, a bit like Hollyfield. We could go and visit it.'

'Why?' she said. 'What would that achieve?'

Adam shrugged. 'I don't know yet, but it's worth a look. You could make some enquiries about sending a mare there. Oh, go on, Aunty Van. We could drive up one day next week.'

'You mean I could.'

'Yeah. And we could try ringing that number. I made a note of it last time I rode up. It might be the number of the stud.'

'And it might not be,' Vanessa sighed, who could not bring herself to share his enthusiasm. She wasn't sure she wanted to find out what it was all about in the first place. In fact, she'd rather she hadn't found out anything at all. She was much happier being left in a state of blissful ignorance. The knowledge that Hank might have been deceiving her was proving a bitter pill to swallow. The fact that she had been taken in by his lies was even worse.

Chapter 14

'There's one thing to be said about the French,' Kate said, savouring the last morsel of mouth-watering mussels in garlic and cream sauce, 'they certainly know how to cook. That was bloody gorgeous.'

The restaurant Lewis had chosen for them was tucked down a narrow and somewhat seedy Paris back street and would have been totally ignored by the casual observer, had it not been for its excellent gastronomic reputation. Reservations had to be made weeks, if not months, in advance, but Lewis had managed to secure them a seat, courtesy of a colleague's unfortunate need to cancel his booking.

'Here's to Matthew,' he said, raising his glass.

'To Matthew,' echoed Rosie and Charlotte, who were thrilled at being invited out to a 'grown-up' restaurant for dinner and were determined to make the most of it.

Ella gave them a rather nervous smile as they chinked their water glasses loudly together. 'Gently does it,' she murmured.

'What did Cheryl have - a boy or a girl?' Kate asked.

She was already on a high, and it wasn't due to the expensive wine she was drinking either. This weekend trip to Paris was a real treat for both her and Charlotte.

She'd been looking forward to spending some quality time with her closest friend for ages.

'A girl,' Ella said. 'They've called her Beatrice.'

'I had an aunt called Beatrice,' Kate said, dipping a piece of bread into the remains of her cream and garlic sauce. 'I used to call her Aunt Beetroot when I was little. She's dead now.'

'I don't think I'll tell Matthew that,' Lewis laughed. 'More wine, Kate?'

'Best not,' she said, placing her hand over the top of the glass. 'Not when I've got Charlotte with me. I need to keep my 'Mummy' head on tonight.'

'Ella?'

'Please - just half a glass.'

She leaned over to gather up the girl's plates. Gastronomic cuisine or not, they had both managed to pick French fries to go with their main course. At least Rosie had eaten part of the dressed and elaborately arranged salad. Charlotte had only nibbled on a piece of frilled cucumber and a carrot baton.

'I've been riding Flossie,' Charlotte told her shyly.

'Have you, darling?' Ella smiled. 'She's a nice little pony, isn't she?'

'Ooh, yes, and that reminds me, I've brought you some photos,' Kate said, rummaging about in her handbag. 'I though you'd want to see them.'

She had planned on getting them out when they arrived at the apartment, but Lewis had been anxious to head to the restaurant, citing traffic as the main reason. It had taken them over two hours to reach the flat from the airport.

'That's Charlotte at the start of the lesson - see, she's looking a bit nervous.'

'I was not.'

Kate smiled, and passed over the next photograph. 'And that's her after she's walked round the school. Oh, and that one's a bit blurred. She was starting to trot, I think.'

'Let me see,' Rosie said. 'Oh, there's Pickle - I used to love riding Pickle, didn't I Mummy.'

'Yes, but you're too big for her now.' Ella passed the photographs on to Lewis, who gave them a cursory glance. He wasn't really interested but felt he should examine them out of politeness.

'And that's Tamsin with Charlotte - that was your second lesson, wasn't it, Charlotte?'

'Yes'

'And that's Flossie again. Oh, and you'll like this one.' Kate leaned back in her chair and waved the photo enticingly in front of Ella's nose. 'This is one of Hank.'

'The American?' Ella grinned. 'Let me see.'

'How much is it worth?' Kate said, hiding the picture behind her back.

'Anything you like from the sweet trolley?'

'Done.'

Kate slapped the photograph down on the table. 'Feast your eyes on him,' she said gleefully. 'How's that for a bit of eye candy.'

Ella lifted the picture up to get a better light. The first thing she noticed was the horse he was sitting on - mainly because she didn't recognise the large chestnut gelding. 'That's not one of my horses,' she said. Kate gave an exasperated sigh. 'All right, I'm looking,' she said, peering closer. The man was about thirty-five, with dark hair and skin that was tanned from working outdoors in the sun. He had a kind of roguish attractiveness about him, Ella decided. She could see why Kate was impressed. 'So, he's the one going out with Vanessa, is he?' she said.

'Apparently.'

'Hmm. He's not her usual type. He actually looks quite nice.'

'I know,' Kate agreed.' And it seems to be serious too - well, according to the girls at the stables it is. They're all dead jealous. Do you know, they all started going to line-dancing classes, so they could impress him, and Vanessa was the best one there.'

'Vanessa?' Ella queried. Her stepsister was normally as clumsy as they come.

'And that's not all. Now they're saying she saved his life.'

Ella glanced sharply across at her. 'How come?'

Kate looked vaguely puzzled. 'Ursula's told you about the shooting, right?'

'No, she bloody well hasn't,' Ella seethed. (God in heaven - what was happening now?) She needed to have words with her stepmother. 'What shooting?'

'Hank got shot when he was out riding. The police think it was an accident - poachers, possibly,' Kate said, taking a small sip from her glass of wine. 'Anyway, Vanessa was the one who found him and stayed with him till the ambulance came, and now they're saying he could have died if she hadn't been there.'

'I don't believe this.' Ella was furious. Ursula hadn't breathed a word of this to her - not one word, and neither had Adam for that matter. If there was some lunatic running round with a shotgun, she at least ought to have been warned about it.

'Did you hear what Kate said?' she fumed, nudging Lewis, who was in the process of showing the girls the dessert menu.

'Uh? What?'

'Hank's been shot.'

Lewis looked baffled. 'Who's Hank?'

'The American,' she groaned, handing him the picture. 'Weren't you listening?'

'No, not really.' He had been preoccupied with guiding the girls away from the exorbitantly priced luxury desserts and settling for something a bit cheaper and simpler (in other words, something they were likely to eat). He peered down at the photograph.

'Can I have the meringue glacony thingy?' Rosie asked, waving the menu at Ella. 'And Charlotte wants chocolate and raspberry ice cream.'

'What did you say this guy's name was?' Lewis said. His brows were drawn together in a puzzled frown. 'Only, I think I recognise him.' He glanced up at Kate. 'Is this the only picture you've got?'

'No, I've got loads,' Kate said, fumbling through the plastic wallet she was holding. 'Here, this is a better one. His name's Hank,' she added. 'Hank Raymond Jefferson.'

'You don't know him, do you?' Ella said, glancing over at her daughter who was giving her an impatient and sulky frown. 'Yes, Rosie, I'll ask the waitress in a minute. Just be patient.'

'He's from Montana,' Kate added, as if that might help.

Lewis flicked through the assortment of photographs and settled on a close-up Kate had taken of the man riding in the sand school. His head was half turned away from the camera, but his profile looked familiar - very familiar.

Ella was watching him with a growing sense of unease. She could see the look on his face. It was as if he was struggling to make a decision.

And he was. He wanted to be certain, but he needed to be one hundred per cent certain, before he said anything.

'Are you having a sweet, Lewis? Kate asked him.

'What? Oh yeah, I'll have what Rosie's having,' he muttered.

'Ella?'

'Coffee, thanks.' Her appetite had suddenly deserted her. 'You do recognise him, don't you?' she said softly. 'I can see it in your face.'

His eyes lifted from the photograph and he met her troubled gaze with one of his own. 'He's not from Montana,' he said. 'No way. And he's not called Hank Raymond Jefferson, either. This man here,' (he jabbed a finger at the picture), 'is called Jed Harrison. He's an actor and a stunt double. I've worked with him a few times. Mainly with horses,' he added. 'He's one hell of a good rider.'

'So, he enjoys working with horses - so what?' Kate said. 'Don't all actors need a second job when they're "resting", as they call it.'

Ella breathed out a sigh of relief. 'Yes, that's right. He could be between jobs.'

'He could be,' Lewis agreed, 'but why say he's from Montana? The man's from Brentwood, born and bred. He's worked in the States,' he added, leaning back to let the waitress place his dessert on the table. ('Merci.' The waitress smiled.) 'He's done a lot of stunt riding out there - big blockbuster movies, you know - epic battle scenes. But he's not worked as an actor for a while, or at least, not as far as I know. He might have done theatre or performed in rep. But why he's calling himself Hank Raymond Jefferson I don't know. I've always known him as Jed.'

'If he's not famous, it seems strange that he uses an assumed name,' Ella said, echoing Kate's thoughts precisely.

'And why pretend to be a cowboy if he's not?'

'Maybe he's trying to impress the ladies,' Lewis said, winking at Kate. She scowled and stuck her spoon into a huge mound of whipped cream. 'There's no doubt he can ride Western and he can do it well enough to convince someone he's the genuine article. It's a pretty good ruse to use, if he wants people to take notice of him.'

Ella wasn't convinced. It sounded a bit fishy to her. 'He is all right, though, isn't he, Lewis?' she said. She didn't like the thought of an impostor pulling the wool over everyone's eyes for malicious or deceitful reasons.

'Yeah, I think so.' He leaned forwards and lowered his voice a fraction. 'Although I did hear he had a spot of bother a few years back, when he lost most of what he earned by gambling. He might have creditors after him, which could account for the change of name. He liked to place a bet or two.'

'Or three, or four, by the sound of it,' Kate said.' No Charlotte, you eat it. You wanted it.'

Ella stirred a spoonful of sugar into her coffee. Whatever the reason, she wasn't happy about it. Anyone who wasn't up-front and honest deserved her suspicions. 'I think I might go home for a few days,' she said.

Kate's spoon hovered halfway between her plate and her lips. A blob of cream dripped onto the starched white tablecloth in front of her. 'When?'

'Mummy, you're making a mess,' Charlotte shrieked.

'I could fly out with you on Sunday night. What do you think, Lewis?'

'Yes, whatever. You do what you think best. You're obviously worried.'

'Mummy!'

'Yes, yes, I know,' Kate said, dabbing at the cloth with her linen napkin. 'It's a good job it wasn't you,' she added, frowning at her small daughter. Both girls giggled, enjoying the spectacle. 'Sunday night might be a bit difficult,' she warned. 'You'd be better coming back on Monday when it'll be easier to get on a flight.'

'I was thinking the same thing,' Lewis said. 'Do you want me to come with you?'

Ella couldn't think of anything she wanted more, but she knew how busy Lewis was at work, especially now that Matthew had flown home to be with his wife and new baby. He was practically running the company single-handed.

'No, I'll be fine. It's only for a few days,' she added,' and then we'll come back. I just want to make sure everything's running as it should be, and after the phone call from Gemma, I think it best that I show up in person. You never know,' she added, 'I might persuade Adam to come over for the remainder of the holidays.'

'I'll believe that when I see it,' Lewis said. 'Wild horses wouldn't drag him away from Hollyfield.'

Which was true enough. Wild horses wouldn't have dragged Adam away from Hollyfield in the middle of the summer holidays. But the search to find the answer to the mystery of Hank's hidden money would.

Early on the Wednesday morning and both Adam and Vanessa were dressed and ready for the drive up to Norfolk in search of the North Hall Farm and Stud.

Vanessa's initial reluctance to go had been partly due to the fact that she didn't want to know what was going on, and partly because Hank was due out of hospital that day. He was bound to think it strange if she wasn't there to meet him, particularly as she'd spent the past few days practically chained to his hospital bed. But Adam had persuaded her that she didn't have much choice in the matter. She had to go - it was as simple as that.

'We've got to find the connection,' he told her. 'And there must be one - it's just a case of looking for it.' He handed her the notice he'd printed for the door of the tack shop. "Sorry. Closed all day for stock-taking". 'There, what do you think?'

'It'll do,' she sighed. 'Come on. Let's get going.'

Two hours later, and they were on the outskirts of Norwich, searching for the road that would take them to the farm.

'Left, Aunty Van. Up there.' Adam pointed to a narrow country lane. 'It's got to be that one.'

'You're sure?' she said, glancing in her rear-view mirror at the car that was cruising along only inches from her bumper. She clicked on her indicator.

'Yes.'

The black car zoomed past her at speed as she braked and slowed to turn left.

'Idiot,' she muttered.

The road was the width of one car. Vanessa hoped they didn't meet anything coming in the opposite direction - like a tractor, for instance. She didn't fancy reversing up the narrow, twisting lane.

She was just about to point out that they must have taken a wrong turning, and that this road wasn't leading them anywhere, when it divided into a forked junction. A huge brown and gold sign proclaimed that North Hall Farm was to the right, and the village of Barnstop was to the left, followed by a "please drive carefully through our village" notice.

'This is it,' Adam said, leaning forwards and staring through the windscreen like a bloodhound on the scent of something interesting. 'Slow down.'

'If I go much slower, I'll stop,' grumbled Vanessa.

The fields were neatly fenced with wooden posts and rails. A couple of horses grazed in the nearest paddock by the road.

'There's the farm,' Adam said, waving his hand to the right. 'See it?'

'I can see it.' Vanessa pulled over onto the grass verge. The wheels bounced over the dry and rutted surface and sank down into what appeared to be a drainage ditch. 'Bugger,' she muttered, revving the engine and reversing backwards.

'You can't park here,' Adam said. 'You're blocking the lane.'

'What else do you suggest?'

'Drive up to the farm. We're here for a look around, remember.'

'I don't think I want to be seen,' Vanessa said. She was rapidly losing her nerve. It was all very well talking about it, but doing it was something else entirely.

'Why? We're not doing any harm. You've got a mare that you want to be put in foal,' he said, sounding a lot more confident and business-like than the thirteen-year- old boy that he was.

Vanessa sighed as she bounced the car back off the verge and hoped she hadn't damaged her suspension in the process.

'You're a prospective owner,' he added, as if she needed reminding of the fact. They'd rehearsed this scenario for the past two hours. 'You need to satisfy yourself that the place will meet your requirements - understand?'

'Yes, yes, okay,' she muttered. 'Though goodness knows what they'll think about us just swanning in here without giving them any warning.'

'That's what the shrewd owner does,' Adam said.

Vanessa parked the car in an area of hard standing beside the main farm building. Apart from the horses grazing in the surrounding paddocks, there didn't seem to be much in the way of life about the place. 'What now?' she said.

Adam clambered out of the passenger seat. 'Well,' he said. 'We can either ring the bell, or we can go for a wander. Personally, I think we should have a look around on our own.'

'But we don't know what we're looking for,' Vanessa complained. It was all very well Adam saying it had to be something that linked Hank to the place, but where to start, that was the problem? Had he worked here? Stolen a horse from here? Planned to take up a job here? What?

She followed her nephew towards the barn area, in the feeble hope that he might find something relevant, never for one moment thinking that he would.

'Bloody hell!'

Adam stopped dead in his tracks and pointed to an adjoining paddock. 'Look, Aunty Van.'

'What?' She squinted against the bright sunlight, wondering what on earth was making him so agitated.

'In the field!' he gasped. 'That horse.'

'The black one?' she said, coming to stand alongside him. 'It's a stallion, isn't it?'

'Yes, but look at it.' He blew softly between his teeth.' That's Midnight Prince's double, I kid you not.'

'Midnight Prince? Isn't that the new stallion at Hollyfield?'

'You bet it is,' Adam said, running towards the rail. 'And this beauty could be his identical twin. Look - he's got the same white fetlock - everything.'

'So?' Vanessa said.

She couldn't understand why Adam was getting so excited. Lots of horses looked the same. It was like cats and dogs. A certain breed produced a certain type.

'Could you tell the difference?' he said.

'I don't know. I can't say I'd noticed…'

'Can I help you?' The voice came from somewhere behind her. Vanessa turned quickly to see a stocky man in muddy green overalls hurrying towards them from the area of the barn. He was wiping his hands on a bit of old cloth.

'Um.' Her mouth opened and shut, but no sound came out of it.

'We were just admiring your stallion,' Adam said, glaring at his aunt.

'Exodus - aye, he's a beauty all right. He's just arrived here. The owner had him sent over from Ireland. See if the Norfolk weather would improve his temperament,' he chuckled. 'Some of the finer breeds don't like the rain and the damp - it affects their performance - know what I mean,' he added, winking at Vanessa, who was wishing a hole would open in the ground and swallow her up. 'Have you got an appointment with Mr Jackson?'

'Um, no - no, we were in the area and we thought we'd take a look around,' she said, trying hard to regain her composure. 'I'm thinking of sending my mare to stud,' she added, picking up the discreet hand signals from her nephew. 'It's a big decision to make.'

'First time, is it?'

'Yes.'

'Uhuh - well, there's two stallions at North Hall, excluding Exodus here. We've got a Welsh cob called William - he's over in the paddock to your right, and we've got a thoroughbred called Minotaur - he's in the stable behind you.'

'I like the look of this one,' Adam said, strolling forwards and leaning on the rail. 'He looks as if he's worth a bit.'

'He is that, lad. Been a good little racer in his time, that one. Perhaps you should see Mr Jackson,' he added, pointing over to the farmhouse. 'He'll more than likely be in, and he can give you all the details.'

'Thanks,' Vanessa said, glancing at her watch. 'Maybe I'll phone and make an appointment for another day. We're a bit pushed for time now. Like I said, we were in the area.'

'Come far, have you?'

'Not too far,' Adam said, frightened lest his aunt gave the truth away. 'We're meeting some relatives for lunch - and we're late, aren't we, Mum.'

'Um, yes,' Vanessa said, trying not to appear as taken aback as she felt. 'Well, nice to meet you. No doubt we'll see you again soon.'

Adam was already beating a hasty retreat towards the car. Vanessa would have walked faster, but for some stupid reason she had put her shoes with heels on, and was finding it difficult to negotiate the hard, rutted ground.

'Who shall I saw was calling?' the man asked.

'Mrs...er...' Vanessa tried hard to think of a neutral name, 'Mrs Jones,' she said. 'I'll be in touch. Bye now.'

She leapt into the driver's seat and slammed the door shut behind her.

Adam was rocking backwards and forwards in his seat like a demented chimpanzee. 'That's it. That is it!' he crowed.

'Oh, do stop it,' Vanessa snapped, reversing rapidly, and then screeching the car forwards onto the narrow track.

'He's going to swap the stallions.'

'You don't know that.'

'I'd say it was pretty obvious. The map, the money - it all fits.'

Vanessa scowled. 'No, it doesn't. You don't just "swap" a stallion and hope no one notices. There are all kinds of formalities - registration papers, identifying marks, vet's papers. It's not that easy, Adam. We could be jumping to conclusions here.'

'Uh uh - no way. You don't want to believe your precious boyfriend's got something to do with it, that's all.'

'I don't want to talk about it,' Vanessa snapped.

'I bet you don't.'

'And I don't want you blabbing off to anyone either. Not until we know for sure.'

'Oh, you mean when Midnight Prince goes missing - because that's the only way we're going to know for sure.'

'No.' Vanessa glared at him.' Adam, let me deal with this, please. I need to talk to Hank.'

'No. You can't.' Adam looked desperate.' Aunty Van, you can't let him know what we've found out. It might be...' He paused. 'It might be dangerous.'

'Who for - me?' She turned the car onto the main road and accelerated away.

'Yes.'

She swallowed back the lump that had risen in the back of her throat. She couldn't believe Hank would hurt her

- that he would hurt anyone. He was kind, gentle, caring. No, she wasn't going to believe this of him. Not until she'd had the chance to speak to him and sort things out.

After all she'd done for him, the least he owed her was the truth.

Chapter 15

Several days in a hospital bed had left Jed feeling as weak as a kitten. He was surprised at how tired he felt - the anaesthetic in his system he supposed - and how everything seemed to require so much effort.

He lay on his bed gazing up at a cobweb that hung from the corner of the ceiling. It was Ursula who had collected him from the hospital that morning and instructed him to rest. He didn't need telling. He was exhausted, and that was just from climbing the stairs. God knows when he'd be fit enough to ride again.

He flicked through the messages that had been left on his mobile phone. Giles was getting anxious - no doubt wondering why he hadn't been in touch. "Jackson's ready for you," he read. (That had been left the day the stallion had arrived at the stud in Norfolk). "Have you picked a time yet?" The final message - "call me", had been left the previous evening.

Sod it, he didn't feel like talking - not to him anyway. He sent him a text message - "Had an accident. Plans delayed but still on track."

That ought to sort it. He laid the phone on the bedside cabinet. The battery was almost done, and it needed to be charged up, but he couldn't be bothered to get off the bed and find the charger.

It was after four, and he wondered why Vanessa hadn't been to see him. Ursula had said something about her going out with Adam for the day, which he found a bit strange considering she'd spent most of her spare time at the hospital. He would have expected her to be waiting for him when he came out.

'Hello?'

The faint cry echoed up the stairs. 'Hank?'

He struggled to sit up and swing his legs to the floor. The gauze padding on his side covered an itching, aching wound.

'Are you decent?'

It sounded like Ursula again.

'Yeah, come on up,' he said.

'I've brought you some dinner,' she said, clumping up the stairs and sticking her head round the door. 'I've popped it in the fridge and you can heat it up later. It's only a hotpot I made earlier,' she said, 'but I didn't think you'd feel like cooking.'

He didn't feel much like eating, either. 'Thanks.'

Ursula was appalled at how poorly he looked. A sickly pallor had replaced his normal healthy complexion and his eyes were ringed by heavy, dark shadows. At this rate he was never going to be fit enough for the Western Riding demonstration. She might need to change her plans, she thought, which was a bit of a pain, since she'd already posted the invitations and invited the press to attend, as well.

'Can I get you anything else - tea, coffee? You ought to drink something,' she added, thinking that a good stiff brandy might do the trick.

'No, I'm fine, thanks.'

'Sure?'

He nodded.

Ursula wondered if she should stay with him, though she'd never been very good when it came to comforting the sick and needy. 'You ought to sleep,' she said. 'You look shattered.'

'Tell me about it,' he sighed. He lifted his gaze. 'Is Vanessa back yet?'

'No.'

His shoulders sagged, and he looked weary.

Goodness, he must be really missing her, Ursula thought. Why she had to go traipsing off today of all days, she'd never know? She'd spent all week pining and moping for Hank, then decided to shoot off with Adam the day he's due out of hospital. 'I'll tell her to call round, when she gets home,' she said. 'She shouldn't be much longer. They've been gone for hours. Adam wanted to visit some farm up in Norfolk,' she explained. 'Don't ask me why.'

She was surprised at the way his head suddenly jerked up.

'Norfolk!'

'Yes.' She let out a heavy sigh. 'I know, it's miles away. I think he said it was some old friend he wanted to see. To be honest, I wasn't really listening. I was more concerned with coming to pick you up.' She patted the end of the bed fondly. 'It's lovely to have you back, Hank. We've been so worried about you.'

'It's great to be back,' he said.

He was struggling to comprehend what she had just told him - that Adam and Vanessa had gone to visit a farm in Norfolk. Why? What for? It didn't make sense.

If Adam was visiting a friend, he could have gone any day. Why this particular day? And why had Vanessa gone with him? He had a bad feeling about this.

'Hank? What are you doing?'

'Getting up,' he said, swaying slightly. He rested one hand against the wall, waiting for the dizziness to pass.

'Oh dear, I don't think you should,' Ursula said.

'I can't lie about all day,' he muttered. 'It's driving me nuts.'

'I know it must be frustrating for you, but...oh dear - Hank, please don't fall down the stairs.' Ursula's voice had raised an octave as she followed him onto the landing.

'I don't intend to.'

He levered himself slowly down to the hall and groped his way towards the kitchen. He'd get himself a drink of water, he decided. That was a start. Then he'd see how he felt. If he was up to it, he intended to go for a walk.

Ursula was delighted to see him on his feet but petrified that he might overdue things. She, more than anyone, wanted him to be fit for the following weekend.

Arrangements for the Barn Dance were well under way. She had booked a highly recommended Country and Western band to play live at the venue and had organised food and drink from a local catering company. Jimmy McPherson and some of his friends from the village had volunteered to clear out the barn. Everything was going according to plan - or at least, it had been until Hank had had his little accident.

And it had been an accident, albeit an unfortunate one. A teenage lad from the next town had been charged with the shooting. He had duly confessed after seeing all the publicity in the newspapers. He hadn't meant to hit Hank, he said, and didn't know he had been hunting rabbits next to a public bridleway.

Ursula had been incensed when it was rumoured that he would get a paltry fine and a few hours community service. As far as she was concerned there were laws to protect the public against that sort of thing, and anyone breaking them should be suitably punished. She, for one, would be making a stand when the case came to court.

She watched Hank pour himself a glass of water from the kitchen tap. His hands trembled slightly, but he seemed steady on his feet.

'You're bound to feel a bit shaky,' she said. 'You've been lying in bed for days. Your muscles will be weak.'

'I'd best start building them up again,' he said, taking a long drink and then wiping his mouth with the back of his hand. 'I've got to earn my keep, somehow.'

Ursula beamed. 'There's no rush,' she lied. 'You take your time.'

Jed leaned back against the worktop and took the weight from his feet.

Putting a brave face on things was one thing - expecting the impossible was another. There was no way he was fit enough to trudge up to the woods - not yet anyway. But he needed to know if the money was still there - or if Adam had found it, as he was beginning to suspect.

'I'll be off now,' Ursula said. 'But I'll tell Vanessa you were asking after her. I expect she'll be down later. Don't forget to heat up that stew. Forty minutes should do it in a medium oven.'

Jed waited until he heard the front door close behind her before collapsing gratefully into the nearest chair. Hell, this was worse than he'd thought. Okay, so he'd lost a lot of blood, but they'd pumped enough back into him. And it wasn't as if he was a nine-stone weakling. He was, and always had been, a fit and active person with tons of energy. Now the slightest exertion exhausted him.

He drained the glass of water and set it back down on the table. He'd done a lot of thinking when he'd been lying in that hospital bed - probably more than was good for him. But it had given him the time he needed to reflect on things, and at least now he was starting to see sense.

He turned and stared out of the kitchen window. A low brick wall enclosed the back yard, and some enterprising person had hung up baskets of trailing blue and white lobelia, and scarlet fuchsias on the gateposts. The track leading down to the stables ran right past the cottage, and beyond it laid acres of paddocks and green fields. It was nice, Jed thought, really nice. A man could do a lot worse than live here.

He flexed his fingers. A vivid yellow and purple bruise marked the back of his hand. His legs ached. Lack of use had weakened his muscles, but that could soon be remedied. He levered himself up off the chair and practised walking round the kitchen table using one hand to steady himself. Easy does it, he thought, as he slowed the pace. He felt like a horse being brought back into work after a period of box rest. Building up fitness took time, but time was what he didn't have. He had the uncomfortable feeling that if he didn't do something about Midnight Prince in the next day or so, Giles would lose patience and pay someone else to do the job. And the way things stood, that was the last thing he wanted. He needed to be able to see this thing through to its rightful conclusion.

Two hours later, and Vanessa was surprised to find him sitting up at the kitchen table tucking into a hearty portion of her mother's hotpot. She had been led to believe that he was at death's door and virtually bed-ridden. Consequently, she had rushed over to the cottage without even dragging a brush through her hair and burst through the door as if it was a dire emergency.

'Hank!' she choked, in disbelief. He looked - normal. Tired, admittedly, and a touch paler than usual, but there was nothing wrong with the way he was enjoying his dinner. Nor in the way he stood up and grinned at her as she burst into the cottage.

'Hi, honey,' he said.

'I thought you were in bed,' she spluttered, glancing back at the door. 'I'm sorry. I would have knocked.'

'That's okay.' He pulled out a chair. 'It's good to see you. I've been wanting to talk to you. Come and sit down. You don't mind if I finish this, do you?'

'Um, no - no, go ahead,' Vanessa said, parking herself on the padded pine chair and wondering if she had misheard her mother. Weak as a new-born kitten, she'd told her. Well, he certainly didn't look that way to her.

'Hank...' she began.

'Jed.' He looked up at her and met her squarely in the eye. His face bore an expression she found quite unreadable. 'My name's Jed - Jed Harrison.'

'Jed?' she echoed, blinking dazedly back at him.

'I'm not from Montana and I'm not even an American.' As he spoke, he dropped the heavy drawl in his voice, and lapsed into an accent that was bordering on Cockney. It was definitely a London accent, anyway. 'I'm from Brentwood,' he said.

Vanessa was speechless. She didn't know what to say; how to react, or whether she should say anything at all. Her whole world seemed to be on the verge of turning upside down. Everything she had believed in was wrong - was that what he was saying? That it had all been a pretence - a lie. That he had hoodwinked her as well as the girls at the yard, to say nothing of her mother, who had taken him on in the first place. And if he'd lied about his identity, had he lied about anything else? How he felt about her, for instance? Had that all been a charade and a fib as well?

'I'm an actor and a stunt rider,' he said, stabbing his fork into a piece of stewed lamb. 'The name 'Hank Raymond Jefferson' comes from a small part I played in a cowboy movie in the States. It bombed at the box office,' he added, chewing thoughtfully. 'That was when Western movies were in decline.'

'Hank - er - Jed.' She corrected herself with difficulty. She was finding this all very hard to take in. 'What's going on? Why are you telling me this?'

'Because,' he said, pausing to lie his knife and fork down and slide the plate to one side. 'Because I think I can trust you.'

'Trust me?' Vanessa echoed, not sure if was hearing things. She gave a hollow laugh. 'You're the one that's been lying to everybody and now you're talking about trust?' She shook her head. 'Come on Hank, Jed, or whatever your name is - I think you've got some explaining to do.'

'It's a long story,' he sighed.

Vanessa folded her arms in front of her. She didn't care how long it took. All night, if need be. 'I'm listening,' she said.

And as she listened, she knew that she'd been right about one thing at least.

This was going to take all night.

Adam didn't take too kindly to being woken up shortly after midnight.

'Come on, get up,' Vanessa hissed, dragging his duvet off the bed and prodding him repeatedly until he opened his eyes.

'What?' he groaned, yawning and blinking sleepily at her? 'What's going on?'

'I'll explain on the way,' she said, tossing his jeans at him.

'On the way to where?'

'North Hall Farm.'

Hank, or Jed, as she was starting to know him, was sitting waiting for them in the horsebox. The physical exhaustion this was costing him was starting to show on his face as Vanessa bundled Adam into the cab and swung up into the driving seat. He looked drawn and tired. 'Evening,' he said, shifting over to let Adam sit beside him.

'You!' Adam choked. He glanced at his aunt, who was familiarising herself with the gears. It had been years since she'd driven a horsebox. 'Aunty Van…?'

'Not now,' she muttered, twiddling with the ignition.

'This is to do with that money, isn't it?' he said, glaring at Jed.

'Partly,' he admitted ruefully.

The engine roared into life, and the horsebox juddered as Vanessa eased her foot off the clutch.

Adam clutched at the side of the seat as they bounced down the track and headed for the road. 'Will someone tell me what's going on?' he said. 'It's about Midnight Prince, isn't it? Something to do with him and that other stallion?'

Jed ignored him. 'Turn right,' he said, pointing.

'I know where the road is.'

'Aunty Van!'

Vanessa swung the wheel round. It was like trying to drive a Sherman tank. She'd forgotten how strenuous driving a horsebox could be. No wonder Jed had needed her help. No way could he have done this on his own.

'Yes, what?' she snapped.

'The other stallion,' Adam repeated, 'the one at North Hall farm. You're going to swap him for Midnight Prince, aren't you?'

'Not exactly,' Jed murmured.

Adam glared at him. 'What do you mean, not exactly?'

'Just what I said,' he muttered, closing his eyes.

It was left to Vanessa to explain what had taken place a few hours previously, when Jed had confessed about his involvement with Giles Peterson and the syndicate that were after Midnight Prince. As far as he could see, he told her, he had no option but to continue with the plan, albeit with a few slight alterations.

'You mean we're going to pretend to swap the stallions,' Adam said, who was warming to the idea by the minute. 'That's cool.'

'Yes, but because Ron Jackson's part of the syndicate, we've got to make it look as if its for real,' Vanessa explained. 'Which is why we've got to pick up Exodus and hang on to him for a few hours before we return him to the stud.'

'Don't you think he'll notice the difference, or lack of it?'

'Would you? You said yourself, he's the double of Midnight Prince.'

Adam thought hard for a moment. 'Yeah, but hasn't Midnight Prince got a tattoo that identifies him. Thomas told me it was on his inner lip. All they have to do is check the number.'

'It's been sorted,' Jed murmured drowsily. He was finding it hard to keep his eyes open. The rolling and rocking motion of the lorry was sending him to sleep as well as any sedative would. 'Jackson's had the same tattoo put on Exodus.'

'What a crook!' Adam seethed.

'There's big money involved when it comes to horse racing. He obviously thinks it's worth the risk,' Vanessa said.

'And talking of money.' Adam's head spun round, and he fixed Jed with an accusing stare.

'Yeah, yeah, it's mine,' he muttered. 'I figured you'd found it. Giles gave me it for expenses.' He gave a dry laugh. 'You'd make a great detective, Adam. Think I'll put it on a winner. What do you say?'

'That there's no such thing as a safe bet.'

'Isn't that the truth?' Jed sighed.

He closed his eyes. With Vanessa doing the driving, and Adam doing the navigating, he decided it was time he tried to get some sleep. He would need all his strength for later.

Fortunately, when later arrived, everything went according to plan. Ron Jackson had been warned of his impending arrival in the small hours, and he had Exodus booted up and ready for travelling by the time Jed drove up to the stud, (with Adam and Vanessa concealed under a blanket in the groom's compartment of the lorry so that he could pretend he was on his own.)

Loading the stallion had, thankfully, been easy. Manoeuvring the heavy lorry was not. He had been grateful to pull off the road a short distance from the farm to let Vanessa resume the driving. He was, as he put it, totally knackered.

'Where to now?' Vanessa queried as she headed back onto the road.

'God knows,' Jed murmured. 'Find a secluded lay-by if you can - otherwise just turn down a side road and we'll wait in a field, or something.'

Vanessa drove for about fifteen minutes, before Adam spotted a picnic area set back in some trees and signposted from the main road.

'How about in there?' he suggested, pointing out the window.

'That'll do,' she agreed, swinging the wheel round. Her shoulders were aching, and she wasn't looking forwards to the drive home.

By the time she had parked up the lorry and turned off the ignition, both Jed and Adam were dozing in their seats and she had a good mind to join them. What else was she going to do for four hours?

She yawned. It was pitch dark, the moon being hidden beneath a bank of low clouds. The air was warm and humid and held the promise of thundery rain.

Vanessa found that she was wide-awake. No matter how tired she felt, it was impossible for her to go to sleep. In the silence of the cab, she could hear the horse's quiet munching of hay, the gentle breathing from Adam, and the faint snores from Jed. His head was slumped sideways against her shoulder and she could feel the warmth of his breath on her face.

Jed Harrison - she mulled the name over in her mind. She didn't know why he had confessed to her, but she was relieved that he had. Hearing it from him first was better than having to force it out of him. And she would have made him tell her the truth, she realised, because she had known, deep down, that something was wrong. It wasn't just finding the money or seeing the other stallion that had roused her suspicions. She had sensed he had troubles from the start.

Her instincts had already told her he was a decent bloke, but with problems of his own. The fact that he'd never wanted to talk to her about his family was one thing. So was the way he seemed guarded about his past. Yet there was no denying that he knew how to handle horses and had a genuine interest in their welfare. He was a good man, she decided - underneath it all - a good man who had been led astray by his weakness for gambling.

She reached up and gently traced her fingers down his face, feeling the firm set of his jaw, the stubble on his cheeks, the soft moistness of his lips.

He sighed. 'Go to sleep, honey.'

'I can't,' she said, but she snuggled into him just the same.

It was rain splattering against the window that woke Vanessa from a surprisingly sound sleep - rain, and the first faint streaks of dawn brightening the purple and pink sky.

'Bloody hell, wake up!' she cried, glancing at her watch and then dislodging Jed from her shoulder. She was shocked that she had dozed off in the first place. 'It's later than I thought,' she added, prodding Adam.

'How late?' Jed groaned, rubbing the back of his neck. A dark shadow of stubble showed on his jaw. His dark hair was tousled, and he looked instantly appealing. Vanessa wondered if he saw her in the same light. She showed him her watch.

'I need a pee,' Adam muttered, pushing open the cab door and heading for the bushes.

Jed caught hold of her arm as she leaned forwards to turn on the ignition key. 'Wait a minute.'

'What?' She glanced sideways up at him. All of a sudden, she was conscious of his closeness, and her heart started to thump faster against her chest.

'I owe you,' he said softly. 'I owe you big time.' He pulled her towards him and kissed her so tenderly, and so sweetly that Vanessa felt sure her heart would burst. 'I couldn't have done any of this without you,' he added. His voice was low and husky with emotion.

'Course you could,' Vanessa said, trying to be light-hearted. 'You'd have found some other mug to help you, I'm sure.'

'You're not a mug. Don't ever think that.' He glanced over at Adam, who was running towards them from the sanctuary of the bushes. 'I need you,' he said, turning back to her. 'And I want you.' He ran his fingers down her cheeks, and she found it hard to meet his searching gaze. 'I really do.'

For now, Vanessa thought. She wasn't stupid. She had the feeling that as soon as they got back to civilisation he would dump her. Problem solved.

Adam scrambled up into the cab and slammed the door behind him.

With a sigh, she started up the engine. 'I'll take it as far as the lane end,' she said, glancing at Jed. 'You can drive the lorry from there.'

Unloading Exodus was marginally easier than loading him, since the stallion recognised the place and was happy to be home again. Jed hoped the stud manager wouldn't notice the horse's uncharacteristically relaxed stance.

'Did you have any problems?' Ron Jackson asked, as he watched him stoop to undo the horse's travelling rug and boots.

Jed shook his head and tried to ignore the gnawing ache in his side. 'No. Everyone was out for the count.'

He straightened up and winced slightly as a jarring stab of pain almost took his breath away. Talk about overdoing things. His only consolation was that he must look as rough as he felt. Like a man who'd been up all night moving horses, in fact.

'I'll put him in his box, shall I?'

'No, I'll do it. You get going,' Ron said. He was as keen to see the back of the horsebox, as Jed was to take it away. He had a reputation to uphold, and handling stolen horses was not part of it.

Jed didn't know how he would manage to raise the ramp unaided, nor how he could turn the heavy lorry around without the aid of power assisted steering. His side was giving him real pain. It took brute force and bloody grim determination to raise and fasten the ramp with the casual air of one who was going about his normal business.

He slumped into the cab and wondered if he had the strength to turn on the ignition, let alone whip the steering wheel round.

'Are you okay?' whispered Vanessa, from her hiding position in the groom's compartment.

'No, but I'll live,' he muttered, gritting his teeth. 'Tell you what, though, I'll be glad when we get back to Hollyfield.'

Vanessa glanced at Adam, who was slouched on the floor and attempting to catch up on his sleep. 'I think we all will,' she said. 'Drive us to the end of the lane,' she added, ducking down out of sight, 'and I'll take over from there.'

'Thank God for that,' Jed muttered, managing a final wave through the window. 'I owe you one, honey.'

'More than one,' she said quietly. 'But we'll talk about that later.'

Chapter 16

Ursula was somewhat peeved to discover that Adam was refusing to get out of bed for breakfast on the Thursday morning, and that Vanessa had failed to come home at all.

If, as she suspected, her daughter was playing nursemaid to the injured Hank, the least she could have done was phone to let her know.

She toyed with the idea of calling in on Vanessa at the Groom's Cottage but decided it might be less embarrassing all round if she caught up with her at the tack shop instead.

In the meantime, she had plenty of things to do at the stables. Getting the girls to put up bunting and balloons in the empty hay barn for a start.

She was expecting an average of about one hundred and fifty people to the American Event and Barn Dance on Saturday and had planned to cater accordingly, with hot dogs, burgers and mixed salads for starters, and American flapjacks, muffins and cookies to follow, served with a generous portion of ice cream. The bill for the bar and accompanying bar staff was costing her a small fortune, but Ursula felt it would be money well spent. Hollyfield needed a bit of a boost every now and then to raise its profile, and with the Western riding event, Ursula thought she had found a real money-spinner that could be milked for all it was worth. If - and it was a big - Hank was fit enough to take part in it. If not - Ursula scowled - well; she didn't know what she would do. Hire another rider, she supposed - someone who knew what they were doing. Unless....

'Tamsin, can your ride Western style?' she called, hanging over the railing to the sand school, having spotted the instructor in the midst of a small crowd of people.

Tamsin was talking to a group of students and did not welcome the uncalled-for interruption. 'Excuse me a moment,' she said to her class, before marching over to the railing. 'What do you want, Ursula?'

'I need a Western rider to perform in the American event on Saturday,' she explained. 'I don't suppose....'

'No.' Tamsin shook her head firmly. 'No way.'

'I'd pay you.'

'That's not the point,' Tamsin said. 'I can't do it. In fact, the only one who's even attempted it round here is Vanessa. I suggest, if Hank's out of action, you ask her. Or Adam. He might like to give it a go.'

Ursula scowled. That was no good. Vanessa had already refused, and Adam didn't have any experience. Oh well, she'd just have to hope Hank was up for it, though she was beginning to have her doubts. He'd looked dreadful when she'd brought him home from hospital. It was to be hoped that Vanessa had managed to work some miracle on him, because otherwise, they were sunk.

Vanessa lay curled up beneath the duvet sleeping like a baby as the sun edged higher in the sky. Beside her, Jed was lying peacefully, not sleeping, but contemplating his future at the stables - in fact, his future full stop.

For the first time in years, he was technically debt free. Giles Peterson had written off the loan he owed him on receipt of the news that Midnight Prince had been exchanged as instructed.

Since Giles' main interest in horses concentrated on their performance on the track and not what their individual habits and idiosyncrasies were, Jed felt sure he would not realise he'd been duped. He'd wanted a black stallion with a white fetlock and he'd got one. If he wanted to believe it was Midnight Prince, then all well and good. Who was he to try and dissuade him otherwise? The stallion had the right marks and conformation. All it lacked was the right breeding. Still, ignorance is bliss, as they say, and it wasn't as if Giles could boast that Midnight Prince was his, not unless he wanted to get arrested for theft. All he and his dodgy syndicate could hope for were future winners and luckily, even they weren't guaranteed.

So, all debts paid, and no laws broken. Now what? Jed rolled onto his side and lay watching Vanessa as she slept. She was perched on the edge of the bed. It had taken all his persuasion to get her into it in the first place; she had been so terrified of hurting him in her sleep.

'I might crush you,' she protested. 'I can lie on the floor for a couple of hours.'

'Get into bed, you silly woman. You're dropping on your feet. I promise I'll yell if you so much as touch me.'

Jed reached out and rested his arm around her middle. He had grown very fond of her over the past couple of weeks. She was what his mum would have liked for him - solid, dependable, and probably honest. He'd had his fill of beautiful and invariably fickle young women. Vanessa had strength of character and a dry sense of humour that appealed to him.

Yeah, he would stick around for her, he decided, if she would let him, although he was beginning to suspect a change of heart on her part. He had detected her withdrawing into herself on the journey home. He couldn't blame her for that. He had given her a whole pack of lies to contend with. She must have been wondering what truth was and what was fiction.

He twirled a curl of her mousy hair around his finger. The scent of lemon and soap made him want to snuggle closer to her, to hold her tight against him. The faint twinge and ache in his side reminded him that it might not be such a good idea.

He rolled over onto his back and continued thinking.

Giles was expecting him to cut and run - to give some sob story about family problems and how he was needed back in the States. Jed didn't want to do that. But if he stayed he would need an excuse to hang around - an excuse that Giles would find credible. He could be making himself indispensable, perhaps, thus ensuring a cast iron alibi should the (non-existent) theft ever be discovered?

That was it, he decided. He would tell Giles that if he disappeared, the finger of suspicion would point to him. So, it would be better if he stayed where he was, for the time being, at least.

Whatever he did, he realised, was up to Vanessa. She might want to shop him. After all, he had kind of steam-rollered her into helping him. He hadn't exactly given her any choice. And he'd lied to her - lied to the whole family. That must have hurt her. She might be tough, but she was innocently trusting too. He'd make it up to her, he decided, if she'd let him. But she might not let him.

Blood was thicker than water, and she had a whole host of family loyalties to consider. If he thought about it rationally, how could she possibly explain to her mother that he wasn't really a cowboy from Montana, but an out of work actor from Brentwood? And, oh yeah, he was only pretending to be a Western riding instructor, and his name wasn't really Hank Raymond Jefferson.

Shit, it was worse than he thought. If he wanted to stay put, he'd need to think up a rational and reasonable explanation for the whole charade - and for the life of him, he couldn't think of one.

But he would, he resolved, glancing sideways at Vanessa as she stirred beneath the duvet. Not only for her sake, but for his sake as well.

'Morning, gorgeous,' he murmured.

Vanessa groaned and opened her eyes. 'It can't be morning. Oh God!' She sat bolt upright. 'What time is it?' She stared, bleary-eyed at her watch. 'Christ!'
She flung back the covers. 'I've got to get to the shop.'

'Can't it wait?' Jed said, levering himself up on one elbow. 'We need to talk.'

His hair was all tousled, and a dark shadow of stubble covered his chin.

Vanessa gazed at his broad shoulders and bare chest and stifled back a sob as she reached for her jacket and boots.

'Vanessa?'

'No. I've got to go,' she blurted, snatching up her bag. She couldn't stay a moment longer. Not now - not after all he'd said and done. Last night she'd been too tired to think straight. Well, she was stronger now, and she knew what she had to do. It was over. Finished with. And the sooner she got away from him, the better.

'Vanessa, wait.'

But she'd gone, slamming the door hard behind her.

'Hello? Hello? Who is this?' Caroline demanded, pulling a face at the phone receiver in her hand. The voice on the other end of the line sounded drunk, or tearful, or both. 'Vanessa?' she said, finally realising that it might be her sister. 'Is that you?'

The hiccuping gulp confirmed that it was.

'What is it? What's wrong?' She paused, listening.

Marcus was sitting at the kitchen table, dressed and ready for work in his smartest suit and tie. He was going in late because he had a court case to attend later in the day, which was, thankfully, nothing to do with the debacle over the gipsy horse. In his hand he held a slice of buttered toast that had Bruno slavering at his feet for crumbs.

Caroline raised her eyebrows at him. 'It's Vanessa' she mouthed. 'Yes, of course I'll come and get you. I'll be there in ten minutes.'

She plucked the toast from her husband's hand as she reached for the car keys. 'Sorry,' she said. 'Got to dash.'

'Your bloody sister, I take it,' Marcus muttered. 'What does she want this time?'

'Sympathy, I expect,' Caroline said. 'See you later, darling. Have a good day if you're gone by the time I get back.'

'I'm not likely to have gone,' he said, reaching for the bread bin and scowling as he removed the end slice of bread from the pack. 'Someone's got to keep an eye on that itinerant horde in the field.'

Marcus still hadn't got over the shock of being called a pillock, or the embarrassment of being herded into a police car with one of the roughest looking gipsies as if he were in cahoots with them. So, he had no intention of going to work and leaving the place empty for them to plunder and pillage at their leisure.

'Don't be long,' he muttered crossly.

'I won't.'

She was back within fifteen minutes, with a tearful and somewhat incoherent Vanessa in tow.

All Caroline had managed to get out of her was the fact that Hank had lied to her.

'I did warn you,' she said, as she reached for the kettle, and waved a curious Marcus away with a flick of her hand. 'Coffee?' she suggested.

Vanessa shook her head. 'I want to go to bed,' she sniffed. 'My own bed, in my own room.' She plonked the keys to the tack shop on the table in front of her. 'Can you open up for me? I don't feel like working today.'

'Me?' Caroline spluttered.' But what about Adam? I though he was helping you in the shop.'

'Not today,' Vanessa said. 'Please, Caroline? I wouldn't ask if I wasn't desperate.'

She certainly looked desperate. In fact, Caroline couldn't remember the last time she'd seen her sister in such a state. She picked up the bundle of keys. 'All right,' she said. 'I'll do my best, but don't blame me if you lose customers.'

'I won't,' Vanessa sniffed.

'And we'll talk later, right?'

Vanessa nodded. She was so exhausted she would agree to anything. Waking up to find Jed staring at her as if she was one of his prized conquests had hurt her more than she cared to admit. She felt humiliated and used by him. What made it worse was the fact that he'd broken her heart. She'd fallen in love with him, and he'd broken her heart. It was the story of her life. Every man she'd ever fallen for had ended up discarding her like a piece of rubbish.

Oh, he'd wanted her to stay. That much was obvious. He wanted to talk. But she'd had enough of talking. She didn't want to hear anymore of his lies and excuses. She wanted to be alone.

As she lumbered up the stairs to her bedroom, even Bruno looked sorry for her, wagging his tail sheepishly, and plodding up the staircase to lie at the foot of her bed.

Vanessa buried herself beneath the duvet. She was worn out, emotionally and physically, and it wasn't long before she was in a deep and dreamless sleep.

The sun was streaming through the curtains and the garden was alive with birdsong. The rainfall overnight had brought a lush freshness to the lawns and flowerbeds. Outside, it was a beautiful day.

Inside, Vanessa slept on.

Jed paid the taxi driver and waited until he had gone before strolling up to the front door of Grey Lodge. He could ring the bell, but he doubted if Vanessa would answer it. He knew she was in there. A trip to the tack shop to see a sneering and haughty Caroline had told him that much.

'She doesn't want to see you,' she said. 'I don't know what you've done to upset her, but it must have been something serious. I've never seen her so distraught.' (She had, but she wasn't going to tell him. It was a known fact that Vanessa generally overreacted when she was in love with someone.)

'It was a misunderstanding,' Jed said. He'd be blowed if he were going to explain himself to Caroline, who was staring down at him as if he was a particularly nasty heap of dog muck. Her snort of derision put paid to any further attempts at conversation anyway. It was obvious that whatever he said, she had no intention of believing him. 'She won't see you,' she repeated, as he stomped towards the door.

Would she not? Well, he'd see about that.

Jed wandered round the side of the house and peered up at the windows. They all seemed tightly shut - apart from one. He gazed upwards. An old oak tree next to the house had one of its branches almost touching the windowsill. If he could climb up, he was sure he could reach in through the small window that was ajar and open the larger one beside it - *if* he could climb up.

He searched round for something to stand on and eventually found a wooden pallet and an old garden chair. The trunk of the tree was fat, huge, and without any perceivable footholds, but once he managed to clamber up the pallet, and then onto the precariously balanced chair, he was able to reach the first thick branch.

He sat astride the bough and leaned back against the trunk, totally shattered. The throbbing round his scar had increased dramatically, and he was alarmed at how light-headed he was starting to feel. This was not the most sensible thing to be doing, the day after his discharge from hospital. On the other hand, he needed to talk to Vanessa. What other option was there?

He shuffled forwards along the bough and then reached up to the next branch. It was an undignified scramble to get his leg over, but he managed it in the end. Now all he had to do was reach the window. As he leaned forwards, the branch dipped sharply and grated across the wall. Jed grabbed at the windowsill to steady himself. Easy does it, he thought, catching his breath. He breathed in deeply and tried not to look down. He was at least fifteen to twenty feet off the ground, and the state he was in, the fall would probably not do him any good at all. It was best not to think about it, he decided, hooking his arm round the branch. He'd done trickier stunts than this in his time.

He wriggled closer to the wall and reached up to the small top window. If he could just force his arm through the narrow gap, he'd be able to release the inside catch.

The relief he felt when the larger window swung open was immeasurable. With a final push, he hauled himself over the sill, and fell sprawling onto the landing on the second floor. For several seconds, he lay where he had fallen, getting his breath back and listening for any sound. Nothing. He sat up and shook his head to try and clear the waves of dizziness.

The corridor stretched in front of him. A narrow wooden staircase climbed up to his left. The bedrooms were further down the landing. He tried to remember which one was which - the first was Ursula's, then there was a bathroom and the next one - that one - he stood up. That was Vanessa's room.

He walked towards the door, his heart thumping. It was slightly ajar. He pushed it open and peered into the gloom of the bedroom. With the curtains drawn it was difficult to see, but it looked as if she was still in bed. He took a step closer.

It was the last thing he remembered before everything went horribly black.

Vanessa stared with terror at the crumpled body lying prostrate on her bedroom floor. The walking stick she was brandishing like a club dropped from her fingers as if it were red hot. Oh my God, she thought, panicking. What if I've killed him?

It had all happened so quickly. She had emerged from the bathroom after a refreshing warm shower to see a hand reaching through the small window on the landing. In a blind panic, she had ducked back inside the bathroom and locked the door. Her heart was beating so fast she thought it was going to burst out of her chest. It had to be one of the gipsies. They'd obviously seen Caroline drive off and were taking advantage of the fact that they thought the house was empty.

Oh my God, what could she do? Get dressed for a start, she thought, frantically pulling on her trousers and polo shirt. She didn't want them finding her naked in the bathroom - no way. Then she crouched with her ear to the door listening to the soft thud of footsteps. Someone was walking past the door. She bit down on her lower lip to stop herself from screaming. She could just stay there, stay hidden, and hope that whoever it was would take what they wanted and go away. Or she could do something to stop them.

She pressed her ear to the door. It sounded like it was only one person. Surely, she could manage one person? Why should he be allowed to roam round people's homes helping himself to whatever he liked? It wasn't right.

Vanessa was justifiably furious. The mood she was in, she was ready for anything. As luck would have it, Ursula had left one of Michael's old walking sticks in an ornate pot stand in the corner of the large bathroom. It was stout and strong with a curved wooden handle. She picked it up and tested its weight in her hands. This would do. This would sort the thief out good and proper.

And it did. She was amazed how the man pitched forwards and fell like a collapsing house of cards onto the carpet of her bedroom, narrowly missing the slumbering Bruno, who was oblivious to all newcomers, and in a doggy dream world of his own.

'Ugh!' She dropped the walking stick with a cry of alarm, momentarily panic stricken over what she had done. The police! She needed to call the police. In a dither, she ran to the door, and then ran back again. What if she'd killed him? What if the police thought she'd used unreasonable force, and condemned her to spending the next few years of her life in prison? Oh my God - what was she going to do?

At this point, the man on the floor gave a low groan. Vanessa recoiled in shock, but then recovered slightly, as she realised, he wasn't dead.

'Don't move,' she said, trying desperately to keep her voice from quivering. 'I've got a gun and…. and I've called the police.'

'What the hell for?' Jed groaned.

'Jed!' Vanessa shrieked, in disbelief.

He had rolled onto his side and was struggling to prop himself up on one elbow. A thin dribble of blood had run down the side of his neck and was staining the white cotton of his t-shirt.

'Jed!' Vanessa collapsed to her knees in front of him. 'Oh God, I didn't know it was you. I thought you were a burglar.'

'I expect you'd have hit me even harder if you'd known it was me,' he said, shaking his head wearily. 'Christ, Vanessa, that really hurt.'

'I'm sorry. I'm so sorry,' She was in a flap again. She hauled a pillowcase off one of the pillows on her bed and tried to dab rather clumsily at the cut on the side of his head. A flood of tears was pouring down her cheeks. 'I could have killed you,' she wept. 'My God, what did you think you were doing? You scared me half to death.'

'Sorry.' He took the pillowcase from her and pressed the cool cotton against the cut. Head wounds usually bled profusely, and this was no exception. However, he didn't think it was too serious.

But the sight of all that blood was not doing much for Vanessa's state of mind, or her self control. Wringing her hands together in frustration, she sobbed, 'I'm sorry, I'm so sorry. This is all my fault. I didn't mean to hurt you.'

'I don't expect it's any less than I deserved,' Jed said, struggling to sit up. He managed to support himself by leaning back against the foot of the bed. Not only was his side aching, but his head was throbbing too.

'What were you trying to do?' she sobbed, somewhat hysterically.

'Trying to see you. Caroline said you wouldn't speak to me…'

'Caroline?'

'I went to the tack shop,' he admitted. 'She was a bit off with me. She said you wouldn't see me, so I guessed you wouldn't open the door to me either. Climbing in the window seemed like a good idea at the time.' He lifted the folded pillowcase from the side of his head. The bleeding was starting to stop. Only a small smear stained the once pale blue and primrose cotton cover. 'You ought to be more careful,' he added. 'That's one heck of a swing you've got there.'

'I was frightened.'

'So, you thought you'd kill first, and ask questions later?'

Vanessa looked mortified. Jed couldn't help smiling at her. 'Hey, it's okay. I survived. And at least I got to see you, didn't I?'

'It's not funny.'

'No.' His expression grew more serious. 'It's not. Vanessa, why did you rush away from me this morning? Was it something I said?'

She gave a short, dry laugh. 'How about everything, Jed? All the lies, the deceit, everything.' She bowed her head. 'Well, you got what you wanted, didn't you? I was a fool to believe I could have meant anything to you.'

'Honey, you've got this all wrong.'

'Stop it!' She clamped her hands over her ears. 'I don't want to hear it, Jed. And don't call me honey. You're a fake,' she added. (Now that she knew he was going to be all right, she was letting rip with her bottled-up emotions). 'You're a liar and a cheat. You wormed your way into my affections for one reason only, to provide a cover for your illegal dealings. I don't know why I don't phone the police right now and tell them what you've been up to.'

'Go ahead, then,' he sighed. 'Go on, phone them, if you think it'll make you feel better, but it won't change the way I feel about you.'

Vanessa sat back on her heels and wiped away her tears with a corner of the duvet cover. She didn't know what to think. How could she trust or believe him, after everything that had happened? And yet, she wanted to - she really, really wanted to.

She rested her hand on Bruno, who was slumbering peacefully by her side, his dark chest rising and falling in time with his breathing. He had to be stone deaf, she decided, or drugged, not to have woken up with all the commotion.

'You ought to see a doctor,' she said quietly. Jed's pained expression was starting to worry her.

'I'll be all right.'

'It's up to you.'

He sighed and leaned his head back against the mattress. He was making a right pig's ear of this. 'Vanessa, I don't want to lose you,' he said. 'That's why I came here. I know I've made a mess of things and I want to try and put things right. I know you'll find it hard to trust me…'

'Oh, you think?' she scoffed.

'Believe me, if I could change things, I would. When I agreed to work for Giles, I was desperate. He offered me a way out. It seemed a simple enough thing to do at the time. All I had to do was swap the stallions over, no questions asked. And then I discovered that the Trevelyan's owned Midnight Prince and I couldn't go through with it. Vanessa, I've worked with Lewis. I like the guy. I wouldn't do that to him.'

Vanessa twiddled her fingers in her lap as she listened to him talk. She was trying to make out she didn't care, but he was making it all sound so reasonable.

'By the time I realised what was going on I'd grown to like you as well. If it hadn't been for that stupid shooting accident, I'd never have got you involved,' he added. 'You'd never have known any of this. I'd have done the supposed swap and carried on as normal.'

'Telling more lies.'

He groaned,' Vanessa, it's only a name. Call me Hank, if you prefer, I don't care.'

'From Montana,' she sneered.

'I've worked there. I've done trail rides. Hell, I've even herded cattle on a ranch. I didn't tell you anything that wasn't partly true. Haven't you ever exaggerated anything before in order to impress someone?' He shook his head wearily. 'What more can I say?'

She gave a small shrug.

Jed sighed. This was getting them nowhere. She was still looking at him as if he had crawled out from under a stone. 'Look, if you think going to the police will help, then fine, we'll go to the police. Except, I think you'll find that no crime has been committed. The stallions weren't swapped. It's only Giles who thinks they were. But please, Vanessa, please believe me when I say I care about you. I do. I really do.'

Vanessa chewed on her bottom lip as she mulled over what he'd said.

She'd never been in this situation before. She knew what it was like to be in love, but normally, it wasn't reciprocated. She was the one being dumped. It gave her a strange sense of power to know that he actually wanted to be with her, that he was prepared to take risks, just for her.

She stroked Bruno's ears, and smiled as he lifted his lazy head and licked her hand, before flopping back down on the carpet again. He hadn't noticed Jed was in the room. Stupid beast.

'What are you thinking?' Jed murmured.

Vanessa wiped her tears away with the back of her hand and managed a weak smile. 'I was wondering,' she said, catching hold of his fingers and squeezing them tight. 'Just wondering, what on earth I'm going to tell mother.'

Chapter 17

By mid afternoon, Ursula was in a foul mood due, in part, to the unreliable behaviour of the staff under her control. Not only had Gemma failed to turn up at the stables as scheduled, but Sarah had arrived late, due to her weekly swimming lesson which she refused to give up, and Maxine had left early to have her highlights put in at the expensive salon in town.

To crown it all, Thomas had chosen that week to take Maisie to visit her sister in Dorset. So, apart from Tamsin, who was already booked up, there was no one left to take charge of the junior jumping class.

'You'll have to do it,' Tamsin told her bluntly. 'Sarah can tack up for you and give you a hand with the poles. I've got a hack to take out.'

'Then I suggest you cancel it,' Ursula snapped, flapping her hand on the duty list. 'There's six people in the jumping class, and only two booked to hack out.'

'They're regular customers.'

'Then they'll understand if you have to cancel,' Ursula said. She was not going to be swayed on this one. It had been years since she had last instructed a jumping class, and she had no intention of doing it again - particularly with the junior riders. Some of the little ponies could be right tearaways. She'd endured enough tears and tantrums with children to last her a lifetime.

'I'm not cancelling the hack,' Tamsin said, her normally calm voice raising a few keys. 'You caused this problem by changing the rest day. If you'd left things as they were, none of this would have happened.'

'Right!' Ursula felt herself start to simmer.' Sarah - you can take the lesson.'

'But Mrs Lloyd Duncan, I'm not qualified to teach,' Sarah stammered, her bottom lip trembling.

'Well now's the time to learn.'

The young girl looked distraught. 'I can't,' she said. 'Not till I pass my exams.'

'That's right,' Tamsin said.' She can't take the lesson.'

'No, but I can,' came a softly spoken voice behind her.

'Ella!' Sarah shrieked, spinning round in delight.

'Ella?' Ursula echoed, taking a step forwards. What on earth? Her face paled at the sight of her stepdaughter, complete with young daughter in tow. What were they doing here? Why weren't they in Paris? Why had no one warned her they were coming home? Her eyes practically bulged out of her head as she saw that Rosie was wearing jodhpurs and looked set to take part in the lesson. Kate and Charlotte were standing behind her, watching the goings on with interest. And Ella did not look in the least bit happy - not happy at all.

Ursula cemented a beaming smile onto her face and took an eager step forwards. 'Ella, darling! What a surprise to see you? You should have phoned.' She took another step rapidly backwards as her stepdaughter came marching towards her. She didn't look as if she was in the mood for polite conversation. 'Um, perhaps I'd better explain….'

'Later,' Ella said, striding straight past her and heading for the tack room. 'Charlotte, Rosie, are you going to help me with the saddles?'

'Yes, yes!' came the excited reply.

'We've been to see Mickey Mouse, Gran,' Rosie announced, proudly pointing out her new sweatshirt as she skipped past.

'Have you darling? How lovely,' Ursula said, breaking into a trot after them. She needed to catch up with Ella, if only to explain that things were not as disorganised as they seemed. Ella, however, was not in the mood to listen.

Ursula simpered in front of her. 'Darling, it was only a little mix up with the duty rota,' she said. 'You caught me when I was in the middle of trying to sort it out. It wouldn't have been a problem.'

'So, I noticed,' Ella replied crisply. 'Since when have we used unqualified instructors to take a lesson? A jumping lesson at that,' she said. 'Charlotte, can you take this to Sarah and get her to tack up Minnie. Rosie, you can manage Blossom. Excuse me, Ursula,' she added, pushing past her stepmother with an armful of bridles and a small jumping saddle. 'I haven't time to chat.'

'No, no, I can see that,' Ursula mumbled, feeling somewhat deflated. 'I'll talk to you later, shall I?'

'No doubt.'

Kate sidled up to her with an amused grin on her face. 'Problems, Mrs Lloyd Duncan?' she asked.

Ursula glared at her. 'Not that it's any of your business. I suppose this is all your doing?' she snapped.

'Moi?' Kate assumed an air of complete innocence that didn't have Ursula fooled for one moment.

With a snort of anger, she turned and went marching back to the house. There was nothing for it but to wait until Ella had calmed down. She was obviously in a bad mood. Foreign travel didn't suit some people. Ella, she decided, was apparently one of them.

'I can't believe you're back,' Tamsin said, with obvious glee.' Honestly, Ella, it's been a nightmare. The woman's power mad. You should see all the changes she's made.'

'I've heard about some of them,' Ella sighed, as she tightened the girth on Starlet's belly. 'Kate's kept me pretty much up to date, haven't you Kate?'

'I've tried,' Kate said, as she loitered by the tack room door and attempted to keep a safe distance between herself and the row of tethered ponies. 'Mind you,' she mused. 'You've got to hand it to Ursula, - she doesn't need to try too hard before she upsets someone.'

'She only has to speak,' Tamsin muttered. (She had not forgiven her for telling her to cancel her instructional hack so abruptly.) 'You know she's organised a Western event for Saturday afternoon, don't you, and now she's lost her star rider? You heard about Hank's injury, right?'

Ella nodded. 'He's the man who was shot.'

'That's right. Well, now he can't ride, and she's trying to get Vanessa or Adam to do the display instead.'

Ella looked startled.' Adam can't ride Western - or at least, I don't think he can.' She looked questioningly at Tamsin, who shook her head. 'So, what's she going to do? Cancel it?'

'Who knows,' Tamsin said, as she undid the head collar of the nearest horse and led it over to the mounting block. 'I'd better get a move on. My clients are here,' she said. 'We'll talk later, okay?'

'Definitely,' Ella said, fastening the strap of her hat under her chin. 'Now then, girls,' She turned to face the assembled group of junior riders. 'Are we ready? Good. You can lead your ponies into the school and we'll use the mounting block to get on them. Rosie, you go first. Sarah, I'll need you to bring up the rear. And Kate,' she added, smiling at her pony phobic friend, 'why don't you get a cup of coffee and bring it over. You might enjoy watching this lesson.'

'Did you know your mother was back?' Ursula said, rounding on Adam who was sprawled on the floor playing his latest Play station game.

'Yeah.'

'What?'

Adam peered over his shoulder at his Gran. She was looking decidedly off-colour, he thought. And drinking gin too, at this time of the day. That was a bit odd. He turned back to his game. 'I said, yeah.'

'And you didn't think to tell me?'

'You weren't here.'

'I was down at the yard,' Ursula snapped. 'Some of us had to work. Some of us couldn't lie about in bed all day.'

More's the pity, thought Adam as he zapped away at his latest enemy on the screen. A long lie-in might have improved his grandmother's mood. She was being rather crotchety. 'Rosie's brought you some sweets,' he said. 'They're on the kitchen table, and I think Mum said she'd put a bottle of champagne in the fridge.'

Champagne? Oh great. Just what she needed right now, a celebratory drink. Ursula stomped out of the lounge and trundled her way upstairs. She could feel one of her heads coming on and decided it might be best if she lay down in a darkened room. Ella wouldn't be back for a while and she might feel better facing her once she'd had a little sleep.

What she didn't expect to face, however, was the sight of Hank and Vanessa draped all over themselves on the lounge settee, when she came back downstairs an hour or so later.

'What are you two doing here?' she said, pushing the door open and observing, with wry amusement, the way they leapt apart like scalded cats.

Hank was looking a lot better, she decided. He had a bit more colour in his cheeks. Though, by the looks of him, he'd nicked himself whilst shaving. There was a nasty smear of blood on the neck of his t-shirt.

'Why aren't you at the tack shop?' she asked, her eyes narrowing sharply on her daughter's flushed face. Vanessa was looking decidedly guilty, she thought.

'Caroline's there.'

'So, who's keeping an eye on Grey Lodge?'

'Um...ah...Bruno,' she faltered.

'The dog? You've left the house empty apart from the dog.' Ursula's voice sounded incredulous.

'We've only just left him, and Marcus should be back from work soon,' Vanessa explained. Her cheeks were scarlet, and she seemed hot and bothered.

It was nothing to how Ursula appeared. Jed thought she was simmering and about to come to the boil, by the look of things.

'Are you all right, mother? Adam said you'd gone for a lie down.'

'Yes, and I had good reason to,' she said. 'Did you know Ella was back?'

'No.' Vanessa's eyes widened in surprise. 'Is Lewis with her?'

'Not as far as I know, but that doesn't mean he isn't,' Ursula muttered. 'It seems I'm the last one to be told about things that go on round here.'

'Ah,' Vanessa said. 'Yes. Actually,' She glanced at Jed. 'There is something we need to tell you, mother.'

'We?' Ursula's sharply plucked eyebrows rose like question marks across her forehead.

'Well, er, Hank, really. Except, that's not his real name,' she faltered. 'He's called Jed.'

'Jed?' Ursula's beady eyes fixed themselves on the man in front of her with a penetrating stare. What on earth was going on now?

'Jed Harrison,' Vanessa said. 'He...er...well, he's an actor, you see, and so he uses an assumed name, so people don't recognise him. Remember when Simon De Silva came to Hollyfield for riding lessons,' she explained. 'Well, if you recall, he used the name Adam Lansing, and no one realised it was him. And that's what Jed does, don't you Jed.'

'Yes.' He nodded. 'I wasn't trying to fool you or anything, but I didn't want you to recognise my name when I was asking you about a job.'

'Never heard of you,' Ursula muttered. She'd been half expecting a wedding announcement; the way Vanessa was behaving. A change of name was hardly in the same league.

'And he's not an American, either,' Vanessa said in a somewhat quieter tone. She looked reassuringly at Jed who managed a half smile. She wasn't sure how well her mother was receiving this news. Her cheeks had gone quite pale and her lips were set in a thin hard line.

'He has worked in the States, though,' she added, as if that would help. 'On a ranch in Montana.'

It was of little consolation to Ursula, who was seeing the complete waste of all the money she had spent on Western tack, to say nothing of the forthcoming American event, which she had organised purely on the grounds that they had a real live Western cowboy staying with them.

It was time, she decided, for another gin and tonic.

Disaster seemed to be heaping itself upon disaster, what with gipsies, shootings, and mutiny amongst the stable girls. Ella turning up at the yard was the icing on the cake. This latest revelation was the cherry on top.

'My reputation will be ruined,' she moaned, slumping into the nearest armchair, and wincing as she found herself perched on one of Rosie's pink plastic ponies. 'I'll be the laughing stock of the village.'

'Rubbish,' Vanessa said. 'If anything, you could use this to get even more publicity. Jed's done a lot of stunt riding in films you know. I'm sure people would be interested in meeting him.'

'What's the use of that if he can't ride?' she snapped.

'I'll be fit enough to ride,' Jed said.' Don't you worry about that.' His sideways glance met Vanessa's concerned frown. 'Saturday's two days away, honey. I'll be in the saddle by then. If you want an American cowboy, Mrs Lloyd Duncan, you'll have one. I promise you that.'

'Oh good,' Ursula said, with more than a hint of sarcasm in her tone. 'Let's hope Equity doesn't come up with any objections, shall we?' She shook her head in exasperation. 'Anything else I should know about, or is that everything sorted for now?'

'Well, there is one other thing,' Vanessa said. 'Seeing as how Jed won't be going back to America after the summer, I was wondering if there was any chance he could stay longer at Hollyfield.'

'What are you asking me for?' Ursula said, draining her glass and looking vaguely puzzled when she realised it was empty. 'Ella's back. You'd better have a word with her.'

'I'm not sure I'm ready for this,' Jed whispered, as he walked arm in arm with Vanessa down to the stable yard. 'Your stepsister might not be so easily convinced as your mother. She's had dealings with actors before.'

'I know, but I'm sure she'll understand,' Vanessa said. In a way, she thought Ella might be easier to deal with than her mother. She would be meeting Jed for the first time, without the alter ego of Hank, the cowboy, to compare him with.

'What if Adam's told her?'

'Adam's thirteen,' Vanessa said. 'He doesn't say much at the best of times - or at least, not to his parents, anyway. I reckon I can keep him sweet,' she added. 'He's pretty keen on learning how to ride Western style too. And really, when you think about it, you haven't done anything wrong.'

'I've still got the thousand pounds Giles gave me,' he said. 'That doesn't feel right. And he's cleared my debts for nothing.'

'He doesn't know that. And besides,' she added, 'he shouldn't have trusted your word. He knew you were an actor. You played a blinder of a part. I've never met such a convincing bloody liar.'

'You reckon?' he said, giving her waist a squeeze.

'Oh yes.' She smiled and rested her head on his shoulder. 'I reckon.'

'That's him!' Kate hissed, nearly spilling her coffee as she jumped up and signalled to Ella to look to her right, where Vanessa and the American had made an appearance at the gate to the school. 'That's Hank!' she mouthed.

Ella swivelled round on the pretext of following the path of one of her young riders. 'Oh, well sat, Jessie,' she called, at the same time as she risked an interested glance in the man's direction.

He was certainly as good looking as Kate's photographs had implied. His dark, unruly hair curled onto his neck, and he was wearing slim fitting denim jeans and a white t-shirt.

Vanessa waved to her, and she smiled and waved back. She was genuinely delighted that her stepsister had found somebody halfway decent at last. The way the man was resting his arm around her waist showed real affection.

'Told you,' Kate said smugly, as she sat back to enjoy the last of her coffee.

But she didn't remain quite as smug for long.

By six o'clock, the story of the "American who wasn't" was all round the yard. It wasn't just Ursula and Ella who had been told the news. Jed had made a point of explaining himself to each and every one of the staff on duty that day.

'What do you mean, he's not American?' Maxine spluttered. She had returned from the hairdressing salon eager to show off her blonde, russet and copper highlights to anyone who was around, and had been flabbergasted when Sarah had come rushing out of Flossie's stable to tell her the news. 'Who told you?'

'He did.'

'He did?' she choked.

'Yes. He's an actor - an actor called Jed Harrison.'

'No!' Maxine was rendered speechless.

'I think he must be a friend of Mr Trevelyan,' Sarah said. 'I mean, he's worked in America in films and things, and I believe he's quite famous. That's why he uses an assumed name when he's 'resting' as he puts it.'

'Resting?'

'Yes, you know - out of work. Ella seemed to know about it, anyway.'

'Ella?' Maxine looked puzzled.

'Of course - you don't know,' Sarah said smugly. She did so like being the first person to pass on the news. 'Ella's back. She took the jumping class this afternoon when you buggered off.'

'I had an appointment,' Maxine retorted.

'Yes well, Ursula was ordering me to do it when Ella turned up, thank goodness. If looks could kill, I'd say Ursula would be long gone by now. Ella was furious.'

Maxine smirked. 'I bet she was.'

'I could have done it, you know,' Sarah said crossly. 'I just didn't want to for insurance reasons. Anyway, you missed all the excitement, what with Ella coming home, and then Jed turning up with Vanessa and telling everyone how he'd been pretending to be an American for weeks. It was great.'

'But he can ride Western, can't he?' Maxine said. 'That's not an act?'

'God no. He's brilliant at it. Apparently, he's worked as a stunt rider in loads of action films.'

'What, well known ones?'

'Yes, I think so.'

Maxine pursed her lips and thought for a moment. She tossed her multi coloured mane over her shoulder and gave an indignant little snort.' What the hell does he see in Vanessa, then?'

Love, actually. Jed had been considering the thought for some time, but at thirty-seven years old, was somewhat sceptical about the idea of falling in love at first sight.

He barely knew Vanessa, yet he'd never felt more contented and in tune with someone in his life. They gelled together. He liked being with her. She was funny and brave, and boy, did she have guts. The way she'd pounced on him when she thought he was a burglar, for instance, was sheer stupidity, but it took a certain strength of character to face up to her fears. She must have been terrified, but she hadn't backed down. And he'd never forget the way she came looking for him when he went missing, and as good as saved his life. Or the long hours she sat with him at the hospital while he recovered from surgery. Or the way she handled the horsebox in the darkest hours of the night, despite knowing he had lied and deceived her. No, she was one in a million all right, and he'd be mad to let her go.

It might have surprised him to know that Vanessa was thinking along the same lines. Not because she was desperate for male attention, (which she was), but because she felt a genuine closeness to him. She didn't have to pretend with him. Jed accepted her for what she was, warts and all. What's more, he even seemed to like her. They got on so well together that she felt as if she had known him all her life.

Ella was the first to comment on it, as they enjoyed a late evening meal together, courtesy of the local Chinese takeaway. It was her treat, seeing as how she hadn't given them any warning she was coming home. The state Ursula was in after three large gins, it was perhaps just as well that she hadn't been left in charge of the catering arrangements.

'I think you look very happy together,' she said, having caught the glances flying backwards and forwards between them throughout the meal.

'Well, it is early days,' Vanessa said beaming happily.

She was wearing a white frilly blouse, with a low-slung leather belt, black jeans and boots. A silver pendant dangled round her neck from a leather thong. She looked quite attractive, Ella thought - and years younger. Normally she wore stuffy business-like suits and tailored clothes that were more suitable for somebody twice her age.

'She's quite a girl, your stepsister,' Jed said, as he handed Ella the bowl of prawn crackers. 'All credit to her, she's one brave lady.'

'There's a fine line between bravery and stupidity,' Ella laughed. 'I don't think I'd be tackling intruders at Grey Lodge.'

'Well, I guess she had the advantage. I had been wounded first. Otherwise, I'd have floored her.'

'Yes, but she didn't know that.'

'No, I didn't,' Vanessa said. 'I thought you were one of the gipsies.'

'Like I said,' Jed chuckled, raising his glass to her.' She's one brave lady.'

'And talking of gipsies,' Ella turned to face Ursula, who was looking rather bleary-eyed at the end of the table. 'What's this I hear about you getting a Court Order served on the ones at Grey Lodge? Why on earth didn't you send them down to Richard Hudson's fruit farm? He's always looking for casual labour, and he's perfectly happy to have them living on his land for the season.'

'Now she tells me,' Ursula muttered, trying with difficulty to spear a battered prawn ball onto the end of her fork.

Adam came to her rescue with the aid of a pair of chopsticks.

Ella watched her son rise to the occasion with a warm smile on her face. It was good to see him getting on so well with his grandmother. 'You haven't been too bored, while we've been away?'

'Who, me?' Adam seemed surprised she needed to ask him.' No, I've been having a great time, haven't I, Aunty Van?'

Vanessa gave him a knowing smile. 'Oh yes, I think I can honestly say he hasn't had time to be bored.'

'I hear you've been doing some Western riding?' Ella said.

'Yeah. It's great fun,' he added, in between mouthfuls of barbecued spare rib. 'It's one of Gran's better ideas.'

Ella laughed. 'So, you think we should start giving lessons at Hollyfield, once Jed's recovered from his injury?'

'Yeah,' he enthused.

'Oh good,' Ursula said, rather morosely. 'I've done something right, at last.'

'No,' Ella said, correcting her quite clearly. 'You should have asked me first.'

The next couple of days flew past. Vanessa, as always, was busy with the running of the tack shop, but Jed was more than happy to sit and spend time with her, when he wasn't instructing Adam in the finer skills of Western riding.

Ella had decided to stay until after the American event on the Saturday, partly because Adam was going to be taking part in the riding display, and partly because she wanted to supervise the return to normal of the duty lists.

Lewis had said he would try to get home for the weekend, so she had more reason than most to be looking forward to it.

Vanessa was just relieved that her mother had taken the news of Jed's duplicity in such good faith. It had amazed her that they had got away with things so easily. Jed was no longer under any obligation to Giles Peterson; he had a bit of spare cash to play around with, and a job at the stables for the foreseeable future. The future, and all it beckoned was looking bright.

Or at least it was until the Friday evening, when Jed received a rather worrying message on his mobile phone. Giles Peterson was coming to see him. Not only that, but he was insisting on seeing him at Hollyfield stables the very next day.

Chapter 18

'He's found out,' Vanessa said in a panic, when Jed showed her the text on his phone. 'He must have. That's the only reason he's coming here.'

They were in Jed's bedroom in the Groom's Cottage, and Vanessa was almost beside herself with worry.

'What are we going to do? If he knows you've tricked him, he might get violent.'

'He won't,' Jed said staring thoughtfully out of the window. 'But he'll know a man who can.'

'Oh God!'

'Hey,' He turned around, surprised at the fear in her voice. 'It'll be okay.'

'How will it?'

Jed shrugged. 'We might be jumping to conclusions. He might have another job for me. It might not be anything to do with Midnight Prince.'

Vanessa did not look convinced. Jed wasn't too happy about it either. Giles Peterson always did something for a reason. Coming to Hollyfield when he'd supposedly stolen their prize stallion seemed madness to him, but who was he to say what went on in the businessman's mind.

'I won't be able to sleep a wink,' Vanessa said. 'In fact, I've a good mind to ask Caroline to run the tack shop for me tomorrow so I can be here in case there's any trouble.'

Jed grinned. 'You'd better bring that stout walking stick with you, then.'

'You may well joke about it, but it's not funny.'

'No,' he conceded. 'It's not.'

In fact, it was anything but funny. He flipped open his phone and read the text message again. There was no doubt about it. Giles was coming to Hollyfield on Saturday to see him. The question was, why?

'No, no, hang the flag from the far beam,' Ursula instructed, watching as Jimmy McPherson perched precariously on a wobbly stepladder in the middle of the empty hay barn. 'We don't want it flapping and frightening the horses.'

'It's looking good,' Ella said, as she watched the proceedings from the huge open doorway.

Ursula had made an arena in the middle of the barn using bales of straw and had organised seating and tables around the perimeter walls. Balloons and bunting in shades of red, white and blue hung from every available beam or hook. The barbecue area was outside the barn, under a huge gazebo she'd had erected in case of rain, and a second shelter housed the portable bar.

Where she'd got the huge American flag from, Ella wouldn't like to say, but it certainly looked effective.

'What time does it all kick off?'

'I put five o'clock on the invitations,' Ursula said. 'I thought that would give people time to watch the demonstration before the barbecue got going.' She came walking towards her, rubbing her hands together gleefully. 'I've got the local line-dancing group from the village hall coming to give a display as well. Did you know Vanessa had taken up line dancing?'

'No, but nothing she does surprises me anymore,' Ella said. She'd seen a huge change in her stepsister over the past few weeks. It was as if she'd suddenly discovered how to enjoy life and was making the most of it.

A pity she couldn't pass on a few tips to her sister, Caroline, she thought, who was turning into a carbon copy of her grumpy husband Marcus.

Ursula had insisted they employ a house sitter to keep an eye on Grey Lodge if they planned to come to the Barn dance. A fact that had not gone down well with Marcus, who didn't see why he should pay, when it wasn't even his house he was protecting. Therefore, he was refusing to come.

Shame, Ella thought. Still, he wouldn't be missed. She was sure Ursula would save him a couple of burgers and a muffin for free. It was the least she could do.

But Caroline kept bemoaning the fact that she would have no one to dance with and complained that it wouldn't be the same without Marcus, (Personally, Ella thought it would be a lot more fun), so in the end, she arranged for one of the teenagers from the village to house sit, on the pretext of looking after Bruno.

None of this would be necessary if Ursula hadn't annoyed the gipsy contingent so much, she thought. It was just as well they were showing signs of moving on. Caroline had reported that two of the vans had left that morning, and the others looked to be in a state of packing up to go.

'Not before time,' Ursula muttered. 'I'd have got that Court order served on them next week. You see if I wouldn't.'

By mid day everything was on schedule. Jed had turned up with Adam in tow and had amazed everyone by getting on Arizona and putting the Quarter horse through an impressive practice display. Adam tried his best to copy him on Lucky, and even Ursula was pleased at how well her grandson had performed.

Things were starting to come together at last.

'What do you think?' she said to Ella, as they walked back to the house for a bite to eat. She hardly dared ask, but she was desperate for her stepdaughter's approval.

'I'm impressed.'

'Really?'

Ella nodded. 'I hate to admit it, but yes, though I still think you should have talked to me about it first.'

Ursula positively glowed. 'Well,' she sighed,' I didn't want to bother you when you were enjoying yourself so much in Paris.'

'Rosie says you took Jed on before we even left for France.'

'Ah - well, yes, maybe I did,' she faltered. 'Though I can't quite remember when it was, exactly.'

Ella knew she remembered as clear as day. With Ursula, some things never changed - the desire to be in control, for one thing.

'When do you expect Lewis to get back?' Ursula asked, deftly changing the subject.

Ella glanced at her watch. 'I'm not sure. Sometime this afternoon, I hope. It depends on how easily he can get a flight.'

'That's not him now, is it?' Ursula said, pointing to the gleaming black car that was drawing into the car park in front of the stables.

Ella paused by the door and looked back. 'No.' She looked closer as a man in a grey suit got out of the car and ground a cigar butt into the gravel with his shoe. 'I don't know who it is, though. Do you?'

Ursula shook her head. 'I've never seen him before. Do you want me to go and ask?'

'No, we'll leave that to Sally,' Ella said, tilting her head in the direction of the reception office. 'Let's go and have some lunch.'

Jed looped Arizona's reins over a tethering rail and unfastened the cinch on the horse's Western saddle. He had seen Giles Peterson's car swing into the car park and knew that the moment of truth was almost upon him. Where was Vanessa when he needed her, he thought? A bit of moral support wouldn't have gone amiss.

He lifted the heavy saddle down and glanced over at Adam, who was doing the same thing with Lucky.

'Keep an eye on this one, will you,' he said. 'I'll be back in a moment.'

The yard was busy with the Saturday pony club youngsters. Tamsin and Gemma were helping them groom the horses, and Jed didn't want anyone overhearing whatever it was that Giles had come to say.

He walked smartly over to the car park and met the businessman halfway.

'You're taking a bit of a risk, aren't you?' he hissed.

'No more than you are,' Giles said, flicking a bit of hay off the lapel of his immaculately pressed suit.

Jed glanced back at the stable yard and ran a distracted hand through his hair. 'What do you want, Giles? You surely haven't come to gloat, have you?'

'Would it worry you if I had?'

'Yes' Jed said. 'I'm trying to keep my head down, here.'

'So, I see.' Giles reached into the inside breast pocket of his jacket and withdrew a folded piece of paper. 'Western riding demonstration,' he read, 'with our own American cowboy. Hmm interesting.' He raised his eyes, 'considering you're trying to keep a low profile.'

'It wasn't my idea.'

'And you've got to keep in character, right?'

'Right.' Jed nodded.

Giles gave him a thoughtful smile. 'Maybe I should hang around and watch.'

'It's by invitation only.'

'How convenient for you.' Giles screwed up the piece of paper and tossed it onto the ground. His lips tightened. 'You're making a big mistake by staying on here. You should have left like we arranged.'

'And have them point the finger of suspicion at me?' Jed hissed. 'Come on, Giles. You know that doesn't make sense. It's better if I keep on working as if nothing's happened. The stud groom's gone on holiday. Everything's sweet. Nobody's noticed anything's wrong.'

'You're sure about that?'

'Absolutely.' It was about the only thing he could be confident about. 'The stallion's settled in really well.'

'Good.' Giles nodded. He folded his arms in front of him and frowned, as if considering the matter. 'Jackson's had no problems up at North Hall either. The difference being that he hadn't had Exodus for long, so it's doubtful if any of the stud staff would have picked up on the difference. And you say the stud manager's gone away?'

'To Dorset.'

'And he wouldn't have done that if he'd had any suspicions.'

'No way.'

'Hmm.' Giles unfolded his arms. 'Right.'

Jed caught sight of Vanessa hurrying towards them out of the corner of his eye. She was dressed in jeans with full leather chaps, a fringed Western shirt and she was carrying a cowboy hat in one hand. A beaming smile lit up her face.

'Oh Hank. Yoo-hoo! Hank!' She waved the hat at him. 'I'm ready for you now.'

'Be with you in a minute,' he called. He glanced back at Giles. 'Sorry, I'm going to have to go.'

'So, I see.' He gave a dry laugh. 'I'd watch yourself with that one, son. She looks like she means business.' He offered him his hand. 'I don't expect to see you again, understand?'

'Absolutely,' Jed said, gripping the older man's fingers and giving them a firm handshake. Nothing would give him greater pleasure.

He waited until the gleaming black car had pulled out of the drive before exhaling steadily and turning back towards the yard. He felt as if he'd been holding his breath for ages.

Vanessa came running to meet him and he gave a whoop of delight as he swung her up in his arms.

'Don't,' she gasped.' You'll hurt yourself.'

'For you,' he laughed, 'I'd do anything.' He kissed her there and then, in front of everyone - the stable girls, the Saturday Club youngsters - everyone.

'You pulled it off, then?' she said, her eyes sparkling.

'Yep!' He kissed her again and again, before releasing her.' Come on, honey,' he said, grabbing hold of her hand. 'Let's get this show on the road.'

'Daddy's back!' Rosie shrieked, leaping down from the cushioned window seat and skipping to the door.

Ella ran to the window and parted the blinds. Lewis was unloading a black overnight bag from the boot of the car he had hired to get him back from the airport.

'You should have phoned,' she said, following Rosie into the garden. 'I would have come and picked you up.'

'What and tear yourself away from all this?' he said, tilting his head at the streamers and bunting decorating the hay barn. The Country and Western group Ursula had hired for the evening were practicing a few numbers and the foot-tapping tunes were drifting out over the paddocks.

Goodness knows what the horses thought of it all, Ella mused.

'Daddy, Adam's going to ride like a cowboy,' Rosie said, tugging at his sleeve. 'You've got to see him.'

'That's why I'm here,' Lewis said, winking at Ella. 'How's it going?'

'To be honest, not bad at all,' she said, linking her arm through his and reaching up to kiss him.

'What about Jed Harrison?'

'Again, everything's fine. He's admitted to using a different name because he didn't want anybody to recognise him.'

'And the reason he said he was American?'

'The same, I guess.'

Lewis didn't look convinced. 'He's not a well- known actor,' he said. 'I reckon he did more stunt and double work than anything else.'

'Whatever,' Ella said. 'He certainly knows how to handle horses and he's a good teacher. That's all I'm interested in. And besides,' she added, smiling, 'Vanessa's really taken with him.'

'Vanessa would be,' he said. 'He's male.'

Ella thumped him lightly on the arm.' Don't be mean. It's not like that. He seems genuinely fond of her.'

'What, Jed Harrison and Vanessa?' he pondered.' This, I must see.'

By five o'clock the seats were well filled in the hay barn, and people were still arriving. Ursula had prepared a timetable of events and was standing at the entrance handing out leaflets to everyone who passed.

In keeping with the spirit of the event, she had dressed herself in a gingham dress and apron that made her look as if she'd stepped out of the set of Oklahoma. A cowboy hat hung from a strand of leather down her back.

Caroline was wearing skin-tight jeans tucked into tan leather boots, and a pale denim shirt that showed off her generous cleavage. Even Marcus, not to be outdone, was wearing jeans with a crease pressed smartly down the front, a checked shirt, and highly polished brown shoes.

'That's a sight for sore eyes,' Lewis whispered. 'Think he'll be any good when the dancing starts?'

'I don't want to think about it,' Ella laughed. 'Come on, there's Kate and Graham. We'll sit with them, shall we?'

Considering that Jed had spent the best part of the previous week in hospital, he gave an outstanding performance on Arizona, and kept up a running commentary as he showed the audience the different skills required. He backed the horse between poles, jogged sideways, pivoted and loped to perfection. Then he introduced Adam into the ring and showed what could be achieved with the minimum of training. Adam gave a remarkable display of neck reining, side passes, and turning on the spot. And then, much to everyone's surprise, Vanessa came riding into the arena, and the three riders performed together, with each horse stopping, turning, jogging and loping in unison.

The audience loved it. Ursula thought she was going to burst with happiness. Caroline was whooping and shouting, and even Marcus looked marginally less miserable.

'I hate to say, it,' Ella whispered, 'but Ursula's done well to put this lot together.'

'Don't say it, then,' Lewis replied. 'Or we'll never hear the end of it.'

The Village Line-dancers were next, and after several complicated routines performed to perfection, they invited members of the audience to join them on the floor. Caroline declined (she hadn't forgotten the last time she tried it), but some of the stable girls were keen to give it a go.

Vanessa sat beside Jed on one of the hay-bales, keeping a watchful eye on Lewis and Ella, who seemed to be enjoying the show.

'Has he said anything to you?' she asked.

'Not yet.'

'What are you going to tell him?'

'The same as everyone else, I guess,' he murmured, squeezing her hand. 'Lewis will understand. You said he'd done the same thing himself with Simon de Silva.' He bent his head closer to hers. 'You did really well, you know.'

She smiled. 'So did you. I'm surprised you could get on a horse, after all you've been through.'

'That's why I make a good stunt man,' he said. 'I bounce back.'

'Well, as long as you keep bouncing back to me,' she murmured, turning towards him.

Jed cupped her cheeks in both hands and gently kissed her. 'Try and stop me, honey.'

Lewis watched them from a discreet distance, both amused and surprised at what he was seeing. It appeared that Vanessa had found her match at last. Well, good for her, he thought. Jed was a decent enough bloke. He was also a brave man - and that wasn't because he was prepared to take Vanessa on, though it would undoubtedly help.

'You're still the best horseman in the business,' he told him, when he finally caught up with Jed. He shook him firmly by the hand. 'I still haven't forgotten how we nearly lost you when we filmed that river scene.'

Jed laughed. 'Me and the horse both.' He had been dreading this moment for what seemed like forever. Lewis Trevelyan was a shrewd and careful judge of character. He knew he wouldn't be able to lie easily to him, and nor did he want to. But to his utmost relief, it appeared that he wasn't there to grill him. He really had just come over to have a chat.

'Are you still up for any parts?'

'You'd better ask my agent,' he chuckled. 'No, seriously,' He glanced across at Vanessa, who had joined the line dancers on the floor. 'I think I'd like to hang around here for a while. See if we can get this Western riding thing off the ground.'

Lewis followed the line of his gaze, and grinned. 'You're sure that's the only reason you want to hang around?'

'It might be,' he said, shrugging slightly, 'or it might not. Let's just wait and see, shall we?'

Lewis found Ella waiting for him with a cool beer at the bar.

'That was some display,' he said, picking it up and taking a long and satisfying drink.

'What, the riding?'

'No, Jed and Vanessa. You know, I think you might be right,' he said, stooping to press a kiss against her forehead. 'I think they're an item.'

'An item?' Adam echoed, pulling a face at him as he strode past. 'Dad, you're so old-fashioned.'

Lewis watched speechless, as his eldest child sauntered across the yard. In his authentic Western gear and low-slung jeans, he was attracting more than a few admiring glances from some of the village girls.

'He called me old-fashioned,' he spluttered.

'Well, you are getting on a bit,' Ella laughed. 'And Adam's growing up fast.'

'I noticed.'

Lewis sighed, and hooked his thumbs into the pockets of his jeans. 'Come on, then, old woman' he said, giving her a conspiratorial wink, 'let's give this line-dancing a go.'

'No way,' she said, shaking her head

'What? Not even for me?'

'Absolutely not,' she laughed. 'I'm leaving that to the experts.'

As if on cue, they watched as Vanessa and Jed joined the line-up. Both moved in unison and mirrored each other's moves. Every so often, they glanced across at each other and smiled.

'It's kind of sweet, isn't it,' Ella said.

'Nauseatingly so,' Kate said, leaning over and taking a handful of nuts from the bowl on the bar. 'And he's such a delicious looking hunk too. Some women have all the luck.' She waved her hand in her husband Graham's direction. 'Still, I don't suppose I did too badly myself, even if he does drive me crazy.'

'I expect it's mutual,' Ella laughed.

Kate glanced down at her, frowned for a moment and then nodded. 'Yep,' she said. 'You're absolutely right. Now then, folks, who wants another drink?'

Other books by the same author include

Green Wellies and Wax Jackets (Braiswick) ISBN 1898030995

The Coach Trip ISBN 9781985097315

A Love Betrayed (Morag Lewis) Robert Hale Ltd ISBN 0709038860

Printed in Poland
by Amazon Fulfillment
Poland Sp. z o.o., Wrocław